HOLIDAY HOSTILITIES

A FESTIVE HOCKEY ROM COM

KATIE BAILEY

Character Cover Art by
CINDY RAS

ELEVENTH AVENUE

1

OLIVIA

May

I've played out this moment—the moment we come face to face again—in my mind so many times over the years that I can barely keep track of my own fantasies anymore.

In one iteration of my deliciously spite-laden daydreams, I have supremely shiny, unfrizzy hair and perfect glass skin, while he, in turn, is sporting a huge new facial wart.

In another, I swan back into his life on the arm of some nameless, faceless NFL player—he's not a football fan, is a hockey freak through and through—who's both taller and broader than he is, and who subsequently challenges him to an arm wrestling competition. Which he loses, obviously.

He was always a sore loser.

One of my personal favorites is the one where he gets on his knees and grovels for me to pay him a lick of attention, but in doing so, slips and faceplants into some readily waiting dirt. Or dog poop. I'm not too picky.

All of them are good, if a little (lot) childish and petty.

But in not a single one of my daydreams about seeing Aaron Marino in the flesh again do I have a massive wedgie.

Clearly, reality can be much crueler than fiction. Because here I am, finally living in this moment, and all I can think is...

Wow, I really should have worn a thong tonight.

Well, that and the very unwelcome—yet very undeniable— observation that those luminous green eyes of his would be ever so pretty if they weren't lodged in the skull of my ex-high school nemesis who's now known as Atlanta's biggest playboy. Well, second biggest, if I'm being accurate. Even I can't deny that Aaron's teammate, Dallas Cooper, wears that particular crown. I've never even met the guy, but his reputation precedes him.

Clearly, hockey players are all cut from the same cloth. And said cloth is a nasty poly-blend that's entirely sweaty and unbreathable and bound to give you a rash. Likely in your nether regions.

My fantasies of seeing Aaron again never made it past my initial moment of retribution. They were mostly just a way to pass time when I was jet lagged and lying wide awake in bed after a long flight. And honestly, my mental vitriol aside, a part of me really did believe that time was a healer. Believed so many years had passed that, when I actually saw him again, my hatred towards the cocky Aaron Marino of my high school days might have dampened into more of a mild distaste for the pro athlete he is today.

But now that we're here and we've locked eyes, the telltale glint in his makes me doubt that very much.

As much as I know I shouldn't stare, I can't help but continue to soak in the sight of Aaron, casually perched on a barstool across the club's VIP area. He's filled out over the years and is more solid and brawny than the teenage version of himself, all lingering traces of boyhood vanished and replaced with one hundred percent *man*. He's grown into his facial features, his strong nose and angular chin annoyingly chiseled, like he's some kind of Greek-god-adjacent scoundrel.

He's hot, *dammit*. Even hotter than I remember.

So much for my dreams of facial warts.

Right now, he's talking to a very pretty brunette in a black dress, but his eyes stay fixed on me. I keep my gaze on him, not wanting to be the one to break first.

We hold our stare for a second.

Two.

Three.

Twenty-seven.

Who even knows?

Time slips away until, finally, he turns towards the brunette and says something to her. She then turns to look at me.

My mouth goes dry as I try to appear cool, confident, casual. Act like I am totally used to frequenting uber-cool nightclubs with teams of professional athletes, and like the slinky silver mini dress I picked out for tonight doesn't suddenly feel gaudy and obnoxious in comparison to the sleek black one Aaron's female companion is wearing.

Bet she *had the foresight to wear appropriately sexy and non-butt-munching underwear.*

I wipe my sweaty palms on my dress and remind myself that I don't have to be this nervous, because I don't have to talk to the man. We can coexist in the same nightclub without crossing paths. He's probably totally indifferent to me being here tonight —which is exactly how I should feel, too.

I look away from Aaron and his date to see the infamous Dallas Cooper knock my brother Jake's elbow before flashing me a flirtatious grin. "So, this is the legendary little sister, huh, Griz?"

"Legendary?" I peer up at Jake, wondering what on earth he could have said about me. My brother is notoriously tight-lipped about, well, everything. "What, did you tell them about the time I won that chili-dog eating contest?"

"No," Dallas says, his dark eyes wide beneath thick lashes. "He did not. No idea why, because that is a *very* intriguing intro."

Jake rolls his eyes at his teammate. "Don't even think about it, Cooper. She's off-limits."

My eyebrows shoot up.

"Excuse me," I interject with a wave of my hand. "I am an adult woman who makes her own decisions."

My older brother was always protective of me, but we're not in high school anymore. I'm twenty-six now for goodness sake. Moreover, we've lived apart for most of the past decade, and I've done just fine on my own.

Yet Jake's lips press in a familiar thin line as he raises one skeptical brow at me. "Says the woman who once decided to eat sixteen foot-long chili dogs and then proceeded to get sick on every available surface—including inside my brand new Camaro."

"That was a very long time ago," I protest.

Dallas's eyes gleam. "Damn, girl. Sixteen chili dogs? You have talent."

"Can it, Cooper," Jake orders before turning back to me. "You can, and should, decide to date *anyone other than* these goons, also known as my teammates."

The "goons" he's referring to are the players for the Atlanta Cyclones, an NHL team who have a decent shot at winning the Stanley Cup this year, according to Jake.

When he told me that, I wiggled my cherry-red metal water cup at him and informed him that I already had a Stanley cup, which earned me a gargantuan eye roll.

"Hey!" Jimmy Jones-Johnstone—affectionately known as "Triple J" to his teammates and the media—pipes up indignantly. "I take grave offense to that." He swivels his head to look at me, an endearingly dopey look on his dimpled face. "Jacob means any of his teammates, except for me. I'm the quintessential 'good guy' sailing in a sea of hockey-player hooligans."

Jake smacks him upside the head. "I was definitely including you in the equation, bonehead."

"But why?" Jimmy sniffs haughtily. "You'd be lucky to have me as a future brother-in-law, Griswold."

"Sounds more like a waking nightmare," Jake grumbles darkly, scratching his beard.

Not the most personable of men, my brother.

"Well, nightmare or not, she's an adult woman who makes her own decisions," Dallas parrots my words with a lazy smile, then flashes me what I can only describe as *bedroom eyes*. The guy's good—too good. I can't imagine how many women have fallen for that look. "So, you up for the best night of your life, Griz's baby sister?"

I wrinkle my nose at him. "Ew, no."

The guys burst out laughing, and Jake flashes a rare grin.

Dallas, apparently unperturbed by my rejection, simply shrugs and winks at me. "Your loss."

He proceeds to break off from our conversation and approach an attractive blond nearby, that flirty expression of his back in place without missing a beat.

Which just goes to show that I was right all along: *Dallas is hot. But I know better than to trust a hot hockey player.*

Involuntarily, my eyes travel back to Aaron, who's staring at me again. I want to be cool. Want to believe that I'm one of those people who rises above it all... but my petulant inner child wins out and I instead flip him off with a sweet smile, trying to ignore the way my heart is nervously galloping in my chest.

"Where are you jetting off to next, Olivia?" asks Colton Perez, another Cyclones teammate who has an impressive head of shiny hair that almost looks like a helmet.

I tuck my hair behind my ears. "Back to London Heathrow tomorrow."

"Whew," he whistles through his teeth. "Busy schedule."

I shrug casually. Like this small talk is totally normal when it's actually pretty surreal to be standing here with all these guys I've seen on TV countless times, playing alongside my brother. "Yeah, it can be pretty tight. Gets even worse when a flight's delayed."

It's not a complete lie.

When I *am* working as a flight attendant, I'm not officially on the clock until the doors of the plane shut and the aircraft is ready for takeoff. So, in that way, delays suck.

But what I don't mention is that I flew into Atlanta earlier today as a passenger, because I had a job interview to attend.

"Is that why you missed our game tonight? A delay?" Triple J asks.

"I was really bummed, because I would have loved to have seen Jake play."

This is entirely avoidant of Jimmy's question, but not a lie, whatsoever. I've never seen Jake play a game for the Cyclones live before. The last game of his that I got to see in person was over three years ago, when he was still playing for the Boston Freeze.

Today, I was hoping to make it through my interview in time to catch the guys' game, and I was pretty choked when I found out my interview slot clashed with the puck dropping.

"Oh, you missed a good one." Colton nods appreciatively. "Marino scored the most beautiful goal in the second."

"With an assist by me," Jake chimes in. "Dream team strikes again."

"Damn right." Colton holds up his hand and my brother high-fives him. "Pity you weren't there to see it, Olivia," he adds.

"Mmm," I say noncommittally, doing everything I can to not look in Aaron's direction again.

While I'm sad I didn't get to see Jake in action, I have to admit that I'm a tiny bit relieved I didn't have to watch Aaron Marino take to the ice to the applause of his adoring fans. He has a literal fan club who call themselves "Aaron's Army," and it's comprised of (presumably braindead) women who wear his jersey and hold up signs that say things like "Future Mrs. Marino" and the slightly more crass "Number 22, I wanna do you!"

Like I said, braindead. There are *way* better players they could be lusting over.

Although, Jake did mention that the Cyclones' captain is retiring at the end of this season and Aaron's being considered to step into the role.

Apparently the Cyclones' management are braindead, too.

But hey, I'm not responsible for other people's poor life choices.

"Let's get a drink," Jake says, and I nod at my big brother. I'm *pretty* sure he's glad I'm here, but like I said, he's not the most expressive. He's the strong and silent type, with a touch of grouchy, while I'm more the back-and-forth quips type. Also with a side of grouchy.

Some real fun genetics we have, clearly.

The two of us sidle off, leaving Colton and Triple J to chat with a pair of beautiful, raven-haired identical twins who recently appeared in the VIP area.

"Singers," Jake tells me as he follows my gaze.

"Thought they looked familiar," I say, now placing them as the hot, new R&B act who have that one song on the radio all the time. I smack my brother on the shoulder good-naturedly.

"Look at you, rubbing shoulders with the rich and famous." I frown. "Although, I guess you're technically included in that bracket now."

Jake huffs a short laugh, scratching at his dark brown beard. "Hardly. I leave the fan clubs to Marino and Sebastian Slater—pair of pretty-boy bastards. I never come to places like this after games. I only came tonight 'coz I thought you'd want to."

I blink, but quickly hide my surprise.

I have to say, I'm touched. Jake always had a particular loathing for places like this, and his coming here for me—coupled with his (albeit misplaced) protectiveness earlier—are how I know he actually cares.

It also reassures me that I've made a good decision, coming here for an interview.

After eight years living in the UK, I've chosen not to renew my work visa and instead look for a job that's based in the States. When the opportunity to interview with AmeriJet and potentially base myself in Atlanta came up, I jumped on it.

So long London, hello putting down some roots after years of spreading my wings.

Plus, given that Jake is perpetually single, and with our mom and dad both remarried with new families, I really want to make the effort to be closer with my brother.

Blood runs thicker than water. And while I know that Jake has a solid support system here (literally—his teammates are all built like brick walls), I like the idea of us being in the same city again. Besides, Jake's closest friend is Aaron Marino, and I really shouldn't allow that idiot to be the main person Jake depends on in Atlanta. Because if Aaron is anything, he's undependable.

I learned that little fact a long time ago.

"Hey, Jake," I hedge as we approach the bar. "What if I had the opportunity to be around more? Spend more time with you?"

"Like, in Atlanta?" he asks, but before I can answer he adds, "What're you drinking?"

"Beer, please."

He looks at the bartender. "Two Dos Equis."

I frown, momentarily losing my train of thought. "Since when do you drink Mexican beer?"

As far as I was aware, Jake's beer of choice was always Miller.

"Since always," Jake answers, almost defensively.

I drop the subject—my brother is one of those people who clams up the more you pry. As I accept my beer from the bartender, there's a tug on my arm and I find Triple J at my side, smiling eagerly. "Everyone went to dance. I ran back to check if you wanted to come, too?"

Jake scowls. "I don't dance."

Jimmy rolls his eyes. "Duh, I know. Which is why I didn't ask *you*." He turns to me with the most sincere expression, like he can't imagine having fun without me. I met the guy about eight minutes ago and he's already talking to me like we're BFFs. "I thought *you* might want to join us. You look more like the dancing type than your big bro."

I laugh, because he's right. Unlike my brother, I love to dance—it's the perfect way to let off a little steam and de-stress. But right now, I'm trying to tell Jake something important.

"It's a compliment," Jimmy adds gravely.

"Well, thank you. I do love to dance, but I, um, think I'll hang out with my brother for a bit." I look over at Jake, who's pulling his phone out of his pocket. "We don't get to see each other much."

"Nah, go ahead and have fun for a bit," Jake says as he peers at his phone screen. "I need to send a text, anyhow."

"If you're sure." Then I tilt my head. And it might be because things have clearly changed and there's a lot I don't know about my brother's life these days, but I have to ask, "Is it anyone special?"

My nosy question is met with resounding silence, Jake's lips locked shut on any possible juicy detail.

Guess some things *don't* change then.

"Come onnnn," Jimmy cuts in, and I get a sudden, vivid mental image of a fluffy golden retriever wagging its tail.

Jake nods at me, eyes still glued to his phone. "Go for it."

Triple J doesn't need to be told twice. I giggle as I let myself get tugged towards the dance floor, taking a few sips of my Dos Equis along the way for liquid courage. Just in case a certain annoyingly handsome hockey player happens to glance my way while I'm out there doing my thing.

Not because I care what he thinks of me, but because the last thing I need is to make a total fool of myself in front of him. Again.

I tip my beer to my lips, taking a huge glug as I'm blindly led into the crowd. But Jimmy loses his grip on my arm as we get into the throng. In the span of a millisecond, not looking where I'm going, I manage to trip over what is most likely my own feet—I've never been the best multitasker—and lose my balance.

I stumble forward, arms flailing wildly, as I teeter dangerously on my heels.

"Oof!" I let out a grunt, which, unfortunately, results in my mouthful of beer exiting my lips in a veritable fountain of spray.

Which, rather fortunately, ends up all over none other than Aaron Marino.

Because not only has he witnessed my unbelievably graceful entrance, but he appears to be the owner of the strong set of arms that just saved me from plummeting face-first onto the sticky dance floor.

Fabulous.

He looks down at me, his hands still on my arms, warm and sure, and then he smiles.

And he looks so handsome, so sincere, that I do the unthinkable and smile back at him.

"If you wanted to get my attention, you could have just said hi." The deep, rich timbre of his voice is unsettlingly familiar, yet completely foreign at the same time.

It punctures my fragile balloon of temporary insanity, and the smile falls off my face. I make absolutely sure that I have my balance before stepping out of his arms, hurriedly wiping away my foam mustache with the back of my hand and shaking off the tingling feeling of his calloused palms on my bare skin.

"Oh, Aaron!" I exclaim sweetly, like I'm suddenly noticing he's here for the first time. "I can't believe it's you! I barely recognized you without your 'I 🖤 MILFs' t-shirt."

He was given that stupid shirt as part of a hazing prank when he was named captain of the high school hockey team his senior year. He was forced to wear it every game day that season, but I don't think the guys were expecting him to wear it *quite* so proudly, with not a hint of shame whatsoever.

Although, in his defense, MILFs loved him, too. I knew this from spending countless hours spectating his and Jake's hockey games and watching all the moms inappropriately swoon every time Aaron looked up at the crowd.

"Come on now, Grizzy." Aaron's eyes crinkle at the corners as he ignores my dig at his former fashion faux pas. Instead, he smirks his stupid face off and makes no attempt to wipe my disgusting mouth-beer off his previously crisp and clean white t-shirt. "You didn't need to literally throw yourself at me, then make up a story like you haven't been glaring at me for the past half hour."

"I was throwing myself at the exit, actually," I retort, wondering if he was always this damned smug, or I just forgot the extent of it. Seems like the years of pro hockey have made him even more pleased with himself. "Felt a little nauseous being in your vicinity."

This earns me a lopsided smile. Insufferable man. "And here I was thinking you were in a desperate hurry to come dance with me."

"Never!" My cheeks burn as I glower at him. I'm 5'9", and in these heels I probably graze six feet, but I still have to look up to meet his stupid green eyes.

"Man, it's good to see you," he drawls as his gaze rakes up and down my body. For a moment, I feel entirely exposed. Naked.

"Wish I could say the same to you," I snap back, which makes his eyes twinkle.

"What are you doing in Atlanta, Lil Griz?" His expression is no longer playful, instead full of what looks like genuine curiosity.

As if I'm going to tell him that, after living abroad for years, I've been feeling more and more isolated as everyone around me settled down with close family and friends, and that now, I'm hoping to move to Atlanta to put down some roots near the only family I have.

"Do we really need to call me that?" I sigh. Jake and I have the last name Griswold, and as he became known as "Griz" with his hockey friends—a nickname which has clearly stuck—Aaron coined me "Lil Griz". Much to my chagrin, everyone referred to me as such until I got out of our hometown in New Jersey and moved to London.

"We really do," he replies with an angelic smile that makes me want to smack him.

So much for being all adult and mature about this.

"There you are!" Jimmy pops up next to me, relief dancing over his features as he confirms that I'm still in one piece and not faceplanted on the dance floor. "Oh good, Marino already found you." He looks at his teammate. "Where'd your date go?"

"Bathroom." He shrugs, like he couldn't care less where his beautiful date is right now.

For some reason, this infuriates me.

"Shouldn't you be with her?" I demand.

"I'm not sure the management of this lovely establishment would take too kindly to a 6′5″ hockey player frequenting their women's restrooms," Aaron smirks. "Plus, *she* might not take too kindly to that either."

I roll my eyes. "If she has any sense at all, she'll escape through the bathroom window and flee."

"Is that what you think," Aaron says, his voice level so it's a statement, not a question. His eyes glint, like he's arrogant enough to believe that I was referring to what happened that night, all those years ago.

Which I absolutely was *not*.

I try not to let it get under my skin. Remind myself that that was then, and this is now.

And now, I'm an adult. An adult with no need to dredge up my teenage petulance, because I have a whole life that has nothing to do with him. A life where my braces are finally off, and I have a career and a straightening iron that actually sort of works.

"You tell me," I say with a smirk of my own.

Just like I don't know today's version of Aaron, he doesn't know the current me. I'm a strong, independent woman who had a momentary lapse in judgment a very long time ago.

And no matter how good he looks tonight, that fact hasn't changed.

It's clearly not the only thing that hasn't changed. Because he goes on to wink at me, and then walk off without a care in the world... to approach the only other redhead besides me on the dance floor. Who, predictably, practically falls at his feet giggling the second she notices his attention.

What a douche.

Luckily, my impending move is about looking forward, not backward.

It's just a pity that "moving forward" means relocating to the city this goon lives in.

2

OLIVIA

November

Getting home at four in the morning after an inbound flight from JFK to ATL, followed by five stops on the red line and a miserable twenty-minute ride on a bus with broken air conditioning, is not the worst thing in the world for me.

I'm used to antisocial hours and late-night public transit, and my new commute in Atlanta isn't half as bad as the two hours I used to spend on the hot, stuffy, overcrowded London Underground every time I got off the clock.

But at least in my previous flat share across the Atlantic, I didn't have roommates who religiously insisted on practicing the bagpipes at six in the morning.

"Noooooo," I groan aloud. It's still pitch dark outside. I roll over onto my stomach, pulling my pillow over my head in a vain effort to drown out the horrific noise. "Not yet. I'm not ready."

"Hey, keep it down!" A crotchety holler carries up through the vents, followed by a flurry of banging noises. That'll be Mrs. Kibitzky, who lives in the apartment below us, tapping on her ceiling with her cane.

Not that I blame her. I completely support her position on the human alarm clock we are both enduring. Because being woken up after two hours of sleep by bagpipe music—more specifically, terrible bagpipe music where the player botches every second note—*is* the worst thing in the world.

There's a moment of blissful silence. And for a shadow of a second, the optimist in me dares to believe that Gregory might've ceased and desisted.

My hope is short-lived.

My roommate has unwrapped his lips from his bagpipes long enough to call out cheerfully in his lilting Scottish accent. "Good morning, Mrs. K! I have a new one for you today. It's called 'Highland Laddie' and I think you'll really enjoy it."

"No! Didn't you hear me, numb-nuts? I said KEEP IT DOWN!" Mrs. Kibitzky's protests are drowned out by a series of melodious-less blasts that shake the floorboards.

With a defeated sigh, I roll sideways and let my feet hit the ground. I'm awake now, so there's no point lying here in a bed of pain. Literally, I think my ears might be bleeding.

As I stand and stretch, my bedroom door flies open.

"It's over!" Romy, my other roommate, announces dramatically, her hand clenched over her heart. She's wearing nothing but a bra, men's boxer shorts, and (bizarrely) knee socks with heeled sandals. "It's really over this time."

"Again?" I ask dryly, reaching for my water cup and taking a long sip. My head feels thick from lack of sleep.

"Aren't you going to ask what happened?" Romy demands, half-yelling over the bagpipes blaring from the next room.

I wasn't, actually. Not because I'm callous or uncaring, but because this is the fourth time this month that she and Elliott have broken up "for real this time." And we're only sixteen days into November.

"He thinks my boobs are too big! Too big!" she continues, mistaking my silence for interest.

I stifle a yawn. "Did he *say* that?"

Romy pauses. "Well, not in as many words."

It takes all of my self-control not to roll my eyes. This time, it's boobs. Last time, it was because she asked him if he'd still be in love with her if she turned into an earthworm, and he said no.

Which I honestly thought was fair.

"But he said he thought Jessica Alba had a great body, and her boobs are way smaller than mine!" Romy sputters.

I stare at my roommate. "Don't you have implants?"

"That's not the point!"

My temples throb. It's *way* too early for this.

"Romy, it's six in the morning," I say as nicely as I can. "I'm sorry you guys broke up again, but can we please talk about this later? I feel a migraine coming on."

"Fine," she huffs. "Can I borrow five bucks?"

"All right." I don't bother to remind her that she "borrowed" ten dollars not two days ago. And another five the day before that. Instead, I grab a wrinkled bill from my wallet and thrust it into her hand as I usher her out of my room and shut the door, willing the migraine to disappear.

My next flight isn't until tomorrow, so today is my oyster. I usually like to start my mornings with a workout, but with so little sleep, all I want is to eat something that's been deep-fried to oblivion.

And there's one person who I know will be awake right now and would likely want to partake.

> Breakfast?

I put my phone down, hoping I'll get a response soon. And, as predicted, my brother texts back immediately.

Absolutely. Essy's?

Hell, yes.

Essy's, short for Esmerelda's Cosmic Cafe, is a retro-style diner that doubles as a fortune teller's den. I think. Esmerelda herself is the owner—a stocky, short woman in her sixties (I suspect her real name is something more along the lines of "Edith"). She's often the one running the floor, clad in a purple kaftan and a lopsided turban as she delivers meals to the wrong tables along with words of "wisdom" she has been prophetically given from the powers that be.

Bizarrely, Essy's is also top-rated for accommodating allergies and dietary restrictions.

It's one of my favorite places in Atlanta so far.

Want me to pick you up?

That would be awesome, thanks Jake.

Sweet, see you in ten.

No time for makeup or a nice outfit, but I ain't gonna complain about a free ride. I don't have a car, and while I'd love to buy one, saving up to get out of this looney bin of an apartment is taking precedence right now.

Public transit and hitched rides, it is.

I pull on a vintage Smashing Pumpkins t-shirt over my sports bra and leggings and brush my teeth, all the while tuning out the racket in my apartment and concentrating on visions of the breakfast bowl I'm going to order—scrambled eggs, duck-fat hashbrowns, extra bacon, extra cheese. Hell, extra everything.

If I'm gonna make it through the morning on this little sleep, I'll need calories. Lots of them.

And then a long nap.

Exactly ten minutes later, I'm rushing down the rickety metal stairs of my third-floor walkup and out to Jake's SUV, tying my red waves into a topknot with a scrunchie.

"Morning!" I say as I duck into the backseat.

Jake's girlfriend, Sofia, twists around in the passenger seat to smile at me. "Hi!"

Yes, I said *girlfriend*. Because Permanently Single Jake is now Loved-Up Relationship Jake. Sofia's existence came as a total surprise when I made my permanent move to Atlanta a couple of months ago. But it did explain my brother's surreptitious texting and his sudden interest in Mexican beer (she's from Monterrey).

She's also (indirectly) the reason for my current living situation.

Not that I hold it against her.

Sofia is the world's nicest person and my brother's polar opposite. She's the best thing that ever happened to him, and while I was shocked when I turned up on Jake's doorstep with a suitcase and Sofia was the one who answered the door with a warm smile of recognition, I'm really happy for him. Even if it meant that I had to move into the first apartment-share I could find on Craigslist.

My initial plan had been to stay with Jake for a week or two until I found an apartment with good transit links to Atlanta's Hartsfield-Jackson airport (or ATL for short). My brother did—regardless of Sofia—offer me his spacious guest room, but I didn't want to cramp his space or third-wheel in his budding relationship in any way. Especially after seeing how cute the two of them are together and how happy Jake is.

Having your baby sister hanging around probably doesn't pave the way for romance.

Which is how I ended up sharing a home with a serial

break-up griever, an honest-to-goodness wannabe-professional bagpiper, and a suspected underwear thief.

Oh, yeah. I haven't mentioned the underwear thief yet, have I?

Guess I'm saving the worst for last.

It's crazy to think that when I moved in here initially, I was hoping it would be a place that felt like home, where I could share the space with people I *fit with*. Like living out my own episode of *Friends*.

Ridiculous, really.

"I can hear the bagpipes from here," Jake says with a wince by way of greeting. "What in the hell is he even trying to play?"

"That one's called 'Highland Laddie,' apparently."

My brother rolls his eyes. "Should be illegal."

I shrug. "Makes a nice change from 'Danny Boy,' which was Greg's flavor of the month until this morning."

"You need to get out of that hellhole. Are you sure you don't want to crash at mine for a while? You know you're always welcome."

"It's not that bad," I assure him as I buckle my seatbelt. "The building security is great." *It isn't.* "And my roommates are just... quirky, that's all." *One way of putting it.* "And anyway, I'm on a red-eye to Frankfurt tomorrow night, so I might get some sleep during crew rest."

Jake snorts. "That's an oxymoron if I ever heard one—going to work to get some actual sleep."

"Not if you test mattresses for a living," I deadpan. Sofia chuckles but Jake, predictably, doesn't laugh (not that I blame him, it wasn't that funny). "You have practice this morning?"

My brother nods. "At nine."

"What about you, Sof? Are you working today?" I ask my brother's gorgeous girlfriend. I still can't believe he landed her; he's definitely punching above his weight.

Sofia is petite and fine-boned, sporting that pixie-like build on which all clothes seem to fall perfectly. She's a fashion stylist with an impressive list of high-powered clients, and it shows. In comparison to my scrubby outfit this morning, she's clad in a rose-pink silk camisole and linen pants, her chin-length dark hair elegantly slicked back off her face, and her minimal makeup flawless.

Meanwhile, I'm 5'9 with a solid frame that my father passed down to both Jake and me. Plus, my unruly red waves will not be tamed, no matter how many times I flat iron them.

I couldn't look as put together as she does if I had literal hours to get ready—and she had mere minutes.

She grins back at me. "I have an appointment at eleven. Unruly politician's wife. It's gonna be a fun one."

"What are you doing up so early, then?" I demand playfully.

"Wanted to hang out with this guy before he hits the road for his away games." She and Jake share an intimate look, and I avert my eyes. She must *really* love him if she's willing to leave her cozy bed this early in the morning to eat greasy fried food at a diner with her boyfriend's little sister in tow.

I honestly can't imagine feeling like that about anyone. I've dated over the years, but nobody's ever looked at me the way they look at each other. Nobody's ever changed their plans for me, or made me want to change my plans for them.

"It won't be long this time, Sof. At least I'll be home for Thanksgiving next week," Jake reminds her, reaching over to squeeze her hand.

Seriously. Who is this guy and what has he done with my brother?

"You're still coming, Liv?" Sofia asks.

"Sure am." When I got my schedule for November, I was shocked to see that I'll be flying in from LA bright and early on Thanksgiving morning, and then will have the next two days off.

When Jake heard that I'd be here, he invited me to watch his game that afternoon with Sofia and have dinner with them afterwards. I readily accepted. I'm enjoying spending time with my brother and his girlfriend.

Plus, this was the reason I chose to come to Atlanta in the first place: to spend more time with family and put down some roots.

Besides, being a flight attendant during the busy holiday season means I'll surely be away for Christmas. It's my first year with AmeriJet, so I'm super likely to get assigned a work trip over December 25th, especially since I managed to score Thanksgiving off. I get my schedule for December sometime next week, and I'm confident I'll be spending Christmas pouring ginger ale at 30,000 feet with no bad roommates in sight.

As if reading my mind, Jake chuckles. "Just don't expect her to come for Christmas."

"Really?" Sofia peers at me. "You don't like Christmas?"

"Ah, I'll probably have to work," I say avoidantly. It's easier than explaining to Sofia that I don't really *do* Christmas.

Might be an unpopular opinion, but to me, the whole "magic of the holiday season" thing is about as real as Santa Claus.

Christmas is simply *not* the most wonderful time of the year. All I remember from Christmases growing up is the distinct feeling of being let down and disappointed. The fighting and arguing. My parents eventually went through a messy and bitter divorce—over Christmas, of course—and forced Jake and me to pick who we'd spend the holidays with.

When each of my parents subsequently remarried, they began to create new Christmas traditions with their new families. Traditions that Jake and I never really fit into.

Jake didn't seem to care one way or the other about the holidays, but I guess I became jaded.

And so, since becoming an adult and moving out on my own, I've always chosen to opt out of Christmas all together. Just like Zooey Deschanel's character in *Elf*, my goal each year is simply to make it through the holiday season with as little fanfare as possible, preferably as far away as possible.

While I'm happy to be living in Atlanta and able to spend more time with Jake, that doesn't change my feelings about Christmas.

And this year, I hope to be eating moo ping skewers at a Bangkok street market, or barbecued bonito on the beach in Bora Bora. Anywhere that I can blind my thoughts in sunshine and breathe in a brick wall of humid heat and pretend it isn't Christmas at all...

"Yams," I say suddenly, changing the subject away from my most hated time of year. "For Thanksgiving, I'll bring yams. And pie."

"Sounds perfect," Sofia replies. She then proceeds to tell me that Jake has been YouTubing how to deep-fry a turkey, and that she thinks his apartment balcony is a terrible place to test this cooking method. You know, in case the whole building goes up in flames. Her concern earns a multitude of protesting grunts from my brother, who insists that he knows how to do it.

Which he obviously does not.

I laugh along with their teasing back-and-forth, and by the time we pull into Essy's parking lot, the sun is coming up and I'm kinda looking forward to a lowkey, burnt-turkey Thanksgiving here in Atlanta with my brother and his girlfriend.

With a smile, I step out of the vehicle.

"That happy to see me, Lil Griz?"

The smile falls off my face when I notice Aaron Marino.

He's lounging against his obnoxious sports car in the next

parking stall, wearing a wolfish grin as he surveys me and my scrubby outfit with glee. He's got those traditional Italian good looks—flawless olive skin, tousled black hair, and strong angles to his bone structure that are juxtaposed with long, sooty eyelashes and full lips that always seem to have a smirk playing on them.

You know, the type of good looks that makes you remember life really isn't fair.

Why on earth does Aaron get *those* eyelashes and I get stuck with little stumpy ones?

"Who invited *you*?" I demand. I cast an eye at Jake, but he's still in the driver's seat talking to Sofia. Why, oh why, would my brother do this to me so early in the morning?

"Good morning to you, too," Aaron replies, his tone smooth as butter. "Although, looks like you've had a bit of a rough start to your day. Did you not get enough sleep?"

He's doing this thing where he *looks* genuinely concerned about my well-being, but I know better than to fall for that. He's clearly taking a dig at my disheveled appearance.

Passive-aggressive prick.

Since moving here and starting my new job a couple of months ago, I've managed to only see Aaron a handful of times (lucky for me). Unluckily, though, in those few interactions, we've pretty much fallen back into our old ways, bickering with one another like children. But we're not children anymore.

I know I should rise above it all, but... *ugh*. The man makes me crazy.

"Had the best sleep of my life actually," I lie cheerily. "And I *was* having a good morning up until, oh, thirty seconds ago."

"When it became a *great* morning, because you saw me," he finishes my sentence (not), green eyes flashing with mirth.

"Agree to disagree," I huff as I turn on my heel and march towards the diner's front door.

Maddeningly, instead of waiting for Jake and Sofia to get out of the car, he follows me.

"I'm having a great morning, too, thanks for asking," he goes on. "Did a workout and got myself nice and stretched out. All while working up an appetite."

He runs a big hand over his torso, smoothing his shirt against his impressive abs. I try not to look at him, I really do. But I inevitably fail.

This fine morning, Aaron's wearing a black t-shirt that shows off every inch of his long, perfectly muscled, darkly tanned forearms, and a pair of black gym shorts that show off a lot of long, perfectly muscled, darkly tanned legs.

As if that wasn't enough, he's also sporting some annoyingly sexy stubble, alongside an even more annoyingly sexy back-wards hat.

The devil has no business looking this good.

"I've officially lost my appetite after that stretching comment," I retort tartly.

He laughs as Jake and Sofia *finally* catch up to us at the front door. Sofia greets Aaron with a warm hug—like she actually likes him or something—and Jake and Aaron do that bro-handshake-thingy all men do.

"Hey, man," Jake says, looking way too pleased to see his apparent best friend, before turning to me. "Hope it's okay I invited Marino."

"Of course it's okay," Aaron says cheerfully before I can reply.

Honestly, I'd take tone-deaf bagpipers and pantie thieves over eating breakfast with this guy, any day.

"Nobody asked you," I mutter.

Aaron ignores this very valid comment, giving Jake an elbow nudge. "Griz and I used to eat breakfast here together at least a couple of times a week before he went and fell head over heels for his lovely lady." He shoots Sofia a little wink, which makes her giggle. "Guess I'll allow it, though. I've never seen him happier."

"Happiest I've ever been." Jake puts an arm around Sofia and tugs her to his chest.

"See?" Aaron smiles at me smugly. "Aren't you lucky I'm here to keep you company while the lovebirds stare into each others' eyes over pancakes."

I grit my teeth. "So lucky."

Sofia claps her hands. "It's like a double date."

"Absolutely not!" I cry as Aaron holds his hands up and says, "It's nothing like that."

Well, there you go. We finally agree on something.

3

AARON

 Talk to me.

Pretty pleaseeeeee.

Come on, Aaron.

I'll make it up to you, if you know what I mean.

😉😉😉

My brows furrow as I stare at the string of texts from an unknown number. Then, I flip my phone facedown on the greasy table—every table at Essy's is greasy, no matter how much they clean them—but it's too late. My screen was on full display, meaning that Olivia saw the incoming messages as they blasted in, one-by-one, and jumped to a million conclusions.

And as luck would have it, Sofia happens to be outside taking a phone call, and Jake has chosen this exact moment to stand up, rubbing his hands on his jeans. "Gotta take a pi—"

"Shh," Olivia cuts him off, "we don't need to know what you're doing in the bathroom."

"Speak for yourself, I was extremely invested," I tell her, which earns me a fantastic scowl.

Jake rolls his eyes at me, then taps the table. "You two behave while I'm gone, k? Aaron, no flirting with my sister. And Liv, no murdering Marino with a butter knife."

"Can't promise anything," she mutters, shooting a murderous glance at my phone. She then levels that same look on me, which makes me chuckle.

"Such a little savage," I tease as Jake disappears to the bathroom, leaving me with no backup for the oncoming Olivia Griswold wrath.

Not that I care. I grin at her, and her hazel eyes narrow at me, pouty pink lips pursed.

I always loved how expressive she was. So much about her has changed since high school, but I'm still able to read everything she's thinking and feeling on her face like she's a walking billboard.

My phone—still facedown on the table—vibrates with a new message. I don't turn it over, instead pushing down my unease.

"What's up, Lil Griz?" I inquire with an innocent smile. I gave her that nickname a million years ago. Mostly because, back in high school, I thought she was insanely hot and it was a good way to constantly remind myself that she was my best buddy's little sister.

A decade later, the name has stuck.

She's still hot, too.

I cut a piece of waffle and dunk it in syrup, followed by whipped cream. Some of the guys on the Cyclones follow strict nutrition plans and count their macros during the season, but I've always been a bottomless pit where food is concerned. My motto is the more, the better. It doesn't seem to matter how healthy or unhealthy, calories just function as fuel to me.

"Everything's peachy with me. *Olivia.*" Her tone drips with sarcasm. "But there's clearly something very wrong with you."

"Nah, I'm good actually," I reply easily, then enjoy the way she looks even more maddened.

Despite all the years that passed without us seeing each other, it took us no time at all to reestablish this equilibrium— the one where I only ever seem to provoke annoyance from her, and for some reason, chase that reaction like a dog chases a freaking tennis ball.

Because oh yeah, she clearly still hates me for what I did back then. Or, more accurately, what I didn't do.

"So, I'm not correct in assuming that the texts coming in are from someone offering to make something up to you with sexual favors?" she demands.

She's cute when she's mad.

Not that I'd ever tell her that.

"You are correct," I confirm. Then, I meet her eyes and point down at my phone. "But as you can see, I am not taking her up on said offer. So honestly, I'm worried that you consider that to be something *wrong* with me. Your moral compass is clearly askew, Grizzy."

"You are the absolute worst," she seethes, her eyes flaring.

"So you seem to think." I shove another bite of syrup-drenched waffle in my mouth.

I'm playing it cool, but those texts have me a little stressed. What I don't tell her is that, at the beginning of this hockey season, a woman who goes by AaronMarinosMistress on social media started sliding into my DMs. It seemed innocent enough until she progressed to lurking around our training facility and even scoped out my house. No idea how she found out where I lived.

I did the only thing I knew to do: *ignored it all*. Unlike some of the other guys, I'd never had a fan with stalker-esque behavior before, and I wasn't too worried about it.

I've been pretty lucky with my fans. I'm flattered to have a group known as "Aaron's Army," and they often turn up to games wearing my jerseys and carrying signs. I've never actually dated a fan, but I always blow them a kiss from the ice, which just makes them scream and cheer louder. It's all in good fun. Tongue in cheek. The media sure seems to love it.

So, yeah. I didn't think too much about AaronMarinos-Mistress...

Until she *proposed* to me.

Outside my house, down on one knee, and surrounded by a million flickering candles which were most certainly a fire hazard on my dry-ass, August-crisped front lawn.

Half of me wanted to turn and run. The other half felt bad for this woman, who I'd never even met—hell, whose name I didn't even know at the time—on one knee in front of me.

The soft half of my heart won out, and so I approached her, gently helped her to her feet, and explained that, while I was flattered, I couldn't accept her proposal.

I was trying to be the nice guy, as kind as possible, while still making sure to be honest and clear about why we couldn't be together. Because never let it be said that I don't learn from my past mistakes.

She thanked me for being honest, and as she turned to leave, I thought I'd done the decent thing.

The next day, though, the story hit the internet. A story in which Brandi (her name, it turns out) painted herself as the jilted ex-lover, and me as the man who crushed her. It didn't bug me too much—like I said, I have a pretty good reputation in general, and most people seem to like me. The notable exception being the woman sitting next to me at this very moment.

Luckily, the whole thing died down pretty quickly, and the media found more exciting things to talk about. But I'm ninety-nine percent sure that Brandi is the "Unknown Number" texting me right now. And while I'm baffled that she managed to get my new number, I'm sure as hell not getting dragged back into that mess just to inquire how she got it.

Olivia pushes her fork around her plate so it makes that awful screeching sound like nails on a chalkboard. When she sees me flinch, she smiles and nods down at my phone. "You can't just discard your dates like used Kleenexes, you know."

"I never dated her."

Her, or anyone else, for months.

"So this woman you *never dated* is randomly sending you suggestive text messages, then?" Olivia's eyes are full of scorn.

"Yes, actually."

Her eyes narrow. "Oh, I get it. You're the *wham bam thank you ma'am* type. The kind of guy who doesn't have the decency to take women on dates and woo them first."

I know I should be bothered by what Olivia's implying, but I have to chuckle. "*Woo* them?"

She folds her arms over her chest. "Am I wrong, Marino?"

"Extremely," I tell her cheerfully, then take a slug of my coffee.

She couldn't be more wrong if she tried.

I've never ghosted anyone in my life, and always treat the women I date with respect, no matter how short-lived the flirtation. But I'm not dating at all right now.

In fact, the last time I went on a date was back in the spring. I remember the day, the time, the setting, everything. Because it was also the night I saw Olivia again.

We Cyclones all went to a fancy nightclub downtown after a game, and I'd arranged to meet my date for the evening there. But then, Olivia walked into the VIP section with her head held high, lit up beneath the flashing lights like some kind of religious vision.

The woman I was on a date with—while beautiful and funny and charming—was a total nonstarter. She had zero interest in me because she was totally in love with someone else.

And I, in turn, was so in shock from seeing Livvy Griswold after literal years, that I could only sit there, stunned and staring, mouth open like a goldfish as I took in that blaze of red hair and slinky silver dress that hugged every one of her curves.

My date ended up telling me all about the guy she was really into, and I spilled a little of my history with Olivia. How we'd known each other since high school, when I became friends with Jake. How we never got along, bickering back and forth as Jake laughed at our inability to get along.

How, underneath all the banter and sparring, I was always kind of obsessed with the fire in her eyes.

It was a weird conversation for a date, that's for sure. But all's well that ends well, because she ended up engaged to the guy she was actually into.

Not long after that, I found out that I was being considered for captain of the Cyclones, and I decided to give that all of my focus. Rearranged all of my priorities and put my dating life on the backburner.

I was officially named captain just as preseason got underway, and ever since, I've been dedicated to my new role. It's a responsibility I don't take lightly, and it's made me realize that I just don't have time for dating at the moment.

More than that, I don't want even a whiff of another scandal attached to my name. The impromptu proposal news was enough without it even being attached to a real relationship. Part of my duty in leading this team is to set aside all potential distractions and focus on the task at hand: getting my team to the playoffs, at minimum.

But I'm sure if I tried to tell Olivia any of that, she'd laugh. Not believe me for a second.

So, instead of saying a word, I swallow my last bite of waffle, make a mental note to change my phone number—again—and look up to see Jake by the door of the restaurant, signaling that he'll meet us outside.

I nod at my friend, then nudge my elbow against Olivia's. "You gonna eat that?"

She blinks at me as I nod towards her breakfast burrito, half of which is sitting untouched on her plate.

Before she can answer, I swipe it, lightning quick, then sink my teeth into it.

"Hey!" she squawks. "I was saving that for lunch!"

I swallow my mouthful of eggs and bacon wrapped in tortilla, raising a brow. "Hours-old soggy scrambled eggs? I don't think so."

"Actually, soggy scrambled eggs are *exactly* what I want for lunch."

I smile at her sheer ridiculousness. "Well, hey, this one's on me. That way, you can order another one to go and let it go soggy just in time for lunch. Deal?"

Her eyes are narrowed slits, her cheeks pink. "You are such a jerk."

"As we have already established." I polish off the remainder of her burrito.

Olivia sighs tiredly. "Shouldn't you be off somewhere practicing hitting a puck into a net instead of hanging out here annoying me?"

I smirk. "Practice? Baby, I don't miss."

When in doubt, act like a jackass, right?

"Try telling that to the six shots you missed last game." She fingers the silver cutlery next to her plate daintily. "And don't ever call me 'baby' again, or I really will stab you with this butter knife, no matter what Jake says."

"Look at you, memorizing my stats," I say with genuine delight. "But you forgot to mention the two I *did* score."

"Lucky breaks," she sniffs, then bites her lip, like she knows what she just said was a lie. They *were* beautiful goals, if I do say so myself.

"Well, make sure to tune in for our game against Baltimore tomorrow night, Livvy." I wink at her. "Because I definitely plan on getting lucky again. Maybe I'll even score one or two for you."

Her grip tightens on her fork. "Please don't."

"You'd be impressed, don't lie."

"The word you're looking for is *horrified*."

"Agree to disagree," I parrot her earlier words back at her as I catch our waitress's eye and motion for her to put the whole meal on my tab.

"I hate you."

"You know what they say, don't you? 'Hate is much closer to love than indifference.' Which means you practically love me."

Her cheeks flare an entirely new, quite pretty, shade of maroon. "In your dreams, Marino!"

And, purely for scientific purposes (AKA to see if I can make those cheeks darken to an even deeper red), I wink at her. "Every night, Lil Griz."

Like I said, when in doubt, act like a jackass.

4

AARON

Practice runs late and I stay behind for a while, practicing my slap shot into an empty net, over and over and over until my wrist aches. And as I do so, I replay every moment of this morning's breakfast in my head.

Particularly the moments featuring a certain fiery redhead.

Once upon a time, on nights before a big game when I was too keyed up to sleep, I'd lie in bed wide awake and find myself wondering where in the world she was. A part of me still can't believe that she's here in Atlanta after so many years of not even catching a glimpse of her face.

Still can't believe that, though she has clearly changed and grown up in some ways, she's exactly the same as she always was in every way that counts.

And her barbed insults and sassy glare still give me life.

Case in point: fueled by our earlier sparring, my shots are like rockets today. One after another after another are hitting the back of the net.

By the time I skate off the ice, I'm absolutely spent from giving one hundred and ten percent. But the "good job, son, way to put in the extra effort!" call from Coach Torres makes it all worth it.

Lead by example.

Those were the words of wisdom said to me by my old captain, Malachi Holmes, who retired at the end of last season. It happened to be a very good season, allowing him to retire on a high. We made it to the conference finals, getting beaten out in game seven after a rowdy match-up with New York. They went on to win it all, beating Denver in the finals for the title of Stanley Cup Champions.

"Win it for me next year, Marino," Malachi told me, clapping a hand on my shoulder after our head coach, Tony Torres, revealed the results of the team vote and officially named me the new captain. "Take home the whole damn thing."

The logical part of me knows that his comment wasn't a literal ask. But I feel the pressure squeezing me daily—I really do want to win it for him this year. Malachi was a great mentor to me, and I want to do him proud now that he's retired.

And not just him.

My dad's dying wish was to see me become captain of this team.

It's all he ever wanted for my career. All *I* ever wanted for my own career. Everything we worked towards. And I want to prove to *everyone*—the Cyclones coaches and management, the fans, my family, the media—that it was the right decision to entrust me with this role.

I want to prove it to myself, too. Silence that little voice inside me that keeps telling me I can't. That my teammates would have been better off voting for Slater, instead.

I grab my phone, check the screen, and immediately regret it. The unknown number has texted again.

> There's no upper limit on what I'll spend by the
> way! Either way, I'll have you…

And as if that wasn't weird enough, there's another message time-stamped twenty minutes later.

> Answer me, Aaron, or I'm going to have to do
> something big to get you to pay attention.

What the actual hell? This is just getting creepy.

I click my phone screen off and head to the locker room. It's empty, but I'm surprised to hear multiple voices carrying from the showers. I figured everyone would be gone by now—we leave tomorrow for two back-to-back away games. When we get back next week, it's our annual Thanksgiving Day face-off against Vegas, which means extra practices in the days running up to the holiday tradition game. I assumed the guys would be making the most of their downtime.

"What're you all still doing here?" I ask as I walk into the shower room, towel wrapped around my waist.

"Captain!" Jimmy Jones-Johnstone cries from beneath a stream of water. "Just the man we've been waiting for."

"Took a hot second," Dallas Cooper mutters.

I snort, stepping into a stall and turning on the water. "Hang on, don't tell me you were all hanging out in the showers together, waiting for me to get here."

Our shower set up features waist-high half-stalls, which means that we can chat while we're showering without a full-frontal nudity fest. But it's not like any of us make a habit of having heart-to-hearts while we're butt-naked.

Jake, who's in the shower stall next to mine, rolls his eyes. "Unfortunately, that is the case."

I have to laugh as I test the water, find it hot enough, and then throw my towel over the wall of my stall before ducking under the stream. I savor the heat on my skin for a moment.

"We have an idea," Triple J says excitedly as he rubs a veritable mountain of foamy shampoo into his hair.

I cast a worried glance in Sebastian Slater's direction. Jimmy's "ideas" are usually the harebrained ramblings of a maniac, and I trust Seb, the team's new alternate captain, to be the voice of reason.

Seb shrugs. "It's actually a decent one this time."

"Seconded," Colton Perez adds from my other side.

"Okay. Hit me with it."

"Teamsgiving!" Jimmy announces proudly.

I raise a brow. "Come again?"

"Teamsgiving," he repeats, not bothering to elaborate.

I look to Seb for help translating.

"We thought we could do a team Thanksgiving dinner next week." Seb explains. "We usually go out together when the game's away, obviously, but it's at home this year, and none of us really have family in town. So Triple J suggested that we start a new tradition."

"Teamsgiving dinner," I repeat slowly.

When Mal was captain and our Thanksgiving games were in Atlanta, he would spend the holiday with his wife Chantal's family. Some of us other guys would hang out from time to time, seeing as most of us don't have family living here, but we've never had an official team event for the holiday.

"Puck doesn't drop til 5pm, though," I muse. "Kinda late to do a big dinner afterwards, and I doubt we'll wanna eat all that before a big game."

I don't mean to sound like a killjoy nor a party pooper, but I'm trying to think about what's best for everyone. Team morale is important, but so is being in the right mindset to win an important game.

"What if we did it on Friday instead?" I suggest.

Jimmy nods eagerly. "You read my mind, Captain. That way, we have the full day to enjoy it."

I look around at the mass of soaped-up, eager-faced men who are looking right back at me. "Is everyone into this idea?"

The guys all nod, except for Dallas, who grins wickedly. "I'm in as long as I can bring a date."

My eyes land on Jake, who's scowling, as per usual, beneath his beard. "Even you, Griz?"

He shrugs. "I'm always happy to go where food is involved."

Fair. The guy's as much a bottomless pit as I am. Might be the thing that first drew us together in high school.

"We'll do it potluck-style," adds Lars Anderssen, our goalie.

"Okay, I'm in," I tell them. Anything that keeps up team morale is a win in my book. If they all like this idea, I like it too. But then a thought occurs to me. "Wait. Can anyone cook?"

"Yes," Lars responds immediately. "I am a great cook. We do not have the Thanksgiving holiday in Sweden, so I will bring a Christmas tradition from my country."

"Bring a couple of the women, too," Dallas says cheekily, earning himself a slap upside the head from the behemoth goalie. "Ouch!" he yelps, but then adds, "I'll bring dessert. I have a great chocolate chip cheesecake recipe."

"You do?" I blink at him, trying and failing to imagine our team's party-boy in the kitchen, baking up a storm.

"What?" He sounds almost defensive. "I love cheesecake."

"I'm making mashed potatoes," Jimmy says, which is a shockingly regular-sounding offering. "And my famous potato-chip-topped potato casserole with ketchup gravy."

Ah, there it is.

Dallas raises his eyes heavenward. "Seriously, do you ever shut up about potatoes?"

"I'm going to be ordering my contribution from a restaurant," Colton volunteers.

"Great idea." I will definitely be doing the same. My nonna taught me how to make pasta from scratch and I can whip up a few Italian family recipes with ease (read: help), but I am totally clueless when it comes to all other cooking. "Who's in charge of turkey?"

I'm shocked when Jake, of all people, throws up his hand, steam billowing off of his arm. "I am. I'm going to deep fry it in a bucket."

"Good luck with that," I say, deciding on the spot that I am going to have precisely zero participation in that activity. Except perhaps providing an extra fire extinguisher or two. Jake is known for a lot of things—he's a stellar defenseman and has a wicked, dry sense of humor underneath his typically grouchy persona. But a good cook, he is not.

"In your backyard," he adds.

"What now?"

Dallas smiles lazily. "Oh, didn't we mention that, Cap? Teamsgiving dinner is at your place."

Fanfrickingtastic.

5

OLIVIA

"Ladies and gentlemen, AmeriJet welcomes you to Atlanta, Georgia, where the local time is 11:37am. For your continued safety, and the safety of your fellow passengers, please remain seated with your seatbelt fastened and keep the aisles clear until the aircraft has come to a complete stop at the gate. Once again, thank you for choosing to fly AmeriJet, and on behalf of all of our crew, we would like to wish you a Happy Thanksgiving."

I hang up the intercom and my smile stays fixed in place until the last passenger has safely disembarked from the plane. Then, I finally turn off my 'customer-service' mode, which is basically just a huge toothy grimace and my soothing, almost-a-human-robot voice.

"Phew." I step out of one of my pumps so I can rub my heel.

"That flight felt like it took fourteen hours, not four," says my colleague and new friend, Jing, as she grabs a trash bag and begins gathering seat garbage. She winces as she deposits what looks like a used bandaid in the bag. "Gross."

"Happy Thanksgiving to us, indeed." I wrinkle my nose as I retrieve my cell phone and flick off airplane mode.

You'd be amazed what people leave in their seats—and we

only do an elementary garbage pick-up. I feel bad for the cleaning crew who come in behind us to properly disinfect the plane. They find the worst of it in all the seats' nooks and crannies. One cleaner told me that she found used underwear stuffed between 36E and 36F once.

Would actually make a great job for my pantie-stealing roommate, Shannon.

Speak of the devil, she texted me during the flight.

> You're away for Thanksgiving, right?

I frown as I type out my reply, idly wondering how long ago she sent the message.

> No, I just landed back in ATL. Going out for dinner but I'll be home later.

Her response is almost instantaneous.

> Oh, okay. I thought you were gone for the holidays.

> For Christmas. But I'm home today.

I still haven't gotten my December schedule, but it should turn up in my email in the next day or two. My phone lights up again.

> I didn't know you were coming home.

My frown deepens at her message, until yet another one pops up.

> If it looks like someone was in your room, it's probably just because I went in there to check that nobody was in there.

Should have guessed.

> Were you sleeping in my bed again, Shannon?

> No, but I think somebody else was.

> The sheets already had makeup on them when I went to check that nobody was in there.

Translation: Shannon was, indeed, sleeping in my room while I was gone. Probably while wearing my underwear.

Which serves as my daily reminder that I need to find a new living situation immediately.

Yesterday's reminder was the e-invite I received from Gregory-the-Scottish-Bagpiper for the "Annual Three-Day Christmas Rave" which will be taking place in our apartment. Because nothing says celebrating the birth of our dear Lord and Savior like EDM music, strobe lights, and ecstasy.

Thank sweet baby Jesus I'll be out of town for that particular atrocity, working somewhere far, far away, I hope. Although I'll have to make sure I lock my bedroom door before I leave. And maybe give poor Mrs. Kibitzky a warning that the apparently "annual" tradition will be continuing this year.

My phone pings again and I'm about to tell Shannon to *get out of my room and stay out*, but it's Jake this time.

> You home yet? Sof has an appointment that might go late so she'll meet you at the game. Your name's on the list, so just tell security who you are and they'll let you through to the box.

Thanks. Good luck today!

I feel like he might actually need it. Since I saw Jake for breakfast early last week, the Cyclones played two games on the road—losing to Baltimore, then tying with Toronto. I'd like to say this was all Aaron's fault, but I'm not *that* petty. Or blind. He scored the only Cyclones goal in either game.

Thankfully, he didn't make good on his threat of pulling a stunt like dedicating a goal to me. Although, a few hours after our breakfast at Essy's, at midday on the dot, I got a delivery to my apartment that consisted of an Essy's breakfast burrito, a can of Diet Coke, and a note that said: *I know you prefer your eggs soggy, but this will have to suffice for your lunch today.*

Which some people might have mistaken for a nice gesture, but they would be exactly that: *mistaken.* Delicious as the burrito was, it was clearly a signature passive-aggressive Aaron Marino move.

Aaron is clearly the same flippant playboy he's always been, and I'd do well to remember that. I saw the way he dismissed his date in the bar a few months ago, just as I saw those texts on his phone the other morning.

It's sad, really, that his neanderthal brain hasn't evolved from his MILF-loving high school days.

"So what are your plans for this afternoon?" I ask Jing as I start helping her with the trash pick-up.

"Hot pot," she says almost dreamily. "My grandma's super secret broth recipe. We eat hot pot every Thanksgiving now, but we also have turkey on the side. And my mom makes pumpkin pie from scratch for dessert because she thinks it's the best American cuisine."

"I love it." I grab a bottle of Prime and toss it in my recycling bag, ignoring the way my chest tightens a little at my own lack of happy memories of my family spending holidays together.

Jing is a third-generation Chinese American, and I think it's awesome that her family gathers to celebrate the holiday while putting their own spin on it.

"Are you still going to the game?" Jing asks as she ties a knot at the top of her trash bag.

"Yup. Sure you don't wanna come?"

Jing loves hockey—well, she loves hockey players, to be exact. The woman has clearly read way too many sports romance books, because she seems to have a very skewed version of what these men are really like.

"I totally would any other time, but... *hot pot*."

"I get it," I tell her as I rummage in my bag for one of my nut-free granola bars—all this talk of food is making me hungry. "I'd probably go for the hot pot, too, under different circumstances."

One of those circumstances being that, since moving here, I haven't managed to make it to a single one of Jake's games. Though, in my defense, I happened to be working during every home game so far.

I'm looking forward to seeing the famous Atlanta vs Vegas Thanksgiving Special in person. When I was living in the UK, I watched every one of Jake's games I could on TV, often staying up until the wee hours. I'm my brother's biggest fan and am endlessly proud of him... even if supporting Jake means supporting Aaron by default.

I can't believe they've ended up on the same NHL team after playing together at school all those years ago. Jake went on to play college hockey at McGill, eventually getting picked up by Montreal, then being traded to Boston, before finally ending up in Atlanta. Aaron, meanwhile, declared for the draft his senior year of high school and went third. He's been playing for the Cyclones his entire career.

"I'm honestly sad to miss it." Jing sighs dreamily. "Blow Dallas Cooper a kiss from me."

This makes me laugh. "My brother would have a conniption."

"Fine. Blow one to Aaron Marino instead."

"I will absolutely not be doing that in this lifetime."

Jing rolls her eyes at me. "I still don't understand how you could possibly think he's not a fine specimen of a man."

"I never said that," I correct her. Objectively, Aaron *is* disgustingly good-looking and I hate that for him. "What he looks like is totally irrelevant to me, because the man is insufferable and lives to make me miserable. Has done so since we were teenagers."

"Still," Jing continues all swooningly. "You'll be sitting with all the players' wives and families in the box at the game, and then you get to just *go* and have dinner with them all after. What a dream."

"Oh, no." I shake my head firmly. "Dinner tonight will just be me, Jake, and his girlfriend. No one else."

With any luck, I won't have to come across Aaron's incessantly annoying path at all today. I'm intending to hurry Jake and Sofia along after the game ends so we can enjoy our dinner in peace.

Besides, I have no idea what Aaron does for Thanksgiving and I don't care to know. Perhaps he doesn't even celebrate because he has male pattern baldness and a micropenis and therefore feels he has nothing to be thankful for.

"Happy Thanksgiving, ladies," calls Benson—one of the pilots—as he heads towards the plane's exit. With his kind brown eyes, he reminds me somewhat of a labrador puppy.

"Same to you, Ben!" I reply, and he winks at me before stepping out, whistling as he goes.

"That guy wants you," Jing hisses under her breath as we stack our trash bags in the galley.

"No, he doesn't."

"He winks at you like he wants you."

I give her a look before retrieving our carry-ons from the staff overhead. "That's what you said about poor old Mortimer, and it turned out he just had a lazy eye."

"Details, details." Jing waves a hand airily as we step off the plane and into the airbridge. "I'm right this time, though."

"Right or wrong, it's never gonna happen."

Ben is really nice, don't get me wrong. Handsome, too. But his reputation precedes him, and I have absolutely zero interest in dating players. No matter the career they have.

"Pity." Jing's eyes linger on Benson's retreating backside. "I think he'd be a total animal in the sack."

"Gross, Jing."

And with that entirely disconcerting thought about a man I work with, I bid goodbye to my crazy friend. Then, I duck into the airport bathrooms to get changed before hopping on the train to the RGM arena.

Nothing like spending my first Thanksgiving back stateside in a frigid, stale-beer-and-ammonia-scented arena, cheering on my big brother while doing my best to ignore the man I cannot stand as he skates onto the ice to the cheers of his adoring fans.

6

AARON

On home game days, we players usually walk into the arena with a swagger to our steps.

And it's not just because we're wearing suits we know we look great in.

Hockey players tend to be a cocky bunch, and I chalk this up to us spending so much time playing for stadiums packed full of fans with our names on their backs.

Honestly, it's a *good* thing. Overconfidence can do wonders for your game. Hockey is almost as much a mental sport as it is a physical one, and I know, from experience, that I need to work as consistently hard on my mental game as on my physical one.

So, no matter how I'm feeling on the inside—no matter how stressed I am that we lost to Baltimore last week when we should have won, and then barely tied with Toronto thanks to my fluke goal late in the third—I show up for a pre-game chat with the media like I own the place.

All thoughts about our shaky start to the season are banished far from my mind. I walk in like a winner. Play it up for the cameras. Answer questions from reporters about my stats, my team's chances in today's game, and my thoughts on how our offense is going to play to win.

Today is our annual Thanksgiving showdown against Vegas, and so I'm also expecting to answer a few questions centered around the holidays and my post-game plans.

But I've never had to deal with a line of questioning quite like *this* one.

"A... cockroach?" I ask, my brows drawing together. I must have misheard.

"Yes," the reporter answers firmly before repeating her question. "Do you, Aaron Marino, feel that you resemble a cockroach in any way, physical or otherwise?"

I realize, quite stunningly, that I did indeed hear her correctly the first time.

"That depends on how handsome the cockroach is," I joke, playing off the absolutely bizarre question with a charming smile.

"It was a regular American cockroach, according to my source." The reporter doesn't smile back. Her head is instead tilted in challenge. "Apparently, the options included cockroach, grasshopper, or small rodent, and she opted for cockroach."

She opted for cockroach.

What in the hell *is this woman talking about?*

I stare at the reporter, wondering for a moment if she has lost her marbles since the last time she interviewed me.

"Well, I'm not sure what cockroaches—or small rodents, for that matter—have to do with this afternoon's game." I try to redirect her questioning onto what actually matters (hockey) and get the interview back on track while pushing down the rising flicker of anxiety in my belly. Falling back on old habits, I shoot the scowling reporter my best flirtatious grin. "Unless we're talking about crushing them. Because this afternoon, we fully intend to crush Vegas. In fact, I'm predicting a shutout."

Media training 101: When in doubt, deflect, deflect, deflect.

Media training 202: Follow that up with charm, charm, charm.

Which is something I'm usually pretty adept at.

Usually.

But the reporter—Sadie something-or-other, who has an evil glint in her eyes that would normally intrigue me because feisty women are my kryptonite—looks less than charmed. Instead, she presses her lips together smugly and I already know that her next question will have nothing to do with hockey.

"Is it true that the woman in question was a member of Aaron's Army with whom you had some—*ahem*—extracurricular relations?"

The flicker of anxiety in my belly evolves into a prickle that climbs up the back of my neck. "I have no idea what you're talking about." I drop all attempts to be charming and opt for the simple truth. "But I think we should get back to talking about this afternoon's game."

"What are your thoughts on the cockroach being fed to an iguana?" Now, it's a bespectacled man from TSN who's been asking me questions about my stats for years. He looks like he's trying not to laugh. "Do you think this was a dig given that you're playing against the Indianapolis Iguanas next week?"

Well. At least *that* question was somewhat hockey related.

I blink at the man, trying not to look too much like a deer in headlights. Well, a big, handsome, suit-clad buck in headlights, because details are important. Paying attention to details keeps you prepared for anything.

And right now, I'm a sitting duck—*buck*—because I have clearly missed some detail that's resulted in me having no idea what on earth these reporters are referring to.

Unprepared and caught off guard. Two things a captain should never be.

I subtly curl my hand and run my fingers over the bracelet on my wrist, letting them move over the soft leather as my jaw tightens almost defiantly. "No idea. But I'd say we have a good chance of beating the Iguanas, especially with the way our defense is able to handle Talbot. He's a great player, but he's no match for Griz and Cooper."

"Still," Sadie presses, that glint in her eyes shining particularly evilly. "This isn't a good look for you."

"What isn't?" I finally ask, my jaw tight.

"You know. The cockroach that was named after you being fed to an iguana earlier today. Doesn't exactly sound like there's tons of confidence in your future as captain." She goes on to smirk. "Is it true that Coach Torres is considering naming Sebastian Slater interim captain until the heat dies down on this story?"

My nostrils flare, my cool expression slipping.

"No," I respond firmly.

Next to me, Seb opens his mouth, but I give him a little shake of my head. Slater jumping in to confirm my response will just make it look like we're denying something. Or worse, make me look incompetent.

When Mal retired a few months back, there was a standing ovation from the media at his post-game conference. He was brilliant, both as a player and as a leader. Commanded the respect of his team and motivated them through every situation. Never had a single scandal or caused a single scene.

I want nothing more than to follow in his footsteps. Be respected as both a leader and a man, rather than being pegged as some loser playboy who can't keep his personal life in check.

So whatever this cockroach story is all about—and whatever

it might or might not have to do with someone from Aaron's Army—I have to crush it. Right here and now.

"Hockey," I repeat, locking eyes with Sadie Something-or-Other. "We are here to talk about this afternoon's hockey game."

Well, Seb and I are here to talk about the hockey game.

Everyone else has clearly lost their damned minds.

7

AARON

"That was... weird," Seb mutters when we finally escape the media circus and are walking the hallway that leads to the locker room.

"That's one word for it," I reply with a chuckle, feeling lighter now that I'm not standing in front of a bunch of cameras with my mouth gaping open like a lizard catching flies.

Or cockroaches, apparently.

"Any idea what they were talking about?" my teammate asks, a bemused expression on his face that exactly mirrors how I feel.

"Nope." I shake my head. "But whatever it was, it sounds made up."

Now that I'm away from the barrage of questions, my head feels clearer. Don't get me wrong, I'm still entirely baffled, but I know for a fact that I haven't done anything "extracurricular" lately that might call my character into question, either on or off the ice.

I'm sure it's nothing.

Although that *interim captain* question was a little rattling.

Seb puts a hand on the locker room door, then shrugs at me. "Let's just forget about it for now and focus on the game."

I nod firmly. "Absolutely."

He pushes open the door and—

"ROACH BOY'S HERE!"

Dallas is currently whooping in delight. Meanwhile, Triple J holds his hands towards Colton and the two men attempt a salsa dance that's both terrible and terrifying as Perez belts out "La cucaracha! La cucaracha!" which makes the rest of the guys collapse in hopeless, side-splitting laughter.

Even the Swedish giant Lars—who might be the most stoic man in the universe—scuttles his fingers in a particularly roachy fashion.

It's a total locker-room looney bin.

Seb sticks his fingers in his mouth and whistles. "SHUT UP, EVERYONE!" he bellows, and a stunned silence falls over the place. Seb is the most Canadian person on the team—in that he's always polite and never yells. At anyone.

I'm actually impressed.

"What Slater means is: can someone please tell us what the hell is going on?" I demand, looking around the room.

"And why Marino's captaincy just got called into question by the media?" Seb adds. He seems almost as riled up about this as I am.

All eyes in the room grow wide as they slide from Seb to me, and I nod. "Whatever Cockroachgate is about, it's got lips wagging."

"Wait, what?" Jake's head jerks up. "It's just some stupid internet story. Your captaincy has nothing to do with it."

"Try telling that to that bloodthirsty Sadie chick out there." I jerk a thumb over my shoulder.

Dallas shudders. "Ooh, yeah. She can be cold as ice."

Jake smirks at him. "Sounds like you know this from experience."

"Oh, I do." Dallas's rueful tone makes me think that Sadie's behavior might have something to do with my teammate.

"Unsurprising." Jake rolls his eyes, then passes me his phone with an article open on the screen.

I scan the story—predictably, a write-up on a trashy news outlet—and my mouth slides into a grimace. "People are... naming cockroaches after their exes?"

"They've been doing it at zoos all over the country," Dallas nods sagely, because of course Dallas would know all about this. "Started as a Valentine's Day revenge thing. Atlanta Zoo picked it up this year as a holiday publicity gig."

I read the tagline from the zoo's website aloud. *"Name a cockroach after a particularly awful ex and gift it to a lizard of your choice this holiday season."* I shake my head. "Sounds idiotic."

"Agreed." Dallas shrugs. "But a few minutes before your pre-game interview, that ex-fiancée of yours live-streamed herself getting to the Atlanta zoo, naming a cockroach after you, and sacrificing it to a lizard. It's clearly getting a ton of shares."

"Super good publicity for the zoo," Triple J adds oh-so-helpfully, which earns him a whack across the arm from Perez.

Meanwhile, I'm totally confused, scrolling further down the article. "Huh? What do you mean, *my* ex-fiancée?"

As I say the words, everything suddenly clicks into place. I stare at the familiar auburn-haired woman on Jake's phone screen, and realize exactly which detail I missed.

AaronMarinosMistress.

Brandi.

Who was definitely never my fiancée, as Dallas damn well knows.

I really should have seen this coming. After the texts last

week got borderline creepy, I changed my number again without replying to her.

This is what she must have meant by "getting my attention."

Hell hath no fury like a woman ignored, it seems.

I scrub my hand over my face, then look around the room. I'm met with the confused, slightly concerned gazes of my teammates. So I straighten up, get my game face on, and channel my inner calm. Present the perfect picture of being totally unfazed.

"Well, guys, lucky for us, all publicity is good publicity. And the more distracted our opponents *think* we are with this story coming out, the more advantage we have to focus and get our heads in the game. So let's go out there and wipe the ice with Vegas!"

The unusually serious atmosphere in the room breaks as the guys laugh and cheer, and morale is successfully restored. My teammates all get back to their pre-game preparations, and I flop down on the bench, still reeling.

I hardly notice when Jake sits down next to me.

"You okay, man?" he asks as he claps a hand on my shoulder.

"Fine, yeah. That was all just a bit insane."

"I'll say." He frowns, squinting at the floor. "But we got your back."

"I know. Thanks." Jake is typically a man of few words, but the words he does say always matter, and I appreciate his support.

He quirks a smile. "It'll be good. Now, I'll leave you alone with your latest creation. What you working on now?"

I chuckle as I pull out my current crochet project: a little red fox with white paws and black whiskers.

"You weirdo," Jake mutters, shaking his head with a grin, and I punch him in the arm jokily. He stands to get ready and leaves me to my task.

This is *my* pre-game prep. A ritual, if you will. I'll crochet pretty much anything before I step out on the ice, but I mostly like to make stuffed animals. They make great gifts for when I visit the children's hospital—my favorite volunteer work. The Cyclones made an appearance there for a charity event two Christmases ago, and I've been going back regularly since. Talking to those incredible kids is the most humbling experience, and I'll be happy to visit them for as long as they'll have me.

Everyone on the team thinks that my crocheting is just a superstition. After all, as well as being cocky, us hockey players are known for our ritualistic superstitions—which can include anything from taping our sticks a certain way, to carrying good luck charms, to, in my old teammate Thomas McNulty's case, listening to "I'm a Slave 4 U" by Britney Spears five times in a row while clutching a rubber snake.

As far as the guys know, back in high school, I helped my nonna with one of her crochet projects the same day I had an important game... and then proceeded to have the game of my life.

While that is where this all started, my crochet habit is more than just a superstitious tradition. It's actually a huge part of my mental game—the best way I know to stop any racing thoughts before I skate onto the ice of a packed arena. There's something about my fingers moving on autopilot that helps my mind go blank so that I can focus on nothing but the game ahead.

And today—despite the unfortunate cockroach incident, and my leadership being questioned, and the Brandi situation—crocheting helps. As my fingers move, my thoughts melt like butter in a hot skillet, reducing in magnitude.

Just like the proposal story, this too will blow over. A cockroach stunt at the zoo does not a substantial threat to my captaincy make, and what really matters now is that I lead by example, like Mal encouraged me to.

Set the intention for us to win, and make it happen.

It's Thanksgiving, for goodness sake, and I'm gonna give us all something to be thankful for.

By the time I've suited up, laced my skates, and stepped out onto the ice at the helm of my team, I'm not exactly feeling better, but I feel equilibrium again. I plaster on my best game face as I wave to the fans and blow a kiss towards the cluster of Aaron's Army groupies in section 110, like I always do. I'm not gonna let one bad apple spoil the bunch, and I really am grateful for their love and support.

But before I turn away from the crowd, I see *her*.

There's a sea of people in the arena, but I'd spot that copper hair and sassy expression a mile away.

Jake told me that she'd be here this afternoon. It's the first time she's in town for a home game, and my buddy was happy his sister could attend. And there she is, in the friends and family box, standing a few feet away from Seb's wife Maddie, and our social media manager, Reagan.

Her expression darkens when she sees me looking at her, and this makes me smile. So much so that I can't help but wink at her.

She looks back at me like she'd like to stab me with the sharpest skate she can find, and I chuckle to myself.

Suddenly, all is right with the world.

8

OLIVIA

According to recent scientific research, octopuses occasionally punch fish who happen to be swimming by for no reason other than spite.

Apparently, the octopus is my spirit animal, because, right now, I'd like nothing more than to punch Aaron Marino in his stupid, pretty face.

He just winked at me.

Winked!

The appalling nerve of this man!

I glower at him, standing down there on the ice like a buffoon.

Our gazes clash and his green eyes flare as a slow grin spreads across his face.

Damn his beautiful, cocky self.

Jake is on the ice now too, also looking in my direction, but I know that he's not looking for me.

I yank my gaze away from Aaron-the-a-hole and focus on my brother. "She's not here yet," I mouth at Jake uselessly while willing Sofia to appear ASAP. I made it past security and through to the box unscathed a few moments ago, but with my brother's girlfriend running late, I don't know anybody here.

And I'm now being regarded with keen interest from other members of the box, thanks to said ridiculous wink from a certain insufferable man.

"Hi!" A pretty, freckle-faced woman with a light-brown bob haircut greets me warmly as she comes to stand next to me. "I'm Maddie Slater."

I recognize the last name—she must be Seb Slater's wife. Lucky for her, because the guy looks like a chef's kiss in human form.

Plus, she seems nice. Friendly. Maybe this won't be too terrible.

"Olivia," I tell her, awkwardly sticking out my hand and smiling back at her. "Jake's sister."

"I figured that's who you were!" Maddie says, then points to the purple-streaked-blond woman on her other side. "This is Reagan."

"Hi," I say, and she gives me a little smile, but her expression is tight as she glances at her phone.

"It's nice to finally meet you," Maddie continues. "We've heard so much about you."

"Really?" I blink. Like I mentioned, my brother is not exactly a talker, and it's a miracle from heaven that he met Sofia and actually managed to form a relationship with her that involved, you know, human adult communication.

"Sure," Reagan pipes up, her eyes darting again to something on her phone screen. "Aaron told me you moved here recently from the UK."

"Oh," I say slowly, wondering if Reagan is Aaron's latest flavor of the week. She seems way too normal to be dating a guy with an ego that large, but I tread carefully, just in case. "Yeah, I arrived in Atlanta last month and I'm renting an apartment downtown." And then, in case she thinks I'm interested in her man or something along those repulsive lines, I add, "Aaron and I know each other through Jake. They've been friends for years."

Okay, the thought isn't exactly repulsive—Aaron has an ego for a reason. The reason being that he's disgustingly good looking in a way that makes me want to simultaneously retch and stroke his biceps.

My neanderthal brain clearly needs to do some serious evolving, stat.

Reagan nods at his hulking form on the ice below. "Do you think he's okay?"

Weird question. But I do know that he gets nervous before games, and he does all these strange superstitious rituals—seriously, the dude used to have a locker full of crocheted animals at school—that he seems to think will help him win. Maybe she's talking about that?

"He's... Aaron." I lift my shoulders, like this statement explains everything.

But for some reason, she nods like this makes sense.

"I wouldn't worry, Reags," Maddie says. "It's just one dumb live stream."

"You're right." Reagan sighs, placing her phone to the side in a definitive sort of way. "So what do you do, Olivia?"

"I'm a flight attendant," I tell her. "I used to work out of Heathrow, but I changed airlines recently, and now I'm based in Atlanta."

Maddie's lips curve upward. "Ooh, has a hot pilot ever swept you off your feet?"

"I wish," I tell her with a chuckle. "Most of them seem to be looking for a good time, not a long time, if you know what I mean."

"Oh, we have a couple of those on the Cyclones." Reagan rolls her eyes.

"I'm aware," I say tightly.

Reagan laughs before she reaches out to grab her phone again. Her eyes widen when she looks at the screen and then she glances down to the ice, where the guys are warming up. Her entire demeanor seems to change in an instant. "On that thought, I, um, will be right back."

She takes off running, but I don't get a chance to wonder about her untimely exit, because Sofia swoops into the box in a cloud of sweet perfume and warm hugs. "Liv, hi! Sorry I'm late." She squeezes me tight, then squeezes the woman next to me. "Maddie, it's so good to see you. I love the new haircut! How's Gray doing?"

"He's so good. He just started smiling. Can't stop grinning at his daddy. It's the cutest."

Maddie whips out her phone to show us a picture of her baby boy. He really is adorable with his dimpled smile and big blue eyes. At the top of the screen, a notification pops up and Maddie winces. "Man, this is really blowing up."

Sofia's face falls. "I just saw. What was that awful woman thinking?"

"I think Reagan just went to her office to do some damage control." Maddie bites her lower lip, then glances at my confused expression. "Reagan's the team's social media manager."

"Right." *Not Aaron's latest woman, then.* But this doesn't quite answer my questions regarding what on earth everyone is talking about. "What happened, sorry?" I don't want to sound nosy, but my curiosity is getting the better of me. Even if this *does* have to do with Aaron Marino.

"Ay ay ay, you'll not believe what's going on with Aaron, so terrible!" Sofia says with wide eyes. Poor silly lamb, she actually likes the man, having met him in the context of "Jake's best friend," and not "Olivia's torturer."

She holds out her phone. "You're gonna lose your mind. Check this out."

I watch the video on the screen for a few moments before I have to clap a hand over my mouth in a vain attempt to muffle the laughter that spills from me.

Ohhhhh, this is *good*.

"Wow. That's, erm... bad," I barely manage through my giggles as the woman in the video shamelessly cheers as a lizard chomps the head off of a cockroach named Aaron Marino.

Happy Thanksgiving to me. Because for this, I am very, very thankful.

Maddie looks at me curiously, her head tilted to one side like a little bird. "You really don't like him, do you?"

"No, I don't," I say simply, not bothering to mince my words. "But don't worry, he doesn't like me either, so it's a mutual kind of dislike."

"Ah, I see," Maddie says in a way that implies that she does not see in the least.

Sofia, meanwhile, has apparently forgotten all about the conversation at hand as she blows a million kisses in Jake's adoring direction.

I also focus my attention on the ice. Seek out number 22 in the flurry of jerseys skating around and warming up. The next time he looks up at me, I give him a big-ass, genuine smile.

It might be exceedingly petty on my part—the childish brat in me winning out again—but I genuinely think it's about damn time that man's way-too-healthy ego took a hit.

Unfortunately for me, though, said ego-hit is short-lived, because within five minutes of hitting the ice, Seb Slater scores thanks to a beautiful assist from Aaron.

Ten minutes later, Perez scores with another assist from the Cyclones captain.

The second period doesn't go as well for the guys, with Vegas scoring twice to tie up the game.

By the end of the third period, we have a nailbiter on our hands. Both teams manage to get a few good looks but don't score, keeping the board at 2-2.

With thirty seconds to go, the crowd jumps to their feet as Aaron dekes out two of the opposing team's defensemen to carve himself a path of opportunity. He's a big guy—6'5, 230lbs, not that I've looked him up—yet he moves so fast, so fluidly, it's practically poetry on ice.

And no, I would never admit that aloud, even over my own dead body.

He outskates the defense easily, lines up his shot, and takes fire.

Scores.

The arena erupts in a deafening roar and it takes me a moment to realize that I'm on my feet with the rest of the crowd, screaming my lungs out for Aaron *fricking* Marino.

As if he can hear my thoughts, he suddenly looks up at me and grins like the devil.

I stare at him, transfixed, for a glimmer of a moment, and then sit my ass down as fast as humanly possible.

9

AARON

I've played hockey for most of my life, and played it professionally for the best part of a decade, and it still amazes me that every single game can be so different.

Sometimes, you're out on the ice and it's the most fun you've ever had. You're amped up, full of adrenaline, and everything—from the acrid smell of rubber and frozen water, to the feel of the ice gliding below your skates, to the bone-rattling sensation of being smashed into the boards—makes you feel invincible. Ready to take on the world.

Other times, it's a grind. No matter how much crocheting you did before the game, you're stressed about what went down with the media and what this might mean for your career. As much as you try to get your head squarely on the ice, your mind is wandering, preoccupied with what you could have said or done differently. Your hair is stuck to your forehead, wet with sweat, your ribs ache from that hit you took last game, and your entire body throbs with the lactic acid circulating in your muscles.

You're not playing for pleasure. You're playing to survive.

Today's Thanksgiving special is one of those games.

Well, it is up until the last few moments, when I catch Olivia Griswold on her feet and cheering after I score. I almost fall off my skates, I'm so shocked.

Her hair's mussed, her arms are in the air, and even from all the way down here on the ice I can see that her eyes are shining... for *me*.

Correction: for the Cyclones. But that's just a technicality, because as per usual when it comes to Liv, I'll take what I can get. And this? This is a world away from the dirty looks and pursed lips I normally get from her.

I'm not sure which I love more.

And I need this motivation right now. Guess that stupid cockroach story got under my skin more than I'd like to admit.

When the game concludes, I skate off the ice reminding myself that at least the stupid cockroach story didn't stop us from getting the W today. I'm glad I didn't let anything going on in my head affect my performance on the ice.

No matter how I feel, playing at my best is a non-negotiable.

I've barely unlaced when there's a sharp rap on the locker room door.

"Everyone decent?" a female voice calls. I'm not surprised that she's here.

I glance around quickly to check that there are no rogue penises on display. "Come in, Reagan."

The Cyclones social media manager peeks her head around the door. "Hey guys. Great game tonight," she says as she carefully averts her eyes from Triple J's currently shirtless chest. Which is kind of funny. For once, our brash social media manager is out of her element—mostly consisting of coercing us into posing for shirtless calendars and dressing up as elves for charity events and the like. Her eyes dart up long enough to meet mine. "Um, got a minute, Aaron?"

I already know what's coming, can feel the prickle of anxiety work its way back into my belly. Reagan is always on top of things, and I'm sure she was doing damage control the entire time we were on the ice. When Brandi's first "jilted ex lover" story hit the internet a while back, Reagan was quick to respond with extra positive social media content about me on the Cyclones account. She's good at her job, and I appreciate all she does.

"Sure." I follow her out the door and into the hallway.

Reagan shifts from foot to foot. Opens her mouth. Closes it. Smiles tightly.

"Spit it out, Reagan," I tell her.

She pauses for another moment before swallowing. "I'm assuming you've seen it?"

"I did, and it's fine," I say as convincingly as I can. *Because we just won the game. Because I have an otherwise good reputation.* "This is just a case of a fan who's gone rogue. There's no real story here. Probably just a slow news day or something. It'll blow over."

"Have you looked at the news since coming off the ice?"

I raise a brow. "No."

She shakes her purple-tipped hair then bites her lip nervously. "Well, you're both right and wrong. The cockroach thing is just a stupid non-starter..."

"I sense a 'but' coming," I say drily.

"*But* all the major news outlets have picked up on Sadie Lincoln's question regarding your captaincy. It's being discussed at length on all the sports networks right now, so I'm sure you'll be getting a barrage of questions about it at the press conference."

Lincoln. That was her last name.

The thought is senseless, insignificant in the face of the information Reagan has just relayed to me. But committing the fact to memory helps me focus on something other than my spiking heart rate.

I earned this captaincy, I tell myself. I've played on this team for my entire career and I've been fully dedicated to the Cyclones. I was the alternate captain before this, and the natural pick to be Mal's successor. People are aware of this. It's just a fact.

"Thanks for the heads up, Reags."

She's picking at her fingernails, looking uncertain. "Tony will likely want to speak with you about this."

"It'll be fine. I appreciate the concern, though," I reassure her with a small smile.

I believe it, too. Because there's no way Coach is gonna buy this.

My teammates have had their fair share of media attention. Dallas has been linked to several famous models. Jake got in an off-ice brawl with the Cincinnati goalie after a game one night. Seb got drunkenly married in Vegas last Thanksgiving.

Coach Torres wasn't the least bit interested in any of it. He's here for hockey. And as long as nobody's had a huge moral failure or done something illegal—and as long as it doesn't affect our performance on the ice—he doesn't give a damn what the tabloids say.

Reagan bounces from foot to foot, still seeming distracted and concerned.

I raise a brow at her. "Is there something else you're not telling me?"

"Well, the gala is in ten days."

Of course. Reagan is worried about the upcoming charity gala. And I get it—this is pretty unfortunate timing.

Every year, the Cyclones have a big Christmas charity event, such as our appearance at the children's hospital two years ago that prompted my regular visits since. Reagan always organizes the whole thing, and puts in months of hard work to make it special. Last year, we were Santa's elves at a toy drive, and this year, she wanted to do something even bigger and better.

And what could be bigger and better than a "star-studded Winter Wonderland event with a huge charity auction," as it's being advertised everywhere on social media?

Last I heard, it's set to raise more money than any of our past team Christmas events. And all proceeds will go to a nonprofit that gives underprivileged kids opportunities to play sports.

Yeah. Reagan really outdid herself this time.

The best part (according to her) will be the auction itself, where they'll be auctioning off... *us*.

Like you're big ol' slabs of meat, were Reagan's exact gleeful words, if I recall.

Which was charming.

And possibly not all together inaccurate.

She still won't tell us what the auction will have us *do* exactly—if we're being auctioned as dates or manual labor or what—but the wicked smile on her face every time the subject gets brought up tells me that she's got something up her sleeve.

Now, though, Reagan's face is lined with worry, and so I put a hand on her shoulder, hoping to reassure her. "If you're thinking that this whole cockroach-captaincy crap could over-shadow the gala, it won't," I promise. "I know how hard you've worked on this, Reags, and it will get the recognition it deserves. And if this whole thing doesn't blow over, I just won't attend. I'll match the donations privately to make up financially for my not being there." I nod firmly. "Either way, I'll make sure that nothing takes away from this event and the cause it's for."

She shakes her head. "As the new captain, you're the main attraction this year. You *need* to be there."

"That would certainly be for the best."

The gravelly voice behind us has us both spinning around.

Tony Torres stands a few paces away down the hallway, his tanned, deeply lined face even more deeply lined than usual.

"Coach," I start, and he holds up a hand to silence me.

"What a joke," he says in his trademark rumble. His face tells me that he's not happy. Not one bit. "I'd never consider replacing you with Slater because of one stupid media story. I trust you and your character, and I assume that whatever went down between you and that woman has been at least somewhat embellished online."

Entirely embellished, I want to correct. But I keep my mouth shut because I'm not a big enough idiot to backtalk Torres right now.

"But the fact is that Sadie Lincoln's ridiculous question has got people talking. And not in a good way. It's like the woman has a vendetta." I remember Dallas's comment earlier and try not to cringe, but Coach wasn't born yesterday. "Something tells me it has to do with damn Cooper not being able to keep it in his pants, as per usual."

I keep my expression neutral, neither confirming nor denying.

"Anyway," Coach goes on, "I just took a call from Dennis— he's in St. Barts right now—and he's requested that we do what we need to do to get this mess smoothed over promptly. He doesn't want to see our new captain being dragged over the coals and the sports networks questioning his competency." He raises a bushy brow at me. "I assume *you* don't want that either, do you, Marino?"

"No, sir."

Dennis Lieberman is the Cyclones GM—and one of the only people who vocally vouched for Slater becoming captain over me. I'd bet my entire year's salary that Coach is mincing a lot of words right now out of kindness, and Lieberman is actually seething while simultaneously crowing "I told you so!" at anyone who will listen.

"Be a good kid and clean up your mess. Get Lieberman off my back by getting the gossip columns off yours. Playing well on the ice ain't gonna be enough to get you back into his good books, so I'm going to need you there at the gala representing our organization and looking every inch the respectable captain. Lieberman will be attending the gala so you better put your best foot forward. Deal?"

"Deal," I say, my voice a lot firmer and stronger than I feel. Which is about four inches tall.

But what Torres is saying makes sense. We just won our game. I simply need to focus on presenting a good image and continuing to win. Then, this will all go away and we can get back to regularly scheduled programming.

Coach claps my shoulder. "Happy Thanksgiving, Marino."

"Same to you, Coach." I nod, my expression as composed as I can make it.

As Coach strides away, there's a sudden a hiss behind my right shoulder. "Yiiiiiikes."

I turn, startled, to look at Reagan. Honestly, I forgot she was here. I attempt to crack a smile. "Come on. That wasn't so bad, was it?"

But she's not even looking at me, she's staring at her phone screen. She swallows thickly. "Aaron. She has a ticket."

My stomach swoops. "What?"

"To the gala. I checked the guest list and Brandi's on there."

"Can't we get her removed? Have her barred?" The suggestion sounds a little extreme, but desperate times call for desperate measures. And I can't take any chances, especially when Lieberman will be there.

Reagan considers this for a moment, tapping her sparkly

fingernails against her chin, but she shakes her blond and purple hair. "I imagine that would make everything look worse. Add fuel to her fire. Give her even more reason—and ammunition—to make you look bad."

"True." I pinch the bridge of my nose, trying to organize my thoughts. "Lieberman is going to lose it if this causes another stir."

"I don't think it will." Reagan now looks thoughtful. "Brandi will likely want to be on her best behavior at the gala, too. She's not going to do anything that might get her kicked out. My guess is that she'll do what she can to get close to you, and that means—"

"Bidding on me in the auction," I finish Reagan's sentence calmly, while internally cursing up a storm as I recall one of Brandi's unhinged texts...

There's no upper limit on what I'll spend by the way! Either way, I'll have you.

Judging by what transpired today, I doubt she's bluffing.

"Yup." Reagan nods. "My suggestion is that you find someone to outbid her, or you could end up on a very risqué date with Brandi."

"Risqué how?!" I demand.

"Don't worry about that part." She waves a hand. "Worry about getting back in Lieberman's good books. Now, I gotta bounce, have a family thing to attend. But I'll see you at your place tomorrow, yeah?"

Oh, yeah. I momentarily forgot that a herd of people are coming over to my place tomorrow afternoon for a Thanksgiving meal l have not started prepping for in the least. I'm now beginning to wonder if I unknowingly broke a mirror and walked under a ladder on Friday the 13th, because luck does not seem to be in my favor right now.

Reagan bounds off towards the entrance of the players' area

where my teammates' friends and family are starting to appear. I paste on a smile before returning to the locker room to get changed, trying to be positive.

I can fix this.

In fact, that's what I'm going to do. Tomorrow morning, I'll come here for an early skate to clear my head and work this out.

But now, I'm going home to eat an entire pumpkin pie while watching Charlie Brown's Thanksgiving. And probably a pecan pie, too.

Bad luck, stalkers, and my captaincy being questioned aside... It's a holiday, dammit.

10

OLIVIA

After the game ends, Sofia dashes off to Jake's place to finish up some food prep, so I opt to go and wait for Jake. I want to give my brother a big hug and tell him I'm proud of him. Tell him that I'm glad I'm here today so we can celebrate Thanksgiving together.

And possibly hitch a ride with him to his place seeing as I took the train here.

But that's beside the point. Mostly.

It takes me forever to get to the ground level, which is mostly due to lining up for the public restrooms (while kicking myself for not peeing earlier in the VIP bathrooms), and then getting thoroughly lost six times. By the time I flash my ID at security and enter the players' area, some of my brother's team-mates have already emerged from the locker room and are greeting their wives, girlfriends, and families. Jake doesn't appear to be out yet, so I hang back, hugging the wall while trying not to feel like a creep.

"OLIVIA!"

I turn to see Jimmy Jones-Johnstone bounding towards me, arms outstretched. He lifts me off my feet in a huge hug, and smacks a kiss on both of my cheeks—I'd like to say it's in that chic, French way, but this is more like being mauled by a pony-sized puppy.

When he finally sets me down, I wobble, slightly dazed by his sheer enthusiasm. "Hi, Jimmy. Good to see you again!"

"Same to you. I've missed you so much."

"Likewise," I tell my apparent best friend, who I have met precisely once, half a year ago.

"I'm making six types of potatoes for the dinner, by the way."

Normally, I'd question such a whiplash of a subject change. But as it's Triple J, I take the conversational detour—and the number of potato dishes he's planning—in stride. "That's nice. You must be feeding a lot of people."

Jimmy nods eagerly. "I'm so excited for you to sample the mashed potatoes. They're my specialty."

"Oh." I realize he has his wires crossed and smile apologetically. "Sorry to miss them. I'm having dinner with Jake and Sofia."

"Yes, exactly." He seems totally unperturbed. "I'll see you there?"

I stare at Triple J for a moment, unsure he heard me correctly. Or maybe he has no family in town, and so Jake invited him to our little get-together? It's possible, though uncharacteristically thoughtful of my brother. Must have been Sofia's idea.

Deciding that this is the most reasonable explanation, I smile like I know exactly what he's talking about. And while six potato dishes seems excessive for our gathering of four people, Jimmy seems like an all-together excessive person and I love that for him. "Great! Can't wait to try the various potatoes!"

As he bounds off, someone behind me clears their throat.

I look over to see Aaron walking in my direction, eyes locked on me. He's freshly showered, his dark hair damp and tousled, and he's wearing a dark red Cyclones hoodie that's made of the softest looking material that I have ever wanted to *not* touch. He looks a little distant, his expression more closed than usual. A far cry from the winking, cocky Aaron who skated onto the ice not two hours ago.

I can't help but wonder what's happened since the game ended and how he's dealing with what appears to be a slight media frenzy. For a moment, I feel a spark of sympathy for him. No matter what I think of the guy, it can't be easy to be raked over the coals for the entire world to see.

"Hello," I say.

He regards me almost warily, adjusting the strap of his gym bag on one broad shoulder. "Hey, Liv."

"Good game tonight," I tell him kindly.

But only because he seems somewhat downtrodden. And it's a holiday.

And he used my real name, for once in his life.

At my words, however, the light in his expression returns and a naughty glimmer in his eyes makes me immediately regret my limp excuse for an olive branch.

"You did seem to be enjoying it. Especially at the end." He smirks.

I arch a brow. "Like I said, it was a good game."

"I'd say you looked just about ready to join Aaron's Army. I can hook you up with a number 22 jersey, if you like," Aaron goes on silkily. His green gaze moves over me and I'm suddenly aware of every single sensation on my skin—my jeans feel too tight, and my shirt feels too scratchy, and my bra feels like something that should be burned, and not just in the name of feminism.

It's all very unfortunate.

"I was merely cheering my brother on," I lie.

"Your brother who wasn't even on the ice at that moment?" Aaron's eyes dance, and I glare at him.

"And my very good friend Jimmy," I say staunchly. "I was cheering for him, too."

"That's no way to speak to the player who scored the winning goal specially for you." He smirks all smugly at me and I have to clench my fist to prevent myself from unleashing my inner octopus.

"Better not say that too loudly, or Aaron's Army might get jealous."

"Well, seeing as you're a proud member—"

"Have you seen Jake?" I interrupt coolly, peering past him like my blood's not currently sizzling in my veins.

Aaron looks like he might ignore my interruption and continue with his idiotic sentence, but he (wisely) changes his tune. "He's still in the locker room. You know Jake loves his long steam showers."

I do. My big brother was always using up all the hot water back when we used to fight over one bathroom.

"Wow. A straight answer for once." I clap my hands together in mock-glee. "Thank you. Now, if you don't mind, I'd like to resume my waiting in peace."

"If you don't want to wait, I could always give you a ride," he says in a low voice that absolutely does *not* result in goose-bumps on my arms.

"That will never happen." By some miracle, my voice manages to sound somewhat normal. I'm about to lord over him the fact that he doesn't even know where I'm getting a ride *to* (and also the fact that he wasn't invited), but he continues, "Suit yourself. Guess I'll see you at Teamsgiving. I hear you're bringing pie."

"Wait, what?" I frown, now entirely confused. "What's Teamsgiving?"

"You know, the big holiday dinner that was dreamed up in the communal showers."

I have no idea what on God's green earth he's talking about, but I do know the last thing I need to be doing right now is picturing Aaron all soaped up and sopping wet in the shower. So I latch onto the words *holiday dinner* and blurt, "You're having dinner with us this evening?"

"I think *you're* having dinner with *us tomorrow* is more correct terminology." He steps backwards with a shrug. "But as you wish."

For a moment, he studies my expression—which is undoubtedly both severely lost and mildly horrified. His full lips then slide into a knowing smirk I do not like one bit. Though it kind of makes the non-feminist-bra-burner in me melt, stupid girl that she is.

"He didn't tell you, did he?" Aaron asks around a deep, throaty chuckle.

"Tell me what?"

"I'd usually say don't shoot the messenger, but I think you might actually shoot me—or knee me in the balls—so I'll let Jake be the bearer of this particular piece of news."

"What news?"

He simply smiles a maddening grin. "See you tomorrow, Lil Griz."

Then, he walks off, whistling cheerfully to himself. I stare at his retreating form (studiously not looking at his backside—take *that*, inner bra-burner) with an ominous feeling gathering in my stomach.

11

AARON

I step onto the pristine, untouched ice and take a deep breath, ignoring the stomachache I currently have from demolishing way too much pie last night.

It's 6am on Black Friday, and as I speed-skate circles around the rink to warm up, letting my body work on autopilot, I try to organize my thoughts.

The stupid cockroach debacle is still haunting me, but more than that, the questions around my captaincy. I know I can't risk further pissing Lieberman off.

As stressed and under pressure as I've felt since being named captain, I still love hockey. I also love this team, and I'm going to do whatever it takes to stay in this role. Getting demoted is not an option.

So, the best thing I can do is to continue staying away from Brandi. It's the only surefire way to avoid giving her any little morsel of a story that she can pass off to the media.

Which means that she cannot, in any circumstance, "win me" at the auction.

I have to throw it. Get someone else to bid on me—using my

own money, of course—and keep on bidding until Brandi gives up.

It might not be a long-term solution, but it's the only one I can think of. For now.

Extinguish one fire at a time.

With that conclusion, I finally feel somewhat at ease.

I skate until there's sweat pouring down my face and my body feels loose and warm, as it always does after a good session on the ice. I make my way to the edge of the rink to grab my Gatorade and check my phone to see that there are twelve missed Facetime calls from my mom.

Normally, twelve missed calls from your mother would be alarming, but in my family, silence is the only thing worth worrying over. I once came back from an all-day training camp to twenty-one missed calls from Mom—turned out she'd run into the mother of my first girlfriend at the grocery store and was struggling to remember her name.

With a chuckle, I call her back, and within seconds, my mom's and my nonna's faces both fill the screen.

"Hi, baby!" Mom greets me. No matter how old—or successful—I get, I'm still *baby* to her. "Happy belated Thanksgiving."

"Hey, Mom. Happy Thanksgiving to you, too. You look great."

And she does. Smiling and happy and relaxed. I love to see it.

"Sorry I didn't get a chance to call you yesterday. Your uncle Dino had a very unfortunate accident involving the crabs he was planning on cooking."

"Is he okay?" I ask, picturing a pot of boiling water upending.

"His butt is out of commission for at least a week!" Nonna

pipes up from behind my mother, her lined face pulled into a grimace.

"Excuse me?"

"Kylie and Sasha took one of the crabs from the bucket and put it on Dino's chair," Mom explains, chuckling. "Long story short, he did not see it."

"The darn thing pinched him so hard, he ended up at the emergency room. Four stitches," Nonna declares.

The mental image is so good, I have to laugh. "Sounds like an eventful Thanksgiving."

"Assolutamente!" Nonna clucks her tongue. "Your uncle Sal decided that the crab deserved to live after putting up such a fight, so he made a detour on the way driving Dino to the hospital. He wanted to go to the docks to set it free in the ocean. He took my car, and there was such bad traffic on the highway that the detour took over an hour and Dino's butt blood got all over my new upholstery!"

At this point, I'm shaking with laughter. "Man, I wish I'd been there," I say as I wipe a tear from my eye.

I take a seat on the bench, feeling a pang of missing my family.

We're a close-knit, rowdy bunch. Always have been.

When I lost my dad to a long battle with MS when I was nineteen years old, my uncles, aunts and cousins wasted no time stepping in and helping us through the dark days. Words cannot express how much that meant, especially as I was playing for Atlanta by then, living a thousand miles away from Mom and Nonna. I'm grateful to know that they have a solid support system back in New Jersey.

My dad was my hero, and I miss him like crazy to this day.

He ran a business with my uncles that had him working long hours, but he always made time for me and came to every game he could. My family made a lot of sacrifices for me growing up, letting my crazy hockey schedule pretty much dictate all of our plans.

I so badly wish that he could have lived to see me become captain of the Cyclones.

Makes me even more determined to make his memory proud.

"Did you do anything nice yesterday, honey?" Mom asks. "After the game, I mean. We watched it on TV while we cooked."

"Just took it easy. Had some pie. The team is having dinner together later today at my place."

For some reason, this makes me think of Olivia. The memory of the expression she made yesterday—the one when she realized she was being kept in the dark as to the change in her Thanksgiving dinner plans—was *priceless*.

I can't help but wonder if she'll turn up today.

A part of me really *hopes so*.

"Dinner?" Nonna peers past Mom with narrowed, scrutinizing eyes. She has the same eyes as me; my dad had them, too. And for the past, I don't know, six to eight years, Nonna has been demanding that I give her a green-eyed great-grandbaby asap. "That reminds me. Have you been making my soup?"

"All the time," I lie. Nonna's Italian Wedding soup recipe is beyond delicious, but I don't really have time in a day to cook.

Nonna sniffs, like she smells a rat. "You look skinny. Tired. Always so hard on yourself and never giving yourself a break. Are you stressed about hockey?"

"Nah," I lie again. I don't need to relay what went down yesterday with the media. They'll just worry for no reason.

"Stressed about that girl?" Nonna throws out.

"I wouldn't say *stressed*," I muse absently, my mind tumbling back to Olivia again and the hilarious look on her face yesterday. I wonder how Jake broke the news to her that she'd be having dinner with me tonight. Well, me and a bunch of other hockey players, but I have a feeling that Olivia only focused on the "dinner with her nemesis" aspect.

"Good." My grandmother tsks. "Silly story, anyway. Nobody will believe such things about you."

"Oh. *That* girl," I say, the penny dropping that they have, indeed, heard about the mess with Brandi.

My mom's eyes narrow. "Who did you think your grandmother was talking about?"

"Uh... nobody."

"Well, are you bringing this 'nobody' home to meet us at Christmas?" she asks with a sly smile.

"No, Mom." I shake my head. "It'll just be me."

"As per usual," Nonna mumbles, which makes me laugh. Her lined face softens. "It'll be good to see you, Nipotino. Christmas wouldn't be the same without you."

"I wouldn't miss it," I promise. I've returned home for the holidays every single year that I've lived in Atlanta. I know how much being together for Christmas means to my family, but I also *want* to be with them.

As I end the call, my thoughts return to a certain holiday dinner I will be enjoying later with another family of mine. Despite my lack of domestic experience, I can't help but feel excited to host my teammates and the girl who lives to hate me.

It's gonna be a good day.

12

OLIVIA

I have never been less excited for anything.

And yes, I know I'm being dramatic.

But as I put mascara on my lashes and gloss on my lips, the girl who stares back at me in the mirror looks incredulous for good reason. Because she is spending the day behind enemy lines.

AKA at Aaron Marino's evil lair.

My brother regrettably failed to inform me that our Thanksgiving plans last night had changed. Instead of our quiet, family holiday dinner, we had pizza in front of the TV. Meanwhile, the pie and yams I made have been repurposed for a huge, potluck-style affair with a horde of hockey players. Hosted by my least favorite hockey player of all.

Jake "forgot to tell me."

Convenient.

Which is how I find myself on Aaron Marino's doorstep at 2pm on Black Friday, flanked by Jake and Sofia, my arms full of food and my stomach fluttering with trepidation. As much as I want to cancel this plan and run away like a coward, I know

Aaron would think that I canceled because of him. And I'm not about to give him that kind of satisfaction.

In fact, I have made a vow to be at my very sweetest this evening. Just to mess with him.

And, hopefully, to make him vaguely wonder if I tampered with his pie.

Which I absolutely did not, but the thought of him *thinking* that I did makes me feel very thankful for this joyous Thanksgiving occasion.

As we wait, I take out my phone and quickly check my email. My December schedule should be out today, and I'm eagerly seeking the silver lining of knowing which far-flung place I'll be in for Christmas.

The door finally swings open to reveal Aaron in the entryway, smiling like a total ass-hat (though he does, unfortunately, have a very cute ass-hat smile). He's dressed up, wearing khakis and a crisp, white button-down shirt that looks like a terrible choice in which to cook (or consume) turkey, but a great choice for showing off that annoyingly perfect olive complexion of his.

"Hey, guys," he says warmly, his lips tipping up further when his gaze zeroes in on me.

"Hey, man." Jake claps Aaron on the back. Sofia then steps forward and gives Aaron a hug, which he reciprocates.

He then turns to me, but doesn't attempt to give me a hug as he did Sofia, thank goodness. Probably because I absolutely would have kneed him in the unmentionables if he had done so, and he knows it. "Welcome. Come on in."

He sounds like a villain enticing us into his lair. All handsome, and ominous, and morally gray, and muscular to boot, and...

No, stop it!

Fricking Jing and her fricking romance books making me almost forget that this stuff isn't meant to be attractive.

While Aaron retrieves the food from my arms in a convincing imitation of a gentleman, I glance around. I'm half expecting to see blood-red paint, and bearskin rugs, and deer heads mounted on the walls, and furniture in the shape of coffins (because I have zero imagination when it comes to villains). But instead, everything is very... nice.

More than nice.

The house is large, but not pretentious, with light Scandi-style floors and an abundance of windows. Throw in the cozy-looking furniture and the selection of houseplants on display and, well, it's eerily similar to what I would want *my* house to look like, in my dream world.

Almost like he had it staged this way, just to taunt me. Which he obviously didn't, but still, I am finding it very difficult to believe that Aaron Marino has such good taste in decor.

As Jake and Sofia make their way down the hallway, Aaron hangs back and falls into step with me.

"What's wrong, Lil Griz?" Aaron looks down at me. The way he towers over me makes me feel positively diminutive, and I'm not sure I like it. "My digs not to your liking?"

"You have a beautiful home," I tell him primly, remembering my vow to be on my best behavior.

Those dratted lips pull up at their dratted corners again.

"Well, you look beautiful in my beautiful home," he drawls.

I roll my eyes at him. "Don't be facetious."

"Take the compliment." His eyes land on mine for one long, loaded moment before he smiles. "You guys are the last to arrive. Everyone else is out back."

He proceeds to direct me down the hallway to the behemoth kitchen, which smells like absolute heaven with scents of cinnamon and nutmeg and vanilla swirling in the air. He deposits my dishes on one of the overcrowded counters—there are countless sheet pans, crockpots, salad bowls, and serving platters taking up every square inch of space that's not crowded with wine and beer bottles and jugs of cocktails.

Overcrowding aside, the kitchen is annoyingly just as classy and perfect as the entryway. The statement piece is the farmhouse sink beneath a picture window overlooking a huge deck and garden, where the other guests are milling around.

Jake is already helping himself to a beer—Dos Equis, like always—from an ice bucket. The host, meanwhile, rolls his eyes at my brother in a jokey tsk-tsk manner and turns to Sofia. "Seeing as your boyfriend appears to have left his manners at home, can I get you a drink?"

She pokes her tongue out at Jake teasingly. "Absolutely, you can."

"Sauv Blanc?"

"Please."

"You know it, Sof," Aaron replies. It's like he's known Sofia for years. He's always had this way about him—he makes people feel like they matter to him. Feel warm towards him.

It's probably why so many women trip over themselves for him.

Well, that and his traffic-stopping face.

Luckily, I am not one of those people who buys into Aaron's ways of wooing people.

I watch as he produces a glass from a cupboard along with a chilled bottle from the fridge—one of those industrial-style ones that I'm sure holds many, many protein shakes. He pours a large glass of wine and hands it to Sof with a flourish, before turning to the stove to stir a simmering pot of gravy like he's Martha freaking Stewart.

At that moment, a couple of hockey wives and girlfriends swoop into the kitchen and Sofia turns to chat with them. Meanwhile, Jake waves at Dallas and Colton through the window, and makes his way out to the deck to join them.

I expect Aaron to follow suit without so much as a backwards glance at me, but he doesn't. Instead, he sets down his gravy spoon and leans against the island, casually crossing one leg over the other.

"Drink, Olivia?"

He says the four syllables of my name slowly, thickly, like his voice is drenched in honey.

And suddenly, a drink sounds like the best thing on the planet. Anything to ease the sudden jangle of nerves brought on by me standing here, in his house, without the buffers of Jake and Sofia.

"Yes." I swallow, then tack on a, "Please."

Because I will not forget my best behavior plan, no matter how weirdly fidgety I'm feeling.

"Beer, right?"

I frown slightly. "What makes you think I drink beer?"

I'm more curious than defensive. Last time Aaron and I were around each other for any significant period of time involving a drink, it was back in *his* high school beer-swilling days, while I was still religiously ordering Unicorn Frappucinos from Starbucks.

Maybe there's a unicorn-frap-to-beer pipeline I don't know about.

"You ordered one last spring," he says, his voice so low that only I can hear. When I look at him even more curiously, he adds, "At the club that night."

The fact that he remembers this makes me feel a little strange—the fact that he remembers seeing me at all, let alone what drink I ordered.

Clearly, he kept that little piece of intel locked away so he could pull it out to use against me when the time was right. Remind me of how foolish I looked when I practically fell on him that night.

Weird thing is, it doesn't feel like he's making fun of me right now.

Not at all.

The cluster of hockey wives are making their way outside, and soon enough, it's just the two of us in the kitchen, locked in some sort of stand-off. The roomy space suddenly feels far, far too small for both of us to exist here at the same time.

"Right." I swallow again, then force my lips to tip up. "The night you ditched your date."

He gives me a closed-mouthed smile, his full lips pulling back to reveal dimples. "Actually, she ditched *me*."

"Ha! I find that hard to belie—"

The glint in his eyes cuts my sentence short. My guffaw is still echoing around the kitchen, mocking me. Because not only was I about to accidentally compliment him, but I was going to do so rather enthusiastically. And he knows it.

His smug expression is smuggening by the second, and so I change course and shrug. "Well, whoever ditched first aside... maybe I want something a little stronger today."

"Margarita?" He jerks a thumb in the direction of a Jimmy Buffet Margaritaville machine in the corner, which is currently churning slushy green liquid.

"Why am I not surprised that you have one of those."

He pats the top of the machine. "I only take her out for special occasions."

"*Her.* Gross." I roll my eyes. "You boys and your toys."

"You want one or not, Lil Griz?" His voice lilts, teasing.

"I do," I admit.

"Say sorry to Margaret, then."

"Who?"

"Margaret." He pats the machine again, then gives me ridiculous puppy-dog eyes. "She took offense to you calling her gross. She's very upset."

I click my tongue. "How original. A margarita machine named Margaret."

"After Margaret Thatcher," he replies, his expression totally serious.

I can't help but snort with laughter. "Oh, yeah. The Iron Lady knew how to party."

"Damn straight, she did."

Aaron busies himself rolling the rim of a glass in salt before pouring in a good helping of the slushy mixture, careful not to spill any on the counter. Still, a little dollop ends up on his thumbnail, which he lifts to his lips to quickly licks off. And I have to admit, a margarita kinda sounds like the *exact* thing I've been wanting all along.

He holds out the glass, but instead of holding it towards me, he holds it above the farmhouse sink.

"Now. Apologize, or I'm tipping this down the drain."

I can't stop the gasp that escapes my throat. "You wouldn't dare!"

"Try me."

I squint at him, trying to work out if he's messing with me, but he squints right back, deadpan.

"Fine." I turn to the red machine, feeling my own face reddening at this ridiculous exercise. But here I am, doing it. Looking like a fool in front of Aaron Marino again, and yet... he's kind of acting a fool along with me. "I'm sorry, Mrs. British Prime Minister of many years gone by."

"She accepts your apology." He nods soberly, then holds the drink out towards me, all gallant-like and with a silly flourish. "One frozen margarita for the lady!"

"Thanks." I accept it, and take a sip to cover my smile.

Aaron grabs himself a bottle of water, and together, we walk out to the deck. I wave to Maddie and Reagan, who are cooing over a baby boy, and offer Dallas Cooper a wry smile after he winks at me roguishly.

"Nice deck," I tell Aaron as I take in the beautiful oasis that is his backyard.

"Built it myself." He glances at me. "I don't know if you remember, but my family has a deck company. Would've been my career, too, if hockey didn't work out."

A memory suddenly captures me of a teenage Aaron sprawled on my bedroom floor, the one and only time he was ever in my bedroom. That night, he was wearing a sweatshirt with a construction-type logo on it. "That's right. What was it called again?"

"Marino's Decks." He shakes his head. "My uncle Sal came up with it. Such a boring name. If I'd gone to work there, I would've petitioned to change it to Big Deck Energy."

I almost spit out my mouthful of margarita. I cough, then recover quickly enough to retort, "Well that would be extremely misleading."

"You're clearly misinformed, Livvy." Aaron flings his arms wide, gesturing at the hardwood below us. "I have the biggest deck in Atlanta. Fact."

I look him up and down and smirk. "More like you ARE the biggest deck in Atlanta."

He snorts with laughter, but before he can reply, Triple J bounces up to us. "What are you two over here whispering about?"

Aaron waggles his eyebrows at me. "My wood."

"His deck!" I practically yell, causing the thinly plucked eyebrows of a nearby hockey wife to shoot up to her hairline. I drop my voice, my cheeks surely fire-engine red. "He means the wood used to build this deck. Not like... any other type of..."

Shut up, Olivia!

I take a gulp of margarita to silence myself.

But Jimmy nods sagely. "He does have a very large deck, this is true."

This makes Aaron howl with laughter. "See, Liv? I told you it was a fact."

"Shut it, or I'll name a cockroach after you, too," I clap back, but Aaron's laughter is infectious, and I find I'm mostly kidding around, my insult delivered with lukewarm heat, at best.

So I'm surprised when Aaron's green eyes flicker and his strong jaw tightens.

It only lasts a fleeting second, but my stomach pinches with regret. I'm about to apologize for going too far, but suddenly, all traces of that pained expression are gone. Replaced by his usual sunny smile and twinkling eyes. Almost as if I imagined it.

"How original," he says, using the same tone I used when I said the words earlier. "Look at you, Lil Griz, jumping on the cockroach bandwagon."

Before I can respond, he fully turns away from me to address the crowd of people gathered in his yard. "All right, team. It's time to eat!"

13

AARON

I shove a forkful of mashed potatoes—made by Triple J—into my mouth and chew. Chew some more. Try not to gag.

Ugh. I hate mashed potatoes in the first place. And these particular mashed potatoes taste worse than usual.

Almost... *oily*.

But Jimmy—who is currently dressed in an orange and red knit monstrosity with a roasted turkey on the front along with the words "Let's Get Basted!"—is looking at me expectantly, so I smile and give him a thumbs-up as I hurriedly reach for my water glass. Down a huge gulp.

"Do you like them, Cap?" he chirps happily. "I added a secret ingredient."

I cough, gasping around the uniquely terrible taste of oily potatoes. "And what would that be?"

Across the table from me, Liv covers her mouth. I assume to hide a smile. Or spit her own potatoes into a napkin.

For a few minutes back there, I forgot about everything and everyone except Olivia. From the moment she arrived at the front door, looking cute as all hell in a short, dark gray t-shirt dress, her hair loose and wavy around her shoulders, she was all I saw.

As I led her inside, my entire focus was on her, barbed banter and sparks flying as we verbally sparred back and forth.

Kind of like old times, but with today's version of Olivia in front of me. She was always gorgeous, tall and leggy and striking with her bright hair and glinting eyes. But she's somehow even more attractive to me now than her teenage self was to me back then.

I love how self-assured she is. How she carries herself with her head high and her lips slightly parted like she has a witty comeback poised on the tip of her tongue at all times.

And then, she had to go and mention the effing cockroach.

I'm used to her trying to insult me—as I mentioned, I kind of live for it—but it was very effective in bursting my flirty-flirt bubble and swiftly reminding me of everything that's going on right now. Despite my problem-solving skate earlier today, the whole situation is still weighing on me.

On instinct, my fingers toy with the bracelet on my left wrist, smoothing the leather down against my skin.

"Horseradish!" Jimmy announces proudly, yanking me out of my thoughts. "Plus some honey. Oh, and a good splash of canola oil."

I do everything in my power not to wince.

"What a creative ingredient list to add to mashed potatoes," I manage to choke out.

Triple J is a great hockey player, and a stand-up guy who'd do anything for the people in his life, but I swear his brain is wired differently. Like he's tuned into some extra-terrestrial frequency that we mere mortals can't pick up.

"J, that is absolutely disgusting." Dallas voices what everyone else is thinking. "Why didn't you just use milk and butter like a normal person?"

Triple J glares at him indignantly. "I wanted to spice things up, add a little je-ne-sais-quoi, you know?"

"I do *not* know." Dallas's face is incredulous. "Haven't you heard of bacon? Sour cream? Grated cheese?"

"And where's the originality in that, Cooper?" Triple J demands. "Who wants to eat boring old potatoes that follow a boring old recipe?"

"Everyone, that's who!"

I can't help but laugh. As the two of them continue to argue back and forth, I push my mashed potatoes to the side of my plate as surreptitiously as possible before digging into my stuffing, which tastes infinitely better.

Questionable potatoes aside, the meal's going surprisingly well. Most of the team is here, along with their better halves and a smatter of sticky-fingered, over-excited children. Reagan came, and so did Stefani—our team chef and nutritionist, and the one responsible for making the incredible stuffing I'm currently shoveling into my mouth.

Laughter rises around the room as people eat and drink and, in Colton and Griz's cases, get a little merry. The two of them have decanted their beers into a couple of the glass pumpkin decorations I bought at Hobby Lobby earlier in a last-ditch attempt to be a good host, and are now having a chugging competition.

Jake wins and, luckily for him, Sofia laughs at his antics instead of publicly disowning him for being a man-child.

All in all, I'm glad Jimmy came up with this plan. All this togetherness is surely good for team morale.

"A toast!" Colton announces grandly when everyone's finished eating, raising his pumpkin high. "To our captain, for hosting us today!"

I smirk. "I don't believe I had a choice in the matter."

"To our captain, for putting up with our B.S." Dallas shouts, and everyone laughs. "May you lead us all to victory this year."

"No pressure," I joke, even as I feel pressure. I shake it off and raise my glass high, saluting my teammates. "To the Cyclones!"

Everyone cheers and raises their glasses (or various drinking containers) accordingly.

"To spending Thanksgiving with all you beautiful people!" Reagan adds.

"To the best hockey team on earth!" Triple J pipes up.

The cheers get louder.

"TO THIS BEING THE SEASON WHEN WE FINALLY WIN THE STANLEY MOTHERF—"

"Kids!" I swiftly cut Perez off. "There are kids here!"

Seb shoots me a grateful look, which is a little funny seeing as his son is, like, two months old and a little blob of a human who can't understand anything being said right now.

"Whoops." Colton grins goofily, swaying on his feet. "I mean, to the Cyclones winning the Stanley FRICKING Cup!"

He looks ridiculously proud of this delayed correction, but nevertheless, everyone gets to their feet and clinks glasses. It's the sort of festive, celebratory scene that would make anyone feel warm and fuzzy inside.

After cheersing everyone in my immediate vicinity, I turn to Olivia. But instead of joining in the celebration, she's chewing her lip while texting with one hand.

Anyone except Olivia, apparently.

"Not going to cheers your favorite hockey player?" I ask her with a waggle of my brows.

"Mmm?" she says, holding out her glass without even looking up from her phone screen. My words must sink in belatedly because her head snaps up, her eyes fix on me, and she smiles slyly. "Jimmy and I clinked glasses already."

Anyone else might have missed it. Might just assume that she was simply distracted by a run-of-the-mill text. But I know Olivia, and I know that, while she has an excellent poker face, she holds all her cards in her eyes...

Sophomore year of high school, she joked about my (very ill-advised and short-lived) faux-hawk hairstyle with a big smile, but those eyes stayed flat. Turned out she'd just gotten a D on a test.

A year later, she laughed about how Arjun Singh turned down her invitation to the Sadie Hawkins dance, but her gaze was glued to the floor to hide the hurt.

That night, my senior year when I tumbled through her bedroom window and we talked on her bedroom floor, her eyes were sparkling and bright. But by the time I left, I'd accidentally extinguished all of those sparks. Let both her, and myself, believe for a moment that we could have something we couldn't. That I could feel something I shouldn't.

A few months ago, when she unceremoniously crashed into me in that club, and her eyes were flashing with the same panic I felt seeing her again for the first time in years.

And, right now, in front of me in my dining room, her smile is fox-like and sexy and cunning, but her eyes are defeated.

Something is wrong. And it's tied to whatever she was just doing on her phone.

Who upset her?

I want to ask if everything's okay, but knowing Olivia, she's not going to volunteer that information in front of all these people. And especially not to me.

So, I try another tactic instead.

"Okay, fine," I say with a shrug, hoping to propel her back into playful mode and take her mind off of whatever's going on. "If not your favorite hockey player in the room, then the sexiest one."

I'm gratified to see the mischief make its way back into her hazel eyes and dance there for a moment before she leans over and extends her glass to Dallas.

My teammate—who has uncharacteristically shown up to dinner without a female companion—gives her his best smile. "Cheers, Griz's little sister."

"Cheers, second best defenseman on the Cyclones," she says silkily, her eyes shining.

Dallas quickly clocks what she's saying—he plays defense on our first line next to Jake, and she's clearly seconding him to her brother. He throws his head back and laughs. "You're mouthier than your big brother. I like it."

Dallas is now donning his bedroom eyes, gazing at Olivia like he's a starving man and she's an all-you-can-eat buffet. This little exchange flares up a protective instinct in me. Makes me kind of want to deck my own teammate. Which is absolutely absurd.

"Hell yeah, she is," Jake crows proudly, more animated than usual thanks to his beer-buzz. And also more obtuse, because he's clearly missing Dallas's not-so-veiled flirting. "And she's right, too."

Liv sits back down and leans forward on the table, her expression triumphant. "Done, Marino. Anyone else you'd like me to clink glasses with?"

I shift forward, too, so my elbows are on the table and I'm mirroring her pose.

"How about a toast to your host for the evening?"

"Fine." She gives me a little smile as she holds up her margarita, still gloating over what she thinks was her win. "Happy now?"

I tap my glass against hers. "Absolutely."

And I am. Because for once, I've actually made her happy, which feels like *my* win.

14

OLIVIA

"And now, we eat the rice porridge!"

Lars Anderssen claps his gargantuan hands together, icy blue eyes glinting with conspiratorial excitement.

We've just finished dinner and are about to partake in what Lars says is a peak Scandinavian Christmas tradition.

And while I'm excited to try Swedish rice porridge, I wish the moment wasn't being overshadowed by the news I just received.

I scowl down at my phone again, but I have no new notifications.

Lars's wife Lena—who I've had the pleasure of exchanging a few words with this evening—smiles cheerily as she produces a literal cauldron from beneath the table. She holds it up for the room to see. "There is a single almond hidden in here. Whoever is lucky enough to find the almond in their bowl is the winner!"

Guess I won't be eating that.

I'll probably stick to the pie I brought. At least I can be sure of its ingredients. Dessert was really the only meal I was concerned about tonight. Although, given Jimmy's apparent penchant for putting literally anything and everything into his potatoes, I did have to double check his "recipes" with him.

And yes, I'm aware that I've just stuffed myself silly on turkey and all the fixings, but I'm a girl who always has room for dessert.

"Ooh, is it timed?" Colton asks, looking genuinely invested. They all do, actually.

These hockey players are a competitive bunch. At the word "winner," they donned their game faces—Jake's eyes are narrowed, Dallas is wielding his spoon, and across from me, Aaron is rolling up his shirt sleeves.

Which is ridiculous. And even more distracting to my already distracted mind, because now, those thick, muscular forearms are on display, veins slicing up his olive skin. A black leather rope bracelet is wrapped around his left wrist. I've noticed it a few times lately, but I haven't thought much of it until now—for a guy who clearly considered his outfit this evening, the bracelet doesn't exactly match his white-shirt-and-extremely-well-fitting-khakis aesthetic.

Must be yet another superstitious hockey thing.

"Nope." Lars shakes his head, then glances around mischievously, looking not unlike a hulking blond leprechaun. "But you're on the right track. It's a game of who can eat the porridge and find the almond the fastest."

"I've always been the fastest at shotgunning beers," Colton boasts proudly, until he scrutinizes the cauldron and its goopy contents. "Though *this* might be a different beast."

"What do we win?" Aaron pipes up.

"Ah, yes, the best part." Lars's eyes widen with excitement. "The winner receives the marzipan pig!"

Of course they do.

It's so totally random that I love it, but it's also another reason I unfortunately can't take part in this seemingly delightful Norse tradition.

"A marzipan *pig*?" For once, even Jimmy looks thrown off.

"Ya." Lena nods solemnly. "It is very good luck to win."

While the guys initially seemed a tad thrown-off at the mention of the marzipan winnings, the words "good luck" act as some sort of trigger. The competition turns even fiercer, the fantastically bizarre prize clearly no deterrent.

I glance at my phone again—still nothing—and look up to find Aaron watching me. "This is no time to be checking your phone, Lil Griz. This is game-face time!"

I roll my eyes. "You really wanna win a marzipan piggie that badly, Marino?"

He looks at me like I'm a total imbecile. "It's not about *what* you win, it's about *being* a winner."

"Duh," Jake adds, drawing out the word like he's a sorority girl. Which gives me final confirmation that he has, indeed, had at least *dos* too many Dos Equis.

Lena begins dishing out portions of the dessert and the Cyclones players all lean forward, eagerly awaiting a bowlful. Meanwhile, I sit back in my chair, moving out of the way of the testosterone-fueled competitiveness.

And that's when my phone buzzes on my lap.

It's my supervisor. *Finally.*

When I got the email about twenty minutes ago from Ameri-iJet HR, I didn't think much of it at first. Until I actually opened the email, scanned next month's schedule and...

How, oh how, am I off for Christmas?!

It still doesn't seem possible. I was so sure that by Christmas Eve I'd be en route to Bangkok or Bora Bora—or Timbuktu, for all I cared—that it took me a few moments to notice the little block of green on the grid, stretching from December 23rd to the 27th.

No matter how many times I refreshed and reopened the email, the block of green remained the same, glaring up at me tauntingly.

I told myself not to panic, not to stress over something I could fix. With my phone propped on my thighs under the table so as to not look completely and utterly rude to the rest of the dinner guests, I've since posted a trade request on our company's internal website, and texted my supervisor and every other colleague I can think of. I've tried to make my messages short and sweet and not nearly as panic-stricken as I'm currently feeling.

Because so far *no one* I've contacted is willing to swap shifts with me. You'd think someone would jump at the opportunity to have the holidays off work, but so far, I'm seeing excuse after excuse. Apparently, AmeriJet pays extra for Christmas shifts, and my colleagues are eager for the dough.

As I open the text from my supervisor, my heart sinks all the more.

There's nothing he can do.

Fricking Christmas, I tell you. I'm legitimately starting to think that Christmas magic *is* real, but it's black magic that's out to get me.

Pressure builds in my temples. On top of my general need to escape for the holidays, I obviously cannot be anywhere near my apartment during the seasonal sacrilege that is my roommates' three-day Christmas rave.

I'm so preoccupied, chewing on my lip and texting Jing to see if she knows anyone else who might like to have Christmas off, that I barely register the bowl placed in front of me.

"Thanks," I say with a distracted smile.

My attention still firmly focused on the three little dots where Jing is typing, I dig into my bowl.

The spoon is halfway to my lips, my eyes locked on a text

notification from a colleague saying that they need the Christmas hours to pay off the "massive inflatable Santa" they're buying this year, when Aaron suddenly stands up, leans across the table, and whacks my spoon right out of my hand.

The cutlery goes flying, hitting the gorgeous, light accent wall with a loud clank and splashing a spray of sticky beige gloop all over the place.

I blink in shock.

"The wallpaper!" I cry, dismayed mostly for the decor and not the sudden loss of my spoon.

"What the hell, man?" Jake jumps up and lurches towards Aaron, like he's going to do... something. Goodness knows what, but something. I doubt he knows himself, because he looks confused as can be.

Aaron doesn't spare my brother a glance. He simply sticks out a big hand, effectively holding Jake at arm's length as he pins me with his gaze.

"You almost kill yourself right here at the table and you're worried about my damn wallpaper?" he demands. His face is like thunder, and I notice he's pale beneath his golden complexion.

The room has gone totally silent, all eyes turned towards us.

My eye twitches. "I... What?"

Aaron opens his mouth, looking exasperated, but before he can say anything, Jimmy pipes up. "Oh, would you look at that. Olivia won!"

I look down at my bowl, which is full of the goopy substance that I now realize is rice porridge.

And there it is, clearly exposed by my spoonful: the almond.

The almond I'd totally forgotten about.

The almond I'm totally allergic to.

Jake's face turns ashen and he swears under his breath. His body language changes as he puts a grateful hand on Aaron's shoulder. "Woah. Thanks, man. Good catch." He turns to address the table. "She's allergic."

My face grows hot.

"I wasn't paying attention," I say, feeling like a goldfish in a bowl, only stupider.

"Oh my gosh, Olivia, I didn't know! I'm so sorry!" Lena wrings her hands, looking distraught.

"No. It was my own fault," I tell her with a shake of my head. My cheeks are on fire from the near miss and also from the embarrassment of causing such a commotion. "I have an EpiPen in my bag, anyway, so nothing terrible would have happened..."

It would have just been really awkward. Even more awkward than this.

Aaron's still looking at me, those green eyes studying my face intently.

I want to thank him. Right after the floor swallows me up. Or I run away. Anything to stop everyone else staring at me.

When Aaron speaks, I expect him to say something snarky, or admonish me for being so idiotic. Both would be entirely deserved.

Instead, he asks, "Are you okay, Olivia?"

His tone catches me off guard. It's soft, low, almost achy in its quality. A world away from his usual faux-charm-inflected dickery. He sounds genuinely concerned for me.

I swallow, nod. "Fine. Fine. Uh, sorry for the ruckus, everyone."

A look of relief flits over Aaron's handsome features, and he grins.

"She was just trying to get me to perform CPR on her," Aaron quips, and his words have the magic effect of breaking the somber tension in the room.

"I'd rather the anaphylaxis," I retort.

Everyone laughs, and my heart calms a little more as I shoot Aaron a grateful smile.

He holds my eyes captive for another moment before he lifts his chin, then sits back down.

As conversations start back up around the table and the marzipan pig prize is presented to Jake on my behalf, the festive atmosphere quickly returns. I put my phone away once and for all, deciding that my work schedule is not worth almost taking myself out.

Lena comes over to chat with me, apologizing again needlessly until I redirect our conversation to something else. And that's when I notice that Aaron—who's chatting with Stefani and Randy Allen, the team's backup goalie—keeps shooting me surreptitious glances. Like he's keeping tabs on me, checking in to see if I'm okay.

A sudden, rather sobering thought occurs to me: Aaron Marino came to my rescue tonight like a knight in freaking shining armor.

Which means I owe him one. Big time.

But even more sobering than that... *How on earth did he remember my allergy?*

15

AARON

When Colton starts trying to waltz with Reagan, and Jake decides the only natural after-dinner activity is to partake in some *Home Alone*-style sledding down my stairs, it's clearly time to call it a night.

One by one, my guests depart into the cool, fall night. Jimmy departs dressed in full motorcycle leathers—*since when does he have a motorcycle?*—and when Stef and Reagan decide to hit up a bar downtown, a couple of the guys offer to go with them. I order an Uber for Colton, and then help Sofia bundle a hiccuping Jake into the passenger seat of his car.

It's kind of cute, watching my oldest friend drunkenly slur, "I love you Sofia, you're the bessssshht" while giving his girlfriend these love-struck, goofy, goo-goo eyes. Sofia rolls her eyes good-naturedly while patting him down to find his car keys. Jake often had a girl on his arm over the years, but I don't think I've ever seen him mushy-sappy like this. Guess love really can change a man.

"You sure you're gonna be okay getting him home?" I ask Sofia. "I can drive you both. Help you get him inside."

She just laughs, waving a dismissive hand. "Don't worry, Aaron. I can handle Jake."

"I believe you," I tell her with a grin. "You want me to hurry Olivia up?"

"No, she said she would find another way home."

"Oh?"

Sof shrugs. "She was pretty insistent."

"Okay, then." I close the door behind her, then tap on the roof and salute her as she drives off.

I watch the retreating taillights of Jake's Rover, wondering what Olivia's plan could be. Most of the Cyclones and their families have taken off already.

My mind immediately (and unfortunately) spins to Dallas. After everyone finished their desserts, I couldn't help but notice the way Dallas and Olivia got to chatting, him topping off her champagne glass as they laughed together cozily.

Maybe Dallas is taking Olivia home. The thought makes my chest clench.

It's none of my business who Olivia Griswold dates, but surely she can see that Dallas is all wrong for her. Don't get me wrong, I like the guy. He's a great teammate and an even better friend, but he's a playboy, through and through. And underneath the hard, prickly exterior she likes to project, Olivia is sweet. Sensitive. Cooper would chew her up and spit her out.

I remind myself that I don't know anything about her dating life these days. I'm just doing what any good friend would do and looking out for my buddy's little sister, but then again, maybe I shouldn't underestimate her.

Maybe she'd be the one to break Dallas Cooper's famously unbreakable heart.

As I step back into my house, I come face to face with the very man I was just thinking about. As my eyes travel over

Dallas, I have to admit the guy has a certain roguishly handsome appeal Olivia could be drawn towards.

Dallas looks up from his phone. "Hey, man. I'm out. Thanks for a great evening."

"Heading home?" I ask as casually as I possibly can, peering over his shoulder to see if Olivia's following him out.

Dallas grabs his jacket off a hook next to the door. "Nah," he says with a devilish grin. "Got myself a little Thanksgiving date."

"You don't say." I'm aiming for jokey sarcasm, but I don't get there. I hate how strained my voice sounds. I cough to cover it, but Dallas gives me a disconcerting look that tells me he sees right through me.

"Have a good one, Cap." He winks, then walks out the door and shuts it behind him, leaving me standing alone in the hallway.

I stare at the front door for a moment before heading to the kitchen, which quite frankly, is an absolute disaster.

Plates are stacked on the island, empty wine, beer, and soda bottles litter the counters, and half-eaten dishes of food are piled haphazardly on the stovetop from where the guys tried—and failed—to help with the cleanup efforts. The dining area, which is open to the kitchen, has more dishes and bottles, alongside stained tablecloths and an array of pumpkin-slash-beer receptacles.

It's a sight that would make any tired, weary man sigh. A sight that would normally have me turn around and go right to bed, committing to deal with the carnage in the morning before Betty, my housekeeper, arrives.

But I don't do anything of the sort, because Olivia is standing in the middle of the mess. She's at the kitchen sink, her back to me, humming to herself as she rinses glasses and stacks them in the dishwasher. An apron is knotted around her waist, and she's pulled her copper hair into a sloppy topknot.

Man, she's pretty.

"You're still here," I say. It's meant to be a question, but it comes out like an exclamation. Which doesn't make me sound unlike an overexcited seven-year-old on a playdate.

She half-turns towards me, pushing back a strand of red hair that's stuck to her cheek. "You're observant."

"Why?" I figured Olivia would be out of here the second dinner was over. I certainly didn't expect her to be standing in my kitchen after everyone else went home.

"I wanted to help. And you clearly need a lot of it right now." She gestures to the mess surrounding us. "So, Marino, feel free to use me any which way you like while you have me."

Her statement, innocent as it was surely meant to be, scorches my blood with such intensity that I have to pause for a moment, remind myself that this is *Olivia* I'm talking to.

So I naturally have to get a rise out of her. "Don't tease me like that unless you mean it."

I enjoy the way her face turns scarlet as she realizes what she implied. She scowls and flicks a dish towel at me. "You are such a perv."

"And yet, you're here with me instead of with Cooper," I retort as I come to stand next to her at the sink, grabbing a wash-cloth to dry the pile of cookware she already washed. I can't help but add, "You guys were chatty tonight."

Olivia rolls her eyes, but I don't miss the way they flicker at the mention of Dallas's name. I don't like this flicker one bit. "I guess we were."

"Talk about anything interesting?" I cannot stop myself. Part of me is itching to know.

Her eyes flicker towards me this time, but they're narrowed.

"We were talking about Ashley, the woman he's gone to meet, since you're so curious."

"Jealous?" I prompt. Which is ridiculous, because if anyone here is jealous, it's me.

"Wouldn't you like to know," she huffs as she turns back to the dishes.

"I'd actually like to know the real reason you're still here," I press, because I work hard, but apparently, the devil in me works harder. "Not that I'm complaining, but you being the last guest to leave tonight is unexpected, to say the least."

Liv looks up, then exhales. "I'm here because I wanted to do something nice to, um, thank you."

"Thank me for what?"

"You know." She chews her lip. "For earlier. The porridge."

My chest tightens once again at the memory of her almost putting that almond in her mouth.

"What happened, Liv?" I ask, my eyes searching hers. I remember, clear as day, how cross-contamination from almonds could give her a rash and hives, and that if she accidentally ate an almond itself, she would have to use her EpiPen.

She ducks her head. "I was distracted."

"By?"

She lets out a long sigh. "Just... work stuff."

She seems agitated, so I decide not to push her further. I have a feeling that there's no way to make light of how she's feeling, and this time, I don't want to. Instead, I grab some plates and begin clearing scraps into the trash.

We work side by side in silence for a few minutes, me diligently scraping plates, her rinsing and stacking them in the dishwasher. It feels comfortable, easy, methodical.

"I'm off for Christmas," she mumbles.

I peer at her. "Off where?"

"No." Olivia shakes her head so forcefully that strands of

her red hair come loose from her topknot. "Like I'm off work for Christmas."

My lips pull up in a half-smirk as I reach up and grab a dirty glass balanced on a high shelf above her head that I noticed her eyeing. "Might just be me, but isn't it a good thing to have the holidays off?"

"I figured I'd be gone somewhere, but I guess I'm stuck at home." She turns her hazel eyes on me, then flicks them heavenward. "My roommates are having a three-day Christmas rave and I was very much hoping not to participate."

I frown. "That's an... interesting way to celebrate the holidays."

"They're interesting humans, to say the least." She snorts.

"Well, interesting can be fun. Maybe you'll love getting dressed up in neon spandex with the roomies."

"Should probably go dust off my glow sticks," she says with a smile, but I know her heart's not in it.

"What about a trip somewhere?"

Liv shakes her head. "That would be ideal, but flying standby around the holidays is a nightmare. Traveling at Christmas is really expensive otherwise, and I'm trying to save up to move to another apartment. You know, because of said raving roommates."

She makes a face, and I chuckle.

"And you can't stay at Jake's?" I ask. Her brother has a super nice condo in Midtown with gorgeous views of the city and a swimming pool on the roof. It also has at least a couple of spare bedrooms, last time I counted.

"Sofia's family are coming from Monterrey." Olivia lifts a shoulder, then begins scrubbing at a pot. "Don't want to crash their first Christmas with her folks."

"Makes sense."

I know better than to ask Liv if she would go home to see

her own folks for Christmas. Jake's not close with his parents or either of their new partners, and far as I know, Olivia isn't either.

I've been friends with Jake since the tenth grade when we started playing high school hockey together, and have known Olivia since she was fourteen. Throughout high school, I don't recall their mom making it to a single one of our games, while their dad showed up at every one for the sole reason of screaming at Jake about everything he was doing wrong on the ice.

Olivia would usually come to our games, too, and I still remember how pale her face would get as she sat next to their father, flinching at his harsh words. Such a contrast to my own parents, who showed up to every game they could, proudly waving banners with my name.

The first thing I did when I signed my first contract with the Cyclones was help my dad retire from the family business and let my uncles continue running it. It was the least I could do given how much he and my mom always supported me.

"Hey, Aaron?" Liv's voice yanks me from my thoughts as I'm putting away the last pot.

I look down at her, still hardly believing that she's standing here in my kitchen. "Yeah?"

She pauses for a moment, fingers playing with the strings of the apron she's currently folding. "How did you remember?"

"Remember what?"

"My allergy."

I meet her eyes. "I remember everything about you, Olivia. Every last detail."

16

OLIVIA

Aaron's green gaze lingers on my face. It feels like all the air has been sucked out of my lungs.

My heart stutters as I try to absorb his words. Words that have caught me entirely off guard because they don't mesh with the mental picture I have of him. Words that simultaneously chill me to the bone and set me on fire.

And suddenly, Dallas Cooper's earlier teasing rings out loudly in my head.

"You're totally into our captain, aren't you?" he asked with delight, rubbing his hands together like I just let him in on an exceptionally juicy secret. All I'd *actually* done is inquire, very casually, if Aaron was feeling okay after yesterday's cockroach debacle.

I told Dallas he was insane.

And this is what I tell *myself* now as I watch Aaron's Adam's apple move in the strong column of his throat, making me swallow the lump in my own.

I need to remember that this is the same Aaron who climbed through my bedroom window one night in high school while he and Jake were trying to avoid getting caught coming back from a party. I let my guard down with him, almost let him kiss me (or maybe I almost kissed him, which is mortifying) before he walked away without a second thought.

Shame on me if you fool me twice...

"I should go," I blurt.

"Oh, okay." Aaron's handsome face is unreadable. "I'll give you a ride."

"No, no. I'll get an Uber or something."

"At this hour? Absolutely not." He gives me a smirk. "Come on, Liv, it's the least I can do. I insist."

There's a note of finality in his tone that makes me nod instead of argue, and I can suddenly see why they made Aaron captain. In so many ways, this isn't the cocky, smirky boy I knew years ago. This is a commanding man who speaks with *authority.*

But then, his grin turns roguish. "Don't want some creep abducting you, do I? Jake would never forgive me."

Instead of making one of my usual acidic retorts to such a dumbass statement, I have to laugh. "Okay, Aaron. Take me home."

⁂

"Your car looks fast," I tell Aaron somewhat idiotically as I buckle my seatbelt. The leather seat is butter-soft and cool to the touch.

I've never been alone with Aaron in a car before, and this, coupled with the general whiplash I'm feeling thanks to his earlier statement, makes me feel the need to say something.

Apparently, a useless observation is the best I could come up with. But in all honesty, I'm impressed. The sleek, sports class Mercedes is unlike any other car I've seen. I mean, the thing looks like it's from the year 2050 and probably cost him more than what I make annually.

Twice annually.

"I love this car." Aaron runs a hand almost affectionately over the steering wheel. I'm momentarily mesmerized by his big, callused fingers moving delicately over the expensive leather.

For a moment, I idly wish that *I* was that steering wheel. Let myself imagine how it would feel for those hands to be moving over me with such assuredness, such confidence.

Sudden heat blossoms in my lower belly and I give my head a shake, horrified by my body's visceral reaction to my mind's very, very inappropriate and uncalled-for thoughts. Aaron is the last person on earth I should be fantasizing about.

What is wrong with me?

"I didn't think you loved anything but yourself," I say archly, but I'm sure my cheeks are twin scarlet beacons that give away the ridiculous fantasy I was just having about him touching me.

That freaking loaded, sizzling moment in his kitchen has clearly sent my head spinning. I need to go home and sleep off whatever *this* is.

Aaron looks over, his mouth pulling at the corners like he's somehow sussed me out. "I make the odd exception."

"Let me guess. The other exception being hockey?"

"Yes," he says lightly as he backs out of the garage. "But people over things, always. I love my mom. My nonna. My team."

"Women," I supply drily.

His smile turns into a full-on grin. "I do love women."

"Were you in love with the woman who named a cockroach after you?" The question leaves my lips before I can think it, and I mentally reprimand myself. When I brought this up earlier, it obviously bothered him, and while I normally wouldn't care about being insensitive towards him, I find myself wanting to go easy on him right now.

"No." His tone is still light, but his smile fixes in place and his stubbled jaw tenses. "I didn't even know her."

"I thought you two were almost engaged." My voice is gentler this time. When I saw the news about the failed engagement, I assumed it was bogus—I've never seen nor heard of Aaron getting serious with anyone. I can't help but wonder if there is a bigger story here.

"You keeping tabs on my dating life, Lil Griz?" he asks cockily, brow arched.

I roll my eyes at him. "Watch the road, bozo. And I can't help it that reading the news about my brother means that I have to see news about you, too."

He gives a soft chuckle, and the sound reverberates through the car, producing goosebumps on my skin. "Don't believe everything you read, Olivia."

After that, we fall silent, save for Aaron's Apple Maps lady directing us to the relative hovel known as my apartment. I shift in my seat, sliding over the slick leather as I will the traffic to disappear so I can get home faster. After spending the last few hours with Aaron, I'm suddenly ready to be alone, far from his proximity and the confusingly enticing smell of his cologne.

Clearly, I'm very tired. I'm usually immune to The Aaron Effect.

Aaron reaches forward and turns the radio up. It's set to a local station, and every hackle on my body raises as I recognize the song playing: "Last Christmas."

Now that Thanksgiving is over and done with, it's officially Christmas music season.

Ugh.

Up ahead, a light turns red, and we grind to another halt.

As George Michael croons that he's once bitten and twice

shy, and how he needs to keep his distance, I'm in half a mind to thank Aaron for the ride and let him know I can take it from here as I bolt into traffic.

But then, he pushes another button on the console to sync his phone up to the car stereo. Thankfully, the Christmas song about a broken heart cuts out and is replaced by none other than Justin Bieber's "Baby."

I turn to stare at him. "You're a Justin Bieber fan?"

Aaron laughs, and shakes his head. "Not really. But you seemed to hate the last song and I thought you might like it seeing as you used to play it to death back in high school."

I remember everything about you, Olivia...

I bite down on my lower lip, trying to force away that pesky warmth again, just as Aaron, tone deaf and overconfident as ever, starts singing along at the top of his lungs, cooing and crooning ridiculously until I have no choice but to laugh.

And then, no choice but to join in. Because as bizarre as this moment is, he's right. I loved this song back in high school, and even now, I belt it out word for word, hitting all the high "oooohs" his deep voice most definitely can't reach.

As the song ends, Aaron chuckles, and the sound is almost... endearing. I have to look out the window to hide my smile.

It takes us the better part of forty-five minutes to get to my place, but by the time we arrive, we've been serenaded by most of Justin Bieber's top hits.

"This is me," I tell him, gesturing towards my building. "There's no parking spots out front, so if you stop here, I'll hop out."

Aaron does not follow my instructions. Instead, he slows down, looks up at the building, then looks back at me. "You live *here?*"

His stunned—and somewhat disapproving—tone gets my hackles raised again.

"Home sweet home." It's meant to be a joke, but the words come out more defensive than I mean them to.

I do, however, manage to refrain from adding "we can't all be rich hockey players" to my defensive response, which I'd like to think is incredibly mindful and illustrates my newfound maturity.

Aaron suddenly jerks the car to the left with so much force, my bag slides off my seat, and he pulls into what is decidedly not a parking spot before turning off the car.

"What're you doing?" I demand.

"Walking you up."

"No, you're not." No way am I going to let him meet my crazy roommates. "You've already driven me home, and that's more than enough. I can take it from here."

As if on cue, two men skulk out of the shadows from the alley right next to us, blatantly ogling Aaron's car as they pull their hoods up.

Aaron's mouth presses into a firm line. "Yeah, no. That's not happening."

"It's fine." I wave a hand. "I come home late all the time from flights." I nod towards the men, now standing on the sidewalk. "Don't worry about those guys. It's probably just Larry and a friend."

"Larry?" Aaron's voice goes up an octave.

"The local weed dealer," I admit.

I only know this because the day I moved into the building, I was wheeling some suitcases towards the front door when Larry stepped in front of me, looked me up and down, and then asked me if I was in need of any broccoli.

I had no idea what that meant, but I assumed that he was not referring to the cruciferous vegetable. A quick google search confirmed that my instincts were correct, and Larry was *not* simply concerned about my folate and Vitamin C intake.

Because of our respective odd-houred schedules, Larry and I have crossed paths a few times. I wouldn't say we're friends, by any means, but we give each other that polite smile-nod greeting people do when they see acquaintances in passing. He even offered to pick the lock on my mailbox when it was stuck one time.

"He's harmless," I add reassuringly. "He's actually a pretty nice guy."

It's obviously the wrong thing to say because Aaron scrubs a hand over his face. "I'm going to be having words with Jake about this," he says darkly.

And then, despite my protests, he throws his door open and stalks around the car to open mine.

Defeated, I get out and check the lines on the road. "You're illegally parked," I inform him.

"I'm aware." He grabs me by the elbow and begins to literally frog march me towards the front door of my own damn apartment building. His grip on my arm is firm, the pads of his fingers digging into my skin, but not hard enough that it hurts.

"Ouch," I say anyway.

He loosens his grip by about one fraction of a millimeter.

"You don't care about getting a ticket?" I ask, looking up at him as I trot along in a vain effort to match his pace.

"No."

"Evening, Olivia." Larry waves at me from where he's still skulking about.

"Hi, Larry."

"Who's your friend? He looks familiar." He peers at Aaron as we pass.

"Oh, he's nobody," I say, flustered.

Aaron just keeps marching for the door.

Once I let us inside, he relaxes a little. Tugs on my elbow so I'm forced to turn and look at him. "Nobody, huh?"

"Didn't want your name associated with a literal drug dealer. Figured that wouldn't be good for your career if the media got a hold of it."

He looks surprised for a moment, but then nods. "That was good thinking. Thanks." His gratitude is short-lived, though, because that scowl is back in the blink of an eye. "But while we're on the subject of names, why does a drug dealer know yours?"

"That's a long, broccoli-filled story."

He stares at me blankly for a loaded moment before shaking his head. "Who are you, Olivia Griswold."

It's clearly a statement, not a question—a rhetorical question, at best—because he doesn't wait for an answer. Instead, he lets go of my arm and makes for the stairs. "What floor are you on?"

"No, no. No need to see me to my apartment." I jog after him. "I'm safely inside now, and you're going to get a parking ticket." My mind whirs with concern, both for his car, and for him meeting my roommates if he keeps to his insistent plan. "What if it gets stolen or broken into or something?"

He barely lifts a shoulder before climbing the stairs. "Good thing I have insurance."

"But you love your car."

"Olivia." He turns around and his eyes meet mine. "I don't give a damn about my car right now. What I *do* give a damn about is getting you home safe. Will you please allow me to do that?"

There's something so earnest about both his tone and his expression that I relent. Probably no use fighting him on this anyway—the man can be stubborn as a mule.

"Okay." I shake my head. "But for the love of all that is holy, *do not* tell Romy who you are, or she will shake you down for every penny you've got on you."

"Who's Romy?" he asks as I direct him out of the stairwell.

At that very moment, down the hallway, the bagpipes start blaring. Old Greg is clearly getting into the holiday spirit, jamming out to "Jingle Bell Rock."

Aaron turns to me, his expression one of total bafflement.

I smile sheepishly. "Sounds like Greg is practicing for the Christmas rave already."

"Right."

He's looking at me with such horror that I have to laugh. "Welcome to the mad house, Marino."

Because if I don't laugh, I might cry.

17

AARON

I wouldn't last an hour in the asylum that Olivia calls home, never mind the months that she's been living there.

She warned me about her roommates, but I did *not* count on a huge guy in a Santa suit—and when I say "Santa suit," I mean the OG *Mean Girls* version, complete with fur-trimmed skirt and thigh-high leather boots—piping away to "Jingle Bell Rock."

I was also not counting on a frantic woman running through the doorway, crashing straight into my chest, and no word of a lie, looking up at me and saying, "Oh, good, you look rich. I need some money to bail Elliott out of jail."

It's all I've been able to think about since I left her place last night... to the sight of a parking ticket on my windshield and a little dent in my driver's side door.

But I haven't given the car a second thought, because through my entire workout this morning, my mind's been stuck firmly on Olivia and how her cheeks stained crimson as she ushered her wayward roommate back into the apartment, stepped inside herself, and then thanked me for the ride home— before she shut the door in my face.

Now, as I walk through our training facility and into the

industrial kitchen where Stefani whips up all kinds of goodies for us, I'm thinking about how this isn't the first time I've unwittingly embarrassed her.

The night in high school when I ended up in her bedroom was worse.

It all happened in a blur. Jake and I were coming home late from a party when we set off the sensor lights in his mom's yard. Jake ducked into the garage, but in a panic, I scaled the nearest drainpipe, and ended up tumbling into Olivia's room.

Instead of doing what I should have done—which was get straight out of there and go to Jake's room—I stayed. We talked. And for the first time ever, we actually got along. Something about the dark of night made us honest, and when she admitted that she'd never been kissed, I was dumb enough to ask her if she'd like to be.

She shocked the hell out of me by nodding, I leaned in...

And reality kicked in.

I left as quickly as I could, and by the next day, we'd gone from casual rivals to full-blown enemies. On her end, at least.

Now, I'm frustrated knowing that she goes home to that dive of an apartment every night. And after meeting her roommates, I can understand why she wants to escape them and their impending Christmas Rave.

In the kitchen, I flick on the lights and head to the fridge. Nobody's here yet—we're not scheduled to review game tape until noon—but I decided to come in early for an extra gym session, and now, I'm starving.

Stef cooks fresh food for us after our practices, but she also usually leaves premade food for us for when she's not here. Today, I help myself to a huge container of overnight oats, a vanilla protein shake, and a couple of those awesome blueberry muffins she makes with the crumbly bits on the top.

I sit at the butcher block table with my spread of food, then slide my phone out of my pocket. I'm surprised, given the early hour, to see I have a new text. Even more surprised to see it's from Olivia.

> Thanks again for the ride last night. And sorry again about my roommates.

I shove a spoonful of oats in my mouth as I text her back.

> It was my pleasure. I always seize an opportunity for some Bieber car karaoke.

> Did your bagpiping friend play 'Jingle Bell Rock' all night?

> He did, yes. Switched it up at 6am today. 'Silent Night' was my alarm clock.

> Ironic. I cannot believe you live with those people.

> Lol and you didn't even meet the pantie thief.

I almost drop my phone.

> There's another roommate? Of the underwear-stealing variety?!

> Unfortunately, yes.

> I fully plan to find a new place by January, by the way. It's my early resolution.

> I hear ya. I'd hate to find out what Regina George plays on the bagpipes for New Years.

I pause for a moment, and then quickly type out one more text.

> Speaking of, did you manage to get your
> Christmas schedule sorted out?

I press send before I can talk myself out of it. It's not like we ever text, never mind texting for small talk, but I'm curious.

The bubbles pop up, then disappear. Once, twice. Three times.

"Marino!"

I look up to see Tony standing in the doorway of the kitchen, clad in a puffy North Face jacket and a baseball cap with the Cyclones logo on it. His face is more relaxed than usual, his lips almost turning upward at the corners. Beside him is an attractive woman who looks to be in her early twenties. She's got long dark hair, deeply tanned skin, and the same piercing eyes as my coach.

"Hey, Coach." I pocket my phone and give him a wave. "Just fueling up after hitting the gym."

"Glad to hear it." He indicates the woman at his side. "This is my daughter, Caelin."

"Hi." I stand from the table and stick out a hand. I've met Coach's wife a number of times but never his daughter. "Nice to meet you."

"Likewise," she responds with a big smile, shaking my hand. "I've heard a lot about you. And the others."

I laugh. "Good things, I hope?"

"Not in the least." Tony snorts, but his eyes are glinting with humor. "Caelin's just come back from Asia."

"That's awesome. Vacation?"

"Backpacking," she replies. "Toured Southeast Asia and Australia, and then taught English in Singapore."

"I'm impressed. Most tropical place I've been to is Hawaii."

"She's a go-getter," Tony says proudly. "But I'm glad to have her home."

"I'll bet." I look over at her. "Are you staying in town for long?"

"At least until the new year. I'm ready for a real Christmas. Last year, I was in Sydney, and a Christmas barbecue on the beach felt wrong on so many levels."

"I can imagine. I'm from Jersey, so even Atlanta doesn't feel like real Christmas to me because it never snows." I chuckle. "Hey, if you're ever at a game, you should find Jake Griswold's sister, Olivia. She's a flight attendant and has been to a ton of places. I'm sure she'd love to chat with you about traveling."

And I'm sure she'd love to meet more like-minded, normal people in this city, given the characters she currently lives with.

"Oh, cool. I totally will."

Coach clears his throat. "Cae, do you mind heading to my office while I have a word with Aaron?"

Caelin says her goodbyes, and Tony turns to me.

"You have a good Thanksgiving in the end?" he asks gruffly.

"Yes, sir. I had the whole team at my place for dinner. Jimmy called it 'Teamsgiving'."

"Checks out." Coach just about rolls his eyes. "How are we looking for the game with New York tomorrow?"

"Team's looking good. Morale is also good. I think everyone's feeling pretty confident about our chances."

"Glad to hear it," Coach harrumphs. "I'm thinking we trash the ice and give the press something to talk about other than rogue puck bunnies creating trouble. Got it?"

"Got it," I say, my hand automatically going to the bracelet on my wrist. I spin it around as I remember that I need to make sure Brandi doesn't win a date with me at the Christmas auction in a couple weeks. Any time spent around that woman will surely just give her more ammunition to create stories about me that'll send fricking Lieberman into revolt.

He nods brusquely. "Don't let me down."

My stomach clenches uncomfortably at his words. "I won't."

"Good. I'll see you in the media room later, then."

Coach leaves the kitchen and I sit back down, suddenly no longer all that hungry. My phone buzzes again.

> I don't know what I'll do about Christmas. But I'll figure something out.

And just like that, I have an idea.

A harebrained idea of Triple J proportions, maybe... but an idea nonetheless.

Before I can overthink it—and risk talking myself out of it—I forget all about my breakfast, dash out to the parkade, and get in my dented car.

Then, I drive straight back to Olivia Griswold's apartment.

18

OLIVIA

I throw my phone down on my bed and groan.

I thought that if I texted Aaron this morning, things might go back to normal and restore our usual equilibrium. You know, the normal where I love to hate him and don't feel like bursting into flames of confusing attraction when he's near me.

Instead, he's now asking about my Christmas plans—which are still derailed, by the way—and I'm really not sure how I feel about his concern.

Any of his concern. Because he was acting strange last night. Almost... protective.

Probably just because I'm his best friend's little sister. He simply felt a responsibility to get me home safe.

Thankfully, I managed to shut the door behind him quickly enough that he didn't need to hear any more of Gregory's bagpiping. Or Romy's proclamation that her on-again, off-again boyfriend, Elliott, was in jail for liberating an entire turkey farm.

And by "liberating," I mean that he drove to a farm on the outskirts of the city and opened every pen and gate door he could find, resulting in a stampede of cows, pigs, sheep, and indeed turkeys, on the I-75.

Then, I walked into my room to find Shannon, in my bed.

Wearing my underwear.

I had to thank my lucky stars that Aaron hadn't insisted on coming inside.

Clambering out of bed, I pull on a black tank top and my favorite gray sweatpants that have lost all the elastic at the waist, and so need to be rolled over on top.

Ratty? Yes.

Comfy as all hell and therefore never going in the trash? Also, yes.

And comfort is going to be key for me today if I'm going to work out a plan to get me through Christmas unscathed. Would renting a campervan and driving myself to Florida be entirely unhinged?

The apartment is unusually quiet. Greg's done with his 6am bagpipe practice, and I can't hear Romy's hysterics. I can only hope that she's out assisting with the livestock round-up on the highway for which I suspect she's at least partially responsible.

I exit my room to find Shannon facedown on the couch in the living room, fast asleep. I'm in half a mind to wake her up and remind her for the ten thousandth time *she has her own room*, but instead, I tiptoe to the kitchen and open my cupboard, hoping to scrounge up breakfast before any more roommate antics begin.

Each of us has our own designated cupboard, and a shelf in the fridge. Well, we're *supposed* to.

This system apparently doesn't matter at all—my food cupboard is suspiciously lacking for having filled it up last week after a big trip to the grocery store. My coffee grounds are depleted, and my nut-free cereal and granola bars have vanished. On my shelf in the fridge is a platter of jello shots that certainly do not belong to me.

I swear under my breath, debating again whether to wake

Shannon up—this time, to interrogate her about who might've been in my cupboard. But, that would mean having to speak to her.

At that moment, there's a sharp knock on the front door.

"Wonder who that could be," I mumble, idly hoping that it's not the police looking for a statement about rogue turkeys. Or the turkeys themselves seeking vengeance for being unceremoniously freed near a highway.

I fling open the door to the sight of a large, well-built frame propped up against the doorframe.

"Aaron!" I say in surprise.

He looks freshly showered and is wearing a black t-shirt with a Cyclones logo and gray sweatpants. That sexy black baseball cap—the one that's always annoyed me with its sexiness —sits backwards on his damp hair, and he's holding two takeout coffees.

"Hi," he says, his face a mask of composure. There's no hint of his usual cocky smirk anywhere.

"What're you doing here?"

One brow rises up and his eyes sparkle teasingly. "You're not gonna invite me in?"

"No!"

"Where are your manners, Lil Griz?"

I open my mouth to retort, but then—

"Is your friend back with Elliott's bail money?!" Romy yells from her room.

"Ugh." I sigh. "Let's talk outside." Without a second thought, I lay a palm flat on Aaron's chest and push him backwards, hard. Of course, the guy doesn't budge an inch at my efforts.

He stands there for a moment, a solid, warm brick wall under my palm, but then, with a grin, he moves back. I step barefoot onto the sticky hallway carpet, shutting the door firmly behind me.

Aaron looks me up and down, his eyes lingering on the strip of bare stomach where my tank top ends and my sweatpants start. When he looks up, I swear I see heat flaring in his gaze, but he blinks, and I think I must have imagined it.

"We match," he says, his voice a little husky as his eyes find mine.

I laugh nervously. "We do."

"I brought you coffee." He holds up one of the cups. "Americano with a splash of oat milk. Exactly what you ordered at Essy's."

I swallow thickly as I accept the cup. "Thanks." My brows pull together as I peer up at him. "So... you came all this way just to bring me coffee?"

"No, I—" He stops, and I watch in fascination as a red blush crawls up his neck. "I have an idea."

"What kind of idea?"

He takes a deep breath, almost like he's summoning strength. It's the same face he makes when he takes a shot on net during a game, I notice.

"Youshouldmoveinwithme."

I blink. My ears must be deceiving me. "Pardon me?"

This makes him laugh. "That might be the most polite thing you've ever said to me." He smiles, looking more sure of himself. More like his regular self. "Would you want to move in with me? Temporarily. While you look for a new place."

"Move in with you?" I squeak.

"Yes." And then, he adds, "You know, pack up your stuff and move it to my place."

I look at him flatly. "I know what 'moving in' means."

He smirks. "Well, I have a very nice guest room you can stay in. Two, actually, so you can take your pick."

At that moment, I realize what's happening. "I don't need your charity, Aaron."

My face is burning. I should have never let him bring me home last night. Because here we are, in the light of day, and the truth couldn't be clearer. Even my arch-nemesis feels sorry for me. So much so that he's offering for me to come live at *his house*.

How mortifying.

"It's not charity." He pauses. Clears his throat. "There's something in it for me, too."

My eyes widen. "I'm not having sex with you!"

This makes him *really* chuckle. "Noted. But no, I didn't come here to ask you to be my live-in sex partner."

"Oh." My face is somehow even hotter. Seriously, the sun's surface can't be anywhere near this temperature. "No. No. I knew that. Obviously."

One side of his mouth quirks up. "Are you planning on coming to the Cyclones Christmas gala?"

I frown, a little stumped by the random question. "No. I don't think so," I reply slowly. Jake and Sofia asked me to come to the event a couple weeks from now, and I am here in Atlanta that night, but super-festive Christmas parties aren't my thing. Obviously.

But strangely, my response makes Aaron smile. "Well then, I want to strike a deal with you: you can stay in my guest suite until you find a new place. And in exchange, you'll come to the Cyclones charity Christmas auction with me."

I narrow my eyes at him, cradling my coffee cup so the warmth seeps through my palms. "Why would you want me to do that?"

He ducks his head a little. "I'm up for auction."

"What a terrific prize." I roll my eyes.

"The *best* prize. But remember that woman who named a cockroach after me?"

"I recall."

"She has a ticket. Word has it that she's going to bid on me, so I'll need you to come as my plus one and outbid her. I'll obviously pay for it, so bid as high as you need to."

"You want *me* to bid to win you?" I burst out laughing. "That's the most ridiculous thing I've ever heard!"

"It might be ridiculous, but it's true." He makes big puppy dog eyes at me. "Please," he wheedles. "Only you can help me."

"That's a bit dramatic, Marino." I lean against the door, enjoying this.

"Olivia, she *proposed* to me."

"Then her winning you might actually be a blessing in disguise," I tease. "Remember that pro hockey player who married the woman who stalked him online? That all worked out pretty well for him, so if your stalker bids on you at the auction and wins the date, it might work out well for you, too. Might even be your ticket to true love."

"Your logic is flawless as ever." His tone is dry as he shakes his head.

I mime taking a little bow.

He smirks. "And when my stalker stabs me to death in my sleep like I'm a life-size voodoo doll, I will come back and haunt the crap out of you."

"Awh. You'd spend your afterlife haunting lil old me?"

"Definitely." His eyes meet mine. "I've always wondered if you're a lacy camisole or flannel pjs type of girl."

His tone is almost gravelly, that lowkey flirty voice of his that normally wouldn't affect me. But nothing about today is normal apparently, and for some stupid reason, my stomach flips, even as I roll my eyes at him. "And you'll keep right on wondering forever, perv."

He smirks, like he somehow knows that he's getting to me. Must be my lack of caffeine intake so far this morning.

"In all seriousness," I continue as I take a large glug of coffee. "Why don't you ask someone you're actually *dating* to come to the auction with you? I'm sure there are many women who'd want to bid on a night with Aaron Marino."

"I said 'date with,' not 'night with.'" He raises a brow cockily. "I know it's difficult, but you gotta get your mind out of that sex gutter, Lil Griz."

"Hey, you want my help or not?" I demand, my face heating. The sex gutter is the last place my errant mind needs to gallop off to. No matter how hot Aaron looks right now, standing in my hallway and smirking at me knowingly.

"I do," he relents. "And it needs to be you. You're the only woman I know who dislikes me."

"Wow. Ego much?"

He shrugs a shoulder. "Just stating the truth."

"I'd say your stalker doesn't like you much either, what with Cockroachgate and all that."

Aaron sighs, his smirky facade dropping.

"It does look that way. The thing is I've had... issues with this woman for a while, and now, she's pulling stupid stunts to try and get my attention. I cannot, in any circumstance, give her what she wants." His jaw is clenched tight, his fingers absent-mindedly toying with the leather bracelet on his wrist. "It needs to be you, because whoever bids on me cannot want to date me for real. I'm not interested in dating at the moment and I can't have any more blurred lines. Can't have any more drama in my life."

From the way he's looking at me, it's clear that he's dead serious about everything he's saying.

Meanwhile, I'm rather shocked to hear that the infamous

Aaron Marino has sworn off dating for the time being. But that's beside the point.

"Being a good captain to the Cyclones is my top priority," Aaron goes on. "And this Brandi stuff is taking away from that. Taking away from all the hard work I've put in to get to this point." His brows draw together darkly. "I can't give her—or anyone else—a chance to get close to me and risk sharing more nonsense story fodder with the media."

I get it. It makes... sense.

For a man as clearly committed to his career, I can understand why Aaron would be doing everything he possibly can to keep his name clean. It's a lot of pressure to be under, especially given his new position as captain.

And to be honest, it's not the craziest proposal in the world. He's obviously correct in that I don't—and will never—want to date him.

Sadly, I think he's also correct in saying I might be the *only* woman who doesn't want to.

"So?" he asks, his tone imploring. "What do you say?"

"I don't know," I say slowly, chewing on my bottom lip.

"You're looking for a place by new year's, right? So it would just be a few weeks. And I have a bunch of away games coming up, so I won't be there half the time. We'll be like ships in the night, other than for the gala. It's a win-win for both of us."

I do like that it's a two-way street—that he needs something from me, too. And the prospect of staying in his gorgeous, welcoming house is tempting.

But living with Aaron Marino? I don't know if I could do that.

Because while he's right that I definitely *do not* want to date him, I do find him dangerously attractive. Still. After all these years.

Living in close quarters with him would be just that: dangerous.

And then, he plays his ace.

"Plus, I'm going home to New Jersey over the Christmas break. You'll have the place all to yourself." He smiles charmingly, like he knows he's about to win. "No Christmas rave."

Dammit. This is even *more* tempting. A game changer, perhaps. The NHL always breaks for Christmas, and this year, the Cyclones play on the 23rd of December and don't play again until the 27th.

The exact dates I have off of work.

Which means that for four entire days during my least favorite holiday of the year, I'd have his gorgeous mansion all to myself. Not a bagpipe or pantie thief in sight.

Just peace, quiet, and a place to escape Christmas, all the while not crashing Jake and Sofia's first holiday season together, nor having to spend the money I need for a new apartment on an actual escape plan.

It's too good to resist.

And he knows it.

I narrow my eyes. "If I say yes, do you promise no funny business?"

He crosses his arms, eyes gleaming. "Define 'funny business.'"

"You know what I mean." My cheeks redden for the thousandth time this conversation. "No stupid jokes or lewd comments. And absolutely no trying to charm—"

"The pants off you?" he finishes with a huge grin.

For a moment, my eyes skate over his handsome, smiling face. The laugh lines around his green eyes. The dark, tousled hair poking out from under his hat. Those perfectly broad and sculpted shoulders, leading to a broad and sculpted chest.

Yes.

"No!" I glare at him. "I was going to say, no trying to charm me into being *friends* or anything. We'll be roommates only, and it'll be a trade. A business agreement. Nothing else."

"Feel free to continue loathing me, Olivia." His eyes are twinkling now that he knows he's got me. "I wouldn't expect anything less."

"That's not what I meant!" I protest weakly, because it *is* what I meant.

"Yes, it is," he says dryly, his green eyes twinkling. "And I promise, I'll stay out of your way. Ships in the night, remember?"

Yes, ships in the night. Between my schedule and his, we'll barely see each other, and I won't have to contend with the weird and uncalled-for attraction I'm feeling towards him these days.

And it's only for a few weeks, until the New Year.

I can do this.

"Okay."

My voice is so quiet that I'm surprised when his expression becomes delighted. "So, we've got a deal?"

He holds a big hand towards me, and I stare at it for a moment. Take in the thick fingers with short and surprisingly neat fingernails, the olive skin, the veins that run along his perfectly muscled forearms. The bracelet around his left wrist.

"Deal," I say thickly, extending my own hand to him. I hear myself saying the word like I'm watching this scene from above, a veritable out-of-body experience. The syllable feels a whole lot bigger than its short, clipped sound.

His hand clasps around mine, almost enveloping it. Even though his palm is warm, a shivering shock jolts through me as his calloused fingertips graze my skin. I wonder if I've just made a deal with the devil.

When I pull my hand away, it's tingling, and Aaron's smil

ing. "Who knows, you might even discover I'm not the worst person in the world, huh?"

I roll my eyes, but I'm smiling. "Doubtful."

"So when are you moving in, Roomie?"

"Don't call me that."

"Suit yourself, Lil Griz."

Ugh.

What fresh hell have I gotten myself into?

19

AARON

December

Early December brings a couple of hard losses for the Cyclones, but then back-to-back much-needed wins on the road—followed by a tie game with the D.C. Eagles on home ice.

It also brings colder weather, and approximately eighty million Christmas lights.

The entire city is aglow, lit up and festive, and I'm totally into it. Atlanta might not be as traditionally 'Christmassy' as my hometown up north, where you're pretty much guaranteed a white Christmas, but it's still a great place to be for the holidays. There's something about carols on the radio, and cheerfully decorated storefronts, and Triple J arriving at practice every day wearing a different ugly holiday-themed sweater that makes things feel generally happy.

We're winning more games, Olivia's coming to the gala to outbid Brandi, and the holidays are upon us. A combination that makes me feel like everything might be okay.

And that's the thought I cling to as I hold on for dear life to my grab handle in Dallas's Ford F150. I'm riding shotgun and am terrified as my teammate takes the gravel roads at breakneck speed. It's an almost ridiculous contrast to the cheerful, uplifting sounds of "Christmas Tree Farm" by Taylor Swift blasting through the truck's speakers.

It was a Jimmy recommendation to "get us in the Christmas spirit for the day ahead." And surprisingly, for the first time ever, Dallas agreed with him.

Despite the literal roller coaster we appear to be on, Jimmy is singing along from the middle of the backseat. He's flanked by Seb and Jake, the latter looking less than impressed with the current choice of music and/or style of driving.

The truck hits another pothole—Dallas doesn't even flinch—and I have a sudden fatherly urge to turn around and ask the guys in the back if they're feeling carsick.

"How much further, Cooper?" I ask as I roll up the sleeves on my flannel shirt.

He lifts a shoulder. "'Bout a half hour."

"Great," Jake mutters thickly.

"Baby, baby, Merry Christmasssss," Jimmy sings.

Seb rubs his temples. "Whose idea was this again?"

"Mine." I have to laugh. "Sorry, man."

When Dallas randomly mentioned at practice this morning that his family owned a Christmas tree farm two hours out of the city, it caused a bit of an uproar. Apparently, our roguish teammate has been holding out on us about his most wholesome of upbringings. In fact, he made the place sound utterly idyllic.

After a lot of team teasing and ribbing about Dallas's newly discovered soft side, I suggested we take a trip out there. Seb and Jimmy were up for it, and I dragged Jake along.

A "nice, peaceful drive down some country roads" (as Dallas described it) sounded like the perfect way to spend my afternoon. I need a Christmas tree for my living room anyway, and we might as well support the Cooper family business.

Plus, I was happy to distract myself from the nervous energy gathering in my body...

Later today, Olivia will be moving in with me.

"As terrible as Cooper's driving is, I'm kind of stoked," Seb says with a smile. "Christmas is my new favorite holiday, and Maddie's excited for a real pine tree."

"My driving is spectacular, Slater." Dallas turns to peer at Seb from over the top of his sunglasses. "And I'll have you know that you're gonna get there in record time, thanks to my superior skills behind the wheel."

As he says this, we hit another huge pothole, and Jake groans as he whacks his head on the window. "Watch the road, you idiot. I'd like to get to the farm alive, if that's okay with you and your *superior* driving."

"Play nice, Griz," I interject in my best 'captain' voice.

"I could drive this road in my sleep," Dallas replies lazily as he drapes an arm over the steering wheel. "Speaking of sleep, I got very little last night."

"TMI," Jake grumbles.

"Actually, it's not. I met a gorgeous brunette at a party and we stayed up late talking."

"Is that what the kids are calling it these days?" I smirk.

He shakes his head. "I swear, it was entirely innocent."

"I once spent all night talking to a woman about meteoroid strikes," Jimmy informs us.

"Sounds... riveting," Seb says dryly.

"So, what's the story?" I ask Dallas. He isn't the type to brag about his conquests or dish dirt on women or anything. We may rag on him for his reputation, but he's a super decent guy. But it is unusual for him to bring up a woman he simply *talked* to.

"I might see her again tonight. Do something chill seeing as we have a game tomorrow." He fiddles with Spotify until Michael Bublé croons at us. Apparently I'm not the only one with a soft spot for the festive season. "You doing anything later, bro? You seemed a bit distracted earlier at practice."

I glance at Jake. "Well, I'm getting a roomie today."

Honestly, ever since we came to our little agreement just over a week ago, I've been waiting for her to get cold feet and call it off. What an absolute turn-up for the books.

I can hardly believe she said yes to my plan in the first place, and the thought of her being in such close proximity is making me feel a whole lot of ways.

So much so, that I figured that a trip out to the farm this afternoon would kill two birds with one stone: give me a distraction until I have to pick her and her stuff up, and give me a reason to decorate my place for Christmas so it's warm and welcoming when she arrives.

Jake harrumphs from the backseat. "Right. Let me know if you need help moving her in."

Triple J claps his hands. "That's right, today's the day! I love Olivia. You two are going to have so much fun."

"We're not teenage girls having a sleepover, J."

"You better not be having any sleepovers," Jake adds darkly.

"Oooh," Seb whistles. "Watch out or you'll end up loved up and locked down, Marino."

"I think I'm the last man alive that Olivia would like to 'love up,'" I reply with a snort. "I just need this Brandi thing to blow over, which Olivia is helping me with."

The gala is days away now, and the guys are all aware of my plan to stop Brandi from winning a date with me. Explaining the situation to Jake, in particular, wasn't that bad in the end— he also thought it best that a woman who wasn't interested in me should bid on me at the auction, and agreed that Olivia fit the bill perfectly.

When it came to telling him that, in exchange, Olivia would be living at my place for the next month, he seemed more concerned. He didn't seem to know how bad things truly were at Olivia's apartment and said she should just come stay with him.

I mentioned that she didn't want to crash his holiday plans with Sofia's family, and he got quiet for a moment before he gave a jerk of a nod.

"She usually spends Christmas alone," he said.

Which might have at least partly fueled my desire to cut down a tree today. The thought of her in my house, alone, over the holidays is a little weird, but if that's how she prefers to celebrate Christmas, I might as well make it as festive for her as possible.

"Word of warning," Seb says, leaning forward to clap me on the arm. "I didn't want a girlfriend either, but then I met Maddie, and in the space of twelve months, I ended up with a wife and a son."

Jake guffaws loudly. "Yeah, but Maddie actually liked you. Liv and Aaron can hardly stand each other, always been that way. Right, Marino?"

"Right," I agree, chuckling along with the others.

But that's not exactly true. I like Olivia, always have.

I just *really* like getting a rise out of her.

"We're here!" Dallas whoops, swerving left onto a beautiful driveway lined with pine trees, all of which are aglow with colored fairy lights.

We soon pull up in front of the cutest place I've ever seen—and believe me, I don't usually think of things like tree farms as *cute*. But this place is storybook adorable, with a whitewashed cottage glowing with Christmas lights, a life-size nativity scene staged in the gardens, and a legitimate candy cane lane that seemingly leads to the area where you cut down your own tree.

As we stumble out of the truck on shaky sea legs—thanks to Dallas's driving—and gather to begin the grand tour of the

Cooper Christmas Tree Farm, I slip my phone out of my pocket to see that Olivia has texted.

> On my way to O'Hare. Flight's on time, and it shouldn't take me long to get home and grab my stuff. I should be at your place around 9pm.

> You ready for a serious roommate upgrade or what?

Her reply comes through almost immediately.

> It's definitely a living space upgrade... the company, I'm not so sure about.

> I can purchase some bagpipes if that would make you feel more at home.

> Or wear your underwear.

> I could've happily gotten through my entire life without that particular mental image.

> I'm just illustrating how much better of a roommate I'll be, that's all 😇

> Okay, okay, it's a roommate upgrade, too. Although I'll never admit to saying that.

> Glad to hear it, because I'm pulling out all the stops to win Roommate of the Year over here. I even made up the master bedroom for you.

I first figured that she would sleep in a guest room, but then realized that one of them has all of my hockey stuff in it— jerseys, framed photos on the walls, memorabilia, and so on— while the other one is chock-full of my crochet projects.

As hilarious as the thought was, I knew Olivia would not enjoy staying in a room basically enshrining my career, nor a menagerie of half-finished crochet animals. And so I came to the conclusion, unbelievably, that giving her the master would involve the least amount of work.

After moving my things to the shrine room, I made up the master bedroom for her with fresh sheets. It's got a huge California King bed and an even huger ensuite bathroom with a steam shower that could probably fit half my hockey team in it (as alarming a thought as that is). I'm sure she'll appreciate the space and privacy after what sounds like a dumpster-fire apartment experience.

My phone rings, and I step away from the group to answer it. "Hello?"

"You don't need to give me your bedroom!"

"Hello to you too, Olivia. Nice to speak with you this fine afternoon."

"I have no time for small talk," she grumbles, sounding not unlike her brother. "I don't need the master. I'll happily take a guest room. Seriously."

"Awh, come on. I thought you'd enjoy sleeping in my bed." I smirk, unable to help myself from prodding at her a little. "My thousand thread-count sheets are an experience everyone needs to have at least once in their lives. After all, they are used to pure physical perfection sleeping on them."

"Are you really bragging about how many women you've bedded, Marino?" Her tone is positively scandalized, and my smile widens.

"I told you to get your mind out of that gutter, Lil Griz." I keep my voice low. "I was talking about myself, actually."

There's a long beat of silence. "I don't know how you even get out of bed in the morning with an ego that inflated. Surely, it's incredibly heavy to carry around."

"Keeps me in that perfect shape you were just talking about."

"I..." She makes a snorting sound, then erupts into laughter. "I can't with you. You're the worst."

"See, you keep my ego in check. We'll be the best room-mates ever."

"We'll be something, all right." Her tone is dripping with sarcasm, but even with the distance between us, I can tell that she's smiling.

"See you later, *Olivia*."

"Not if I see you first, *Aaron*."

Laughing, I end the call, now almost excited for her to move in.

This Christmas season is sure going to be interesting.

20

OLIVIA

I walk towards my departure gate at Chicago O'Hare slowly, pulling my wheeled carry-on suitcase behind me and trying to ignore all of the wreaths filled with twinkling lights that decorate Terminal 3. The tinny sounds of "Walking in a Winter Wonderland" carry from the convenience store on the left, and wafts of peppermint mocha emanate from the Starbucks on my right.

It's like the spirit of Christmas got drunk and threw up all over the airport.

Kind of makes me want to throw up, too.

But if I'm being honest, that might be less about all the Christmas paraphernalia and more about the nervous knot that's growing in my stomach.

"You're going to need to tell me again," Jing says as she bounces along next to me. She has a candy cane pin on her uniform blazer and she's sipping a gingerbread latte. "how did you end up agreeing to live with Aaron FRICKING Marino?"

I still have no idea.

"I'm not living with him," I correct her. "I'm staying at his house until the new year while I search for an actual place to live."

"That's living with him!"

"No, it's not. I'm a *guest*." I protest. "Besides, I'll be working a bunch and he has several away games, so we'll barely see each other."

"Living with the Italian Stallion himself," Jing says with a sigh.

"Jing, nobody calls him that!"

"If they don't, they should." She winks at me. "And FYI, I'd saddle up that horse in a hot second if I were you."

"You are unbelievable," I mutter, even as more nervous anticipation tightens in my core.

It's been just over a week since Aaron turned up on my doorstep with a crazy proposition that I, even more crazily, accepted.

Today is move-in day. When I land in Atlanta later this evening, I'm only going back to my apartment to collect my things. And, if I'm being honest, my thoughts. Which have been disturbingly close to the so-called "sex gutter" since he informed me I would be sleeping in his bedroom.

Although, by Jing's remarks, I'm not the only one having inappropriate thoughts about my brother's best friend.

As much as I will admit that I'm attracted to Aaron physi-cally—and as much as he actually makes me laugh with his ridiculous big-headed comments, and surprises me with his random acts of kindness—I cannot even begin to go there. Ever.

We agreed that I'd move in on the first Sunday in December, just a few days before the gala. This would give me time to give notice to my crazy roommates and to pack up my things before a slew of back-to-back flights.

In the end, telling my roommates I was leaving was easy: Gregory nodded and asked me if I'd like to buy a commemorative CD of his bagpipe music, Romy wailed hysterically for about thirty seconds before getting distracted rummaging through my bag to steal gum, and Shannon immediately called getting my room after I left.

Crazily, it might be Larry I miss the most about that place.

The relief I feel at moving out is palpable, but the pressure is now on for me to find a new, reasonable living situation for the new year.

Because from tonight onwards, I'll be sleeping at *Aaron's* house.

In Aaron's *bed*, to be exact. A fact which I will definitely not be sharing with my lovely friend Jing.

"Come on," Jing grabs my elbow and tugs me forward. "We don't want to be late for your flight to Babeville."

"Is that what they're calling Hartsfield-Jackson International Airport these days?" I ask with a roll of my eyes.

She giggles and slaps my arm as we walk through the departure gate to board our plane.

***

The flight goes by in the blink of an eye, and before I know it, we've landed, disembarked, and are walking through the airport.

Jing is at my side again, chatting a million miles a minute about a hot military man she has a date with tonight, when she suddenly stops in her tracks and squeals. "Oh. My. Gosh."

Oh my gosh, indeed.

Aaron is standing under the Arrivals sign in the middle of a huge crowd of people awaiting their loved ones. He's easy to spot: he's half a head taller than anyone else in the vicinity, and about a hundred times more handsome with that face that could, and just did, stop traffic.

"He came to pick you up!" Jing squeals. "Aaron Marino is

here to pick you up from the airport. I can't. I simply can't." She starts to stagger around like a drunken sailor. "I'm going to need smelling salts to revive me, because I'm swooning away."

People are giving us very strange looks—Aaron included—so I wrap my hand around her bicep and yank her towards me. "Stop swooning, you madwoman!" I hiss under my breath. "They're going to pull you aside and search your bag if you keep falling over your feet like that."

Jing promptly straightens to her full and tiny height. "Good thinking. I will swoon inwardly instead." She turns big eyes on me. "Can you introduce me?"

"Can you be normal if I do?"

"I can try."

"Try really hard, because I don't need him to—"

A throat clears behind us, and I turn to see Aaron looming over us. He looks even more gorgeous than usual, his hair windswept and his cheeks rosy from the cold. He's wearing dark jeans, vintage-looking sneakers and a gorgeous olive green jacket that makes his eyes glow. "Am I interrupting something?"

"Yes!" I say, just as Jing says, "Oh, no. No, no, no."

Aaron looks from her to me, and he quirks a brow.

"Nothing important," I relent, then cock my head. "What are you doing here?"

"I'm picking you up from work." Before I can say anything, he turns to Jing. "Hi, I'm Aaron. OIivia's new roommate."

"I know who you are," Jing says, all breathy and sounding nothing like herself. She has stars in her eyes, their brown depths positively shimmering.

"Nice to meet you...?" He holds out a big hand, and Jing snaps to sudden attention.

"Bing." She winces. "Uh, Jing. I'm Jing."

Aaron looks at me, a little bemused, and I clarify. "Her name is Jing. She is a fan of yours, as you can clearly see. But she's not picky when it comes to the Cyclones and is a fan of all of you, so don't let it go to your head."

"Wouldn't dream of it."

As he shakes Jing's hand, Aaron gives her a lopsided, all-too-humble smile that I should loathe, but instead makes my insides prickle in an all-too-pleasant way.

"I could've taken the train to the apartment, grabbed my bags, then bussed to your place," I say.

"What kind of a man would I be to allow that?" he replies while winking at Jing, who simply gazes back at him in adoration. She might have a new favorite Cyclone. "My schedule's open this evening, so I'm at your service to help you move."

"Well, that's... kind of you," I say.

And I mean it. Because the prospect of lugging my suitcases around on public transit was not exactly something I was looking forward to.

"Happy to help." He shrugs. "What about you, Jing? Need a ride?"

Jing—who is meeting her date shortly for margaritas at a Mexican joint by the airport—looks like she's all but forgotten the poor guy's existence. "I, um... No, actually. Which is a pity."

I have to hold back a laugh at Jing's downtrodden expression. "A real pity," I agree—Jing would probably be a great buffer for Aaron's whole charming, "I'm at your service" persona right now.

All too soon, we're outside the airport saying goodbye to Jing (the brat hugged me and whispered "get it, cowgirl" in my ear). Aaron then somehow gets ahold of my suitcase handle and I end up trotting after him (and my suitcase) all the way to short-term parking.

"Over here," he says as he directs me to a behemoth truck that I'm impressed he managed to squeeze between the lines of a tiny parking spot.

"What's this?"

"I borrowed Dallas's truck in case you had a lot of stuff to move."

"Oh." I blink in surprise. "Good thinking."

He unlocks the truck. "Least I could do, Lil Griz. You're doing me a bigger favor helping me with this Brandi thing."

I raise a brow at him. "All I have to do is bid on you at a Christmas auction."

"No, you're saving me. Seriously," he says dryly. We climb into the truck, and Aaron turns the key in the ignition so the engine roars to life. "You know what Brandi did today?"

"*Today?*" I repeat, surprised. I kinda figured the whole Brandi thing died down after Cockroachgate and my bidding on Aaron at the auction was mostly a precaution. I pull on my seatbelt. "The saga continues?"

"The saga continues," he confirms solemnly. "With the woman in question turning up to our practice this morning in a bikini." He shakes his head. "A bikini. At an ice rink. In December."

"Maybe she was planning on using the hot tub or something," I suggest, cocking an eyebrow. "I'm assuming that luxurious players' area of yours has one."

"It does. But Brandi was wearing a giant fur hat and fur boots with her bikini, so I'm not sure that was her intention. I'm honestly not sure *what* she wants."

"Wow. She's, um, determined."

"That's one word for it." He scrapes a hand over his stubbled chin, then throws the truck in reverse. "I got my ass to the locker room pretty quick so we didn't cross paths, but I did see that she was holding up a sign that said 'Roses are red, violets are blue, I came to your practice to say I still love you!'"

"That's insane," I say.

He quirks a smile. "Decent rhyme, I thought."

"I don't know how you do it." I wrinkle my nose. "I'd be so freaked out if that was happening to me."

"Just part of being in the public eye, I guess." His tone is nonchalant, but I notice his jaw is tight as he speaks. "At least she didn't post about it on social media this time."

I've never directly followed news about Aaron (because why would I?), but he does seem pretty private with his personal life. Any information I've seen about his potential relationships were mostly speculations made by the media, and not actual announcements or statements he's made himself. I don't think he's ever even soft-launched a woman on his Instagram.

As someone who protects her own privacy fiercely—I couldn't stand having three roommates in my business, never mind the general public—I find myself feeling sympathy for his situation.

It's a foreign feeling for me when it comes to Aaron.

It makes me itchy.

"So, Lil Griz, now that you're moving in," he says, his voice quite a bit lighter. "Do you have any stalkers or boyfriends that *I* need to be aware of?"

"Negative."

"To the boyfriends, or the stalkers?"

"Both."

He smiles like this pleases him, and I roll my eyes. "I'm not saying that like there's an opening, you creep!"

I reach out to slap him playfully on the arm, but his reflexes are quicker than mine and even while driving down the freeway, he easily catches my hand in his.

The contact sets off sparks on my skin. He gives my hand a little squeeze and his fingertips find my pulse point. I wonder if he can feel my heartbeat hammering way too fast. The edge of his fingertip drags over my wrist, and a shiver racks through me.

Self-consciously, I pull my hand out of his grip and busy myself retying my ponytail.

Like he didn't just touch me like that.

"You look good in that uniform by the way." His eyes flicker to me. "I like it."

I dip my head to hide my flushing cheeks as I smooth down the navy skirt I've always thought was extremely unflattering on my hips. "Probably just reminds you of that old Britney Spears video where she's dressed as a sexy flight attendant. Jake had her poster up on his wall; I assume you had a whole assortment of similar ones."

Aaron turns off the freeway and into the neighborhood I'm about to leave behind. "Nah, I was always more into redheads."

"Ha, ha." My voice feels suddenly thick and I hope he can't hear it.

He illegally parks the truck right where he illegally parked his car the last time he dropped me home and turns to look at me, his eyes burning into mine with undeniable heat this time as he says, "I'm not joking, Olivia."

And then, before I can say anything at all, or even catch my damn breath, he gets out of the truck.

21

AARON

"What happened in here?!"

Olivia's standing in my doorway, packed suitcases at her feet, and her mouth is hanging open as she surveys my handi-work. She looks...

Appalled. Straight up appalled.

I know my tree decorating skills are not exactly on par with The Rockefeller Center's, but up until this moment, I was quite proud of the ten-foot Fraser Fir I whacked down myself at the Cooper Christmas Tree Farm. It was too big to fit through my front door, so I helped the delivery guys drag it through the French doors around the back of the house.

It was also a pain in the ass to put up. My living room might have vaulted ceilings, but it was a struggle to get the massive thing to stand upright. But after I hauled out a step-ladder—making a mental note to never let Coach find out I was on a ladder, lest I be hung, drawn, and quartered—and covered the tree with twinkly lights and ornaments, I have to say it looks pretty damn festive.

Obviously, though, Olivia disagrees. Looking at her face

right now, I'm reconsidering my actions—I've never before seen a freaking Christmas tree conjure up so much horror.

I flash her a teasing smile. "Not sure you're aware, but we're past spooky season. We're now closer to a holiday called Christmas. Maybe you've heard of it? Involves a baby in a barn and some sheep and a trio of kings and whatnot?"

Her horrified expression quickly changes to a flat glare, leveled my way. "I have heard of it, yes."

"Good, good." I take off my Timberlands and place them in the closet, and then hang up my coat. "Well, you might also be aware that many people choose to put a tree up in their home to commemorate this holiday."

She doesn't reply, merely flicks her eyes heavenward.

"Your resting Grinch Face is showing, Liv." I chuckle.

"And your Holly Jolly Weirdo Face is showing, Marino."

"Olivia Renee Griswold. I did not peg you for one of those Scroogy miser types who can't stand good cheer," I chide, teasing.

"Christmas is just so.... *Christmassy*," she grouches, and I'm about to retort when I catch a flicker of something in her eyes.

The memory of her shifting uncomfortably in my car when I put on Christmas music suddenly pops into my mind. And another memory; of Jake saying that she prefers to spend Christmas alone. Which I thought was a little odd, but I'm now wondering if there's more to it.

Does she actually not like the holidays or something? Is that why she prefers to spend them by herself?

Our eyes hold for a moment, and she looks away.

"We can redecorate the tree to be less Christmassy," I propose. "We can even get some little hockey player ornaments in my likeness that you can deface in any which way you prefer."

She smiles like a Cheshire Cat. "That sounds like my kinda festive. Sign me up."

I grab her suitcases in each hand. "Shall I show you your room? I'll get the rest of your stuff from the truck after."

Without waiting for her response, I start walking towards the stairs. But she doesn't follow. I look back to see her gawking at me.

"You coming, Lil Griz?"

"How on earth are you doing that?" she asks in lieu of answering my question.

I raise a brow at her. "Doing what?"

"Holding an entire freaking suitcase in each hand like it's nothing!" She looks almost indignant, and I smile.

"This *is* nothing," I snort, although I'm not gonna lie, I do flex my biceps a little. For effect, obviously. "What does a suitcase weigh, like fifty pounds?" She rolls her eyes at me, and I wink. "I could lift this in my sleep."

"Bully for you," she says, but I don't miss her glancing at my flexed biceps for a glimmer of a moment.

This only spurs me on. I can't get enough of that addictive, annoyed spark in her eyes. Even if it means summoning every bit of inner jackass I have in me. "If you want to be really impressed, after we get you settled in, we could go to the gym and I'll show you what I can actually lift."

"Your ego is bigger than that damn Christmas tree." She groans, but she's laughing as she passes me on her way to the stairs. "This way?"

"Yup," I tell her. But as she prances up the stairs in front of me in that uniform of hers, my throat gets tight.

It's probably not ideal to be staring at your new roommate's butt on the day she moves in, is it? Especially while she's wearing that ridiculously sexy flight attendant skirt.

What was AmeriJet thinking, giving its employees such scandalous uniforms?

Although, now that I think about it, I've been on hundreds of AmeriJet flights over the years, and have never once been tempted by—or even noticed—said skirt.

Olivia just wears it so damn well. It's hard *not* to notice.

I try to focus on her long, red ponytail instead, but by the time we get upstairs, I'm a little flustered. And it has nothing to do with the weight I'm carrying.

Trying to look cool and casual, I tip my head to the right. "I'm staying down there, and you'll be over here."

She squints her eyes at me, like she has me sussed out. "Lead the way."

As I push open the door to my bedroom, I can't help but wonder what she might think of it. I find myself hoping she'll be comfortable here.

When I bought this house, I hired a decorator and gave him a vague rundown of what I wanted it to look like. He managed to bring what little info I gave him to life better than I could have ever imagined.

I love how it all turned out, and for some reason, I hope Olivia likes it, too.

Setting down the suitcases, I flick on the light. She gasps.

I'm gratified to see her mouth hanging open the same way it did when she saw my Christmas tree, but this time, her face is less appalled, more amazed.

"*This* is your room?" Her eyes are big and round as she takes in the space, and it suddenly occurs to me that *Olivia Griswold is in my bedroom.*

"What were you expecting, an upside-down coffin or something?"

"Yup." She smirks. "Or maybe a dark, creepy little cave. Like where Gollum lives."

"Nerd," I tease her.

"Takes one to know one," she shoots back, taking a seat on the bed.

"Well, make yourself at home. And by the way, I keep my handcuffs in the drawer by the bed, if you so..." I trail off at her horrified expression. "*Kidding*, Livvy."

"Oh," she says on an exhale. "Yeah. Duh."

I give her a teasing smirk. "I'll go unload the rest of the stuff from the truck."

She stands from the bed. "I'll give you a hand."

"No need. Probably good for me to climb those stairs a few times. Gotta get those glute workouts in, right?"

Liv rolls her eyes with a loud sigh. "Obnoxious as that was, thanks. I'd love to take a shower."

"Should have everything you need in the ensuite," I say, nodding towards the bathroom to the right, which I've stocked with all of Maddie's recommendations. Although Lord only knows what a hair mask is.

Olivia gives me a little smile before opening one of her suitcases and rummaging through her clothes. Meanwhile, I walk back towards the staircase, doing everything in my power not to think about the fact that Olivia Griswold will soon be in my shower.

I'm unsuccessful, and I almost trip on the first damn stair.

22

AARON

After I've deposited the rest of Olivia's things outside my—uh, *her*—bedroom door, I duck into my new bedroom to change into sweatpants and a hoodie. Then, I head to the kitchen, where my other project for the evening awaits.

I ran out of time before I had to grab Olivia from the airport, so the counters are a mess of carrot peels, spilled pastina, and parmesan rinds. I set to work cleaning everything up before I turn on the burner under the soup pot. I might have had to call Nonna three times during this preparation process, but I think I pulled it off.

Nonna's Chicken Pastina soup—fondly known as Italian Penicillin soup—is one of my favorite foods on earth and making a vat of it today seemed like a great idea for two reasons:

One, my nonna totally saw through all my B.S. on the phone the other week and knows I haven't been making it.

And two, I thought Olivia might like a home-cooked meal because airplane food is the pits.

That is, if she wants some. The bubbling soup smells amazing, if I do say so myself, but Olivia's had a long day and is currently in the shower. Which I'm still absolutely not thinking about.

After she's done, she's probably going to go straight to bed. Not sit in my kitchen and drink soup with me, for goodness sake.

This isn't an episode of *Friends*.

My phone buzzes on the counter, and I reach for it. It's Jake.

> Everything go okay?

> Yup. She's all settled in. Think she went to bed.

> Thanks again for doing this. Watch out for her, okay?

A flicker of unease moves through me, because some of the thoughts I've been having this evening would probably make him want to murder me in cold blood. But I brush it off. Offering her a hot meal counts as watching out for her, right?

> I will.

> Good, I trust you. Off topic, are you wearing a tux to this gala thing? Reagan said it was black tie, and Sof insists that means a tux.

Glad of the conversation change, I ladle myself a huge bowl of soup, grab my phone, and plod to the living room, texting as I go.

> Dude, it definitely means tux. And the gala is around the corner. Did you not buy or rent one yet? You better get on that because it can take a while to get them altered.

"Hey."

The soft voice coming from across the living room startles the crap out of me, and I jerk my head up from where I'm typing. Unfortunately, my hand jerks too, and I give myself a shower of scalding hot soup.

"Agh!" I yell, dropping the bowl so it hits the floor and breaks. But this is the least of my worries as the broth seeps through my sweatshirt, scorching my skin. "And also ow!"

Quick as a flash, I whip off my hoodie. I'm left standing in the living room in nothing but a pair of gray sweatpants, stranded amongst shards of broken bowl and a sea of soup.

Olivia is standing at the side of the room, staring at me with her eyes bugging. Despite my little spill, I can't help but notice that her hair is wet and braided over one shoulder, her skin is free of makeup, she's got her glasses on instead of her contacts, and her current outfit confirms my suspicions: her pajamas consist of flannel pants and a baggy t-shirt.

Not gonna lie, that's my new favorite kind of pajama.

A trickle of liquid runs down my bare chest, and I wipe at it with my hoodie. I notice that Olivia's gaze follows my hand.

She swallows. "Um, you okay over there?"

"Soup!" I blurt out uselessly, then explain myself. "I made you soup. My grandmother's recipe."

Her eyes meet mine, a little glazed, and she gives her head a slight shake. "That doesn't really answer my question."

I clear my throat. "I'm fine, just a little embarrassed you witnessed that."

"Are you kidding?" She grins. "Hearing Aaron Marino scream like a little girl might be the highlight of my year."

This makes me properly belly laugh. "Glad to be of service. And the good news is, I think my reflexes were quick enough to save me a second degree burn." I shrug. "Guess I've seen one too many horror movies."

Olivia raises a brow. "You like horror movies?"

"No. But I've suffered through many over the years—your brother is obsessed with them."

"I am, too," she says. "My guilty pleasure."

She lowers her eyes, letting them rake over my chest and torso. Not gonna lie, her gaze on my skin feels hotter than the soup. "Second degree burns or not, you'd better get a cold compress on that."

"Right after I clean this up." I gesture to the mess surrounding me.

"I'll help," she replies. And this time, I accept.

A few minutes later, I've picked up all the shards of what was previously my favorite bowl, and Olivia's mopped up the floor. It occurs to me that this is the second time in the span of a month that Olivia Griswold and I are in my house together, cleaning up.

Talk about being domestic. Normally, I'm not home enough to do this type of thing.

We head into the kitchen, where I deposit the last shards in the trash, and I nod at the pot of soup. "Help yourself. I'm gonna grab a clean sweater."

Olivia's eyes find my bare chest once again, and she points at one of the stools beside the counter. "Sit."

I raise a brow. "Is that an order?"

"Yes." Her gaze is unwavering.

"I'm used to giving the orders, not taking them," I say with a smirk.

"Sit your ass in the chair, Marino."

I sit my ass in the chair.

"Good boy." She smiles in satisfaction and I have to laugh at her smug expression. "Where do you keep the clean cloths?"

"Second drawer on the left of the sink."

She opens the drawer and retrieves a couple of cloths, and as she runs them under the faucet, I realize what she's doing.

"Ah, that's not necessary, Liv. I'm a big boy. I'm sure I'll be fine."

"Your skin is currently rivaling a tomato's." She tuts as she comes to stand in front of me. "You ready for this?"

I skeptically eye the cloth she's holding towards me. "You know what you're doing?"

"Yup. I'm trained in first aid as part of my job."

I give a little nod. And so, she gently places a cloth on my chest, smoothing it out so it hugs my pecs.

I inhale sharply—more so at the sensation of her hands moving across my skin than anything else. I'm glad when she winces, misinterpreting. "Ooh, sorry, did I hurt you?"

"Not at all."

I sit stock still as she smoothes another cloth over my shoulder, and a third on my ribs. The cool cloths feel amazing on my hot skin, and I try to hold my breath so I don't audibly inhale again. Or breathe in her sweet-smelling body wash and shampoo.

Or do something completely insane like grab her and kiss her...

I can't believe how consuming the thought of that is right now.

I blame the damn shower.

"There. All done." She steps back, and I let out a sigh that's equal parts relief and frustration.

"Thank you, Olivia."

"You're welcome."

I clear my throat. "You settling in okay?"

"Sure." She pauses for a moment, wrinkling her nose before she adds, "Thanks again for letting me stay."

"Anytime." I quirk a grin. "I was ready to throw you out after you grinched out about my Christmas tree, but you've redeemed yourself."

I expect her to make a smartass remark in response, but instead, she glances at the tree in the living room and frowns. "Sorry about that. Christmas isn't my favorite."

This confirms my earlier suspicions, and I feel a little bad for calling her a grinch. Twice.

"Don't be sorry," I tell her.

She lets out a sigh. "I'm sure Jake mentioned to you that our parents got divorced at Christmas time, and it was, well, messy."

I knew their parents were divorced—had been since before I even met Jake—but he never told me any details. In contrast, I was blessed to have parents with a loving marriage full of mutual respect, but I know a lot of people who are kids of divorce, and how hard it was on them.

"That must have been difficult."

She lifts a shoulder, but then a shadow falls over her eyes, and for a moment, her guard slips as she adds, "Nah, it was almost a relief when they finally went their separate ways and stopped constantly screaming at each other."

"Were Christmases a little better after that?" I ask haltingly, wanting to give her space to express how she feels.

"Yeah." Her pretty eyes flutter closed behind her glasses, like she's replaying a memory in her mind. But then, she exhales. "Well, no, actually. Not really. By the next Christmas, my mom was remarried to a guy who had no time for Jake and me, and my dad got arrested for drunk and disorderly behavior." She looks up at me suddenly, and her expression shutters again. "Christmas isn't ever really the same after you've spent it trying to get your dad bailed out of jail."

I swear under my breath, finally understanding her desire to hunker down for the holidays, alone. I get the sense she must do this every year—just ride it out until it's over, trying to pay the festive season as little heed as possible.

It's such a clear, polar opposite to how me and my family

normally spend this time of year, and I wish I could do something to make it better for her. Make this Christmas a little brighter.

But if I've learned anything about Olivia Griswold, it's that she knows what she likes. And even more so what she doesn't.

"I'll be out of your hair soon enough to give you time to yourself over the holidays," I say, nodding towards the corner of the living room. "In the meantime, though, I'll take down the tree."

"No, please don't." She shakes her head with a dry laugh. "I can only imagine how much work it was to move that monstrosity in here. My personal beef with Christmas shouldn't stop you from celebrating it in your own house."

She gives me one of those determined looks of hers and I study her, trying to read her face. "About the gala," I say gently. "I don't want you to feel obligated if it'll bring back painful memories for you. I can find someone else to come, or just ditch, and you can obviously still stay here—"

"Aaron," she cuts me off. "I'm a grown ass woman. I might not like Christmas, but I can go to a party." Her eyes light up. "Plus, I kind of want to get a peek at this infamous Brandi."

The joking tone in her voice indicates that her walls are back up and our serious conversation is over. For now, at least. Because I kind of liked talking to Olivia so openly and honestly. Kind of liked seeing what lies behind her guarded exterior.

And I'm not ready to part ways just yet. "Okay, well, thanks. I appreciate it, in advance." I give her a smile. "In the meantime, do you want to eat soup and watch a scary movie with me? Not an ounce of Christmas cheer, just a bunch of decapitations and stabbings?"

She laughs. "I thought you'd never ask."

23

OLIVIA

The morning after I move into Aaron's house, I wake up to a sound that is foreign to me...

Silence.

Sweet, beautiful *silence*. And it's made even better by the fact that I'm lying in the most comfortable bed I've ever slept in. Times a million. I'm talking fluffy cloud pillows, and the best mattress, and yes, I must admit, Aaron's sheets are incredible.

Aaron's sheets.

With a start, I sit up, my blood heating as I remember my dream:

Aaron Marino, shirtless in his kitchen, wincing as I dabbed cold washcloths on him like I was Florence Fricking Nightingale. But then, the dream version of this event became a lot less PG than the actual occurrence.

Not a dream, but a nightmare, really.

"What is wrong with you?" I hiss at myself as I hurriedly shake away the remnants of Dream Aaron. Usually, my nightmares are more along the lines of going to work naked and everyone laughing at me. Or being in a room full of people who all know each other and I'm the only person who knows nobody, sticking out like a sore thumb.

This nightmare was a brand new one, and I freaking caused it by putting myself in the firing line of that insane physique of his.

I also blame the damn thousand-thread-count sheets. Even crisp and clean, they have the lingering, delicious smell of *him*.

Rolling out of the massive bed before I can focus too much on said scent, I notice the clock on the nightstand. It's *11am*?

Holy. I've had a 6am alarm clock for months now in the form of Gregory's bagpipes. Apparently, I've been needing to catch up on sleep.

I plod to the ensuite bathroom, which is stocked better than a Sephora, surprisingly. At first, I thought that the fancy lotions and shampoos must be remnants of some of Aaron's former, ahem, *companions*. But upon further examination (i.e. relentless snooping), I discovered that all the bottles and jars are unopened. Well, apart from that really nice conditioner in the shower that I may have accidentally on purpose used last night.

I brush my teeth and examine myself in the mirror. I'm running a brush through my hair and reaching for my moisturizer when I remember that I don't care what he thinks about how I look.

But as much as I try to tell my brain that, my body only wants to recall the heat in his eyes last night when I came downstairs. It was unmistakable as he took in my freshly-showered self, standing there in what I made sure were my least sexy pjs.

And then, he fed me soup.

Delicious, but favored by sick people and the elderly. Ergo, universally recognized as the world's least sexy food.

Unless you're Aaron Marino, of course. Because while I was wallowing in soupy, pajamaed unsexiness, he managed to turn the moment into something more exciting than a *Magic Mike* show.

I put down my brush and make my way downstairs in search of caffeine. The house is dead quiet, aside from the sound of my bare feet padding across the gorgeous oak floors.

In the kitchen, I'm surprised to find a note on the island, accompanied by what looks like a handful of darts. Which is weird.

> O—
>
> I left early for practice, hope I didn't wake you. Will be gone for most of the day so you have the place to yourself. Help yourself to anything in the fridge or cupboards, and make yourself at home.
>
> —A
>
> P.S. I've made some changes to the Christmas tree, if you need some entertainment for your day ahead.

What on earth did he do to the tree?

And do I really care?

Your resting Grinch face is showing, I can almost hear Aaron taunting me, and against my better judgment, it makes me smile.

I pad around the kitchen, grabbing myself a coffee and feeling mildly relieved that he won't be around today.

I can hardly believe that I blurted out all my family woes about Christmas to him last night. All that bare chest vicinity clearly short-circuited my brain for a minute.

Although honestly, he was really nice about the whole thing.

Afterwards, we hung out for a couple of hours, watching two slasher movies back-to-back and playing dirty word scrabble—basically just scrabble, but you can swear. Aaron is apparently a master at this game, and took the W with the word "douche" on a triple word score.

And he never did put a shirt on. Which was... distracting, to say the least.

But all in all, it wasn't the worst night ever. By a long shot.

Aaron's note in hand, I make my way to the living room.

And there, in the middle of his huge, gorgeous tree decorated with a million gold and red Christmas decorations, is a dartboard.

It's hanging off a large branch, and upon closer examination, I have to laugh, because he's taped pictures of random Christmassy things—and pictures of himself—to the board.

I grab my phone and snap a picture, then text it to him.

> You are a ridiculous man, Aaron Marino.

Morning, sleepyhead. Or afternoon, at this point. I thought there'd be multiple darts in the middle of my forehead by now.

> Might have slept in a bit. But thank you. This is an excellent addition to your decor.

Figured you might want something you can take out all your holiday hostilities on.

> This gift makes me feel the warmest and fuzziest I've felt about the holidays in a long time.

Probably due to the pictures of my handsome face on the dartboard.

I pause briefly, searching, waiting for the annoyance and indignance I usually feel towards Aaron and his ridiculous remarks, but I come up empty.

Instead of replying, I pocket my phone and head back to the kitchen in search of carbs and more caffeine.

Humming, I open the fridge to find three cartons of Oatly and a huge case of canned Diet Coke. There's also tortilla wraps, eggs, bacon, sausage, veggies, and everything one might need to make breakfast burritos.

Hm. Aaron must love them as much as I do.

I then head to the pantry, where there's a neatly stacked shelf full of snacks.

All clearly labeled "nut free."

> Did you, by chance, buy me snacks and Diet Coke?

Possibly.

> You didn't need to do that!

Sure I did. I remember how hangry you can get.

> I don't know whether to be flattered or offended.

Oh, it was purely selfish on my part. Last thing I needed was a hangry houseguest on my hands.

I let out a chuckle, rolling my eyes as I reply.

> Wow, that was a lot of alliteration.

> People do say that I have a way with words.

> Humble as always. But thank you for the snacks.

> You are most welcome. We can eat some tonight while watching Saw III.

> You assuming I don't have plans?

> On the contrary, I'm assuming you do have plans. With me. And Jigsaw.

I grin at my phone screen, then suck in a sudden, sharp breath. Because the feeling that's currently rising up in me as I text Aaron?

It's the opposite of annoyed or indignant.

In fact, it's downright... *fluttery*.

24

AARON

One week into living with her, and it's like Olivia Griswold has infiltrated all areas of my life.

Not that I'm complaining.

It's just... surreal to go from not seeing her for years, to waking up every day and finding her *everywhere*. Her shoes in the entryway, her coffee cups in the dishwasher, the smell of her shampoo on the couch pillows. Diet Coke cans are stacked neatly in the recycling, and there's a cardigan draped over a barstool in the kitchen.

Yesterday, I found a pink hair tie in my hockey bag. No idea how it got there, but it sure ain't mine.

It made me smile, though, because I like to see that she's making herself at home. I want her to feel comfortable at my place, treat it like it's hers for the next two and a half weeks until the new year rolls around and she moves into a new apartment. Although, as much as she's been looking, I'm not sure if she's found anything she likes yet.

"Get your head out of your ass, Marino!" Coach Torres hollers at me as I miss an easy pass from Perez who plays left wing. He used to be on a line with Slater and Holmes, but when Mal retired, I moved into his old position playing right wing on the first line.

"Sorry Coach," I call as I skate over to scoop up the puck from where it's settled against the boards and continue on with the drill we're running. Forcing my head back onto the ice and into this practice, I snap the puck to Seb, who's skating up ahead.

We're practicing our tails off today after a rough loss to Toronto last night. But for some reason, I'm not feeling quite as anxious about it as I usually would, the negative words in my mind about my performance not as loud and consuming as normal.

Maybe it's because we've also had a few wins recently, and our current standing in our conference is better than it's been all season.

Or maybe it's because Olivia was in Atlanta last night and came to the game. I gave her a ride home afterwards and we watched the fifth *Saw* movie together.

Well, *she* watched it, while I watched her watching the movie.

Seriously, the sight of her enthralled face as people got sawed up on-screen was way more entertaining than the movie. And the fact that she happily scarfed down popcorn while watching was downright impressive—all that gore makes me lose my appetite.

But strange snacking habits aside, I like Olivia's company. She's just as witty and funny as I remember. Snarky, with her sweeter side rippling just below the surface. And knowing what I do now about her family situation, it explains so much of the harder exterior she presents when she's feeling vulnerable.

I don't know if it's the holidays coming up or what, but I have to say, after living alone for years, it feels pretty cozy to have someone to sit with in the evenings by the flickering light of the Christmas tree.

Frick. Maybe I need to get a dog or something when she moves out.

A big, goofy golden retriever, perhaps.

Or a cat. One of those fluffy ginger ones. I'd be a great cat daddy, I am sure.

"All right, bring it in!" The blast of Coach's whistle shakes me from my feline train of thought, and as we all skate to the edge of the ice, Triple J comes up alongside me.

"Hey, Cap. What color is your tux for the gala?"

Right. The gala is tomorrow, and it's been the talk of the locker room all day. Reagan's been hyping it up on the Cyclones' social media pages, and everyone's pretty excited for an excuse to get all dressed up and dapper-looking.

"You mean my bowtie?" I frown at my teammate. "I'm going with classic black."

He shakes his head like I'm being really, really slow. "No. Your *tux.*"

"Um, also black, J. Like most tuxedos." I narrow my eyes at him. "You going powder blue? Or orange, like in *Dumb and Dumber*?"

I'm obviously joking, so I'm a little startled when he nods. "Blue *was* my top choice, but I also have green, and I thought that might be more festive. I just wanted to double check that nobody else is wearing a green tux." Triple J chuckles. "That would be so embarrassing if two of us showed up wearing the same color."

"Yeah. *That's* what would be embarrassing," Dallas says from my other side. Jimmy gives him the middle finger, and Dallas smirks and adds, "Maybe I'll have to dig my green tux out of my closet so we can match after all."

Triple J looks appalled. "You wouldn't dare!"

"I think you'll be fine in green, J," I cut in. "Very... unique." I mean it, too. I'm one hundred percent sure that Dallas is way too vain to turn up to a black-tie gala in a comedy tuxedo.

"I rented one with those penguin coat tails," Colton jumps into the conversation. "Think I might get a top hat to go with it."

"Get a monocle, too, and people will think you're the monopoly man," Seb tells him with a cheeky wink.

"The pants are too tight on mine," Jake grouches, his bearded face screwed up in horror. "I finally picked one up and thought I was done worrying about it, but like Marino warned me, the woman at the store insisted I had to get mine taken in. She was wrong, though, because now I can hardly walk in those stupid pants."

Looking at him right now, his face all pouty, I can see the resemblance between him and Olivia, clear as day. They normally look nothing alike—Jake is a beast of a guy, whereas Olivia is strikingly pretty. But this particular facial expression he's making serves as an excellent reminder that the woman I'm currently enjoying living with is my best buddy's little sister.

"I'm sorry for your hardship," Seb tells Jake smugly. "If it helps, I look great in mine."

"Same," I add cheerfully.

"Ladies!" Coach thunders, clapping his meaty hands together. "When we're all done talking about our fashion choices, can we please get back to talking about hockey?!"

"What are *you* wearing, Coach?" Jimmy asks innocently, and we all have to cover our laughs with an array of coughs. I swear even Torres' lips twitch at the corners.

As Coach goes over the next drill, I find my mind drifting again, returning to Olivia. I can't help but wonder what *she'll* wear to the gala, and I'm intrigued to see what she looks like dressed up. A week or two ago, I would've guessed she'd spite-dress in her rattiest sweatpants or something in an effort to protest Christmas or make me look bad at the gala (joke's on her, she still looks stupid hot in sweats). I can't imagine she'll wear that sexy silver mini-dress she wore at the club a few months ago.

Last time I saw her properly dressed up was at my senior prom. She looked totally stunning in a poofy, frothy-looking thing, or so my teenage self thought. She went to that prom with Daniel Davis from marching band.

And despite repeatedly insisting to myself that I wasn't, I was jealous as all hell.

This time, she'll be with me.

Coach blasts his whistle again, and we all skate onto center ice. But Dallas nudges me in the ribs with a knowing smirk I don't like one bit. "Think your girl will give me a dance at the gala?" he asks under his breath.

"No," I hiss back, and my neck prickles with embarrassment as his smirk grows. I try to cover and correct myself. "Doubt she'd wanna dance with the likes of you."

"So, no issues calling her your girl, huh?" Dallas's smirk is taking up his entire face at this point.

"Not my girl," I retort hurriedly. "Roommate. Jake's sister. Plus one."

He cocks a dark brow. "Keep telling yourself that, bro."

And with that, he skates off to take his position, leaving me alone with the ever-growing sensation that I'm wading into quicksand. That I'm starting to fall back into those old feelings I had for Olivia...

The ones I never allowed myself to feel, let alone act on.

I unconsciously glance towards the box where she was sitting during last night's game. Her face fell after the final buzzer, and she looked so cute in that moment that my first thought was not that we'd just lost a game, but that I got to go home with her afterwards.

Yeah, scratch that.

I'm not sure I ever stopped having those feelings for her.

25

OLIVIA

Confession: I have never been much of a girl's girl.

This is not, in any way, because I don't want to be.

It's also not because I don't enjoy other women's company. And it's *certainly* not because I like the attention of men so much that I find other women a threat. A pick-me girl, I am not.

Truth is, I often find groups of women intimidating. In London, I had a couple of female friends, but avoided the big flocks of flight attendants who would go out together when we were staying in far-flung destinations.

At my new job, the only person I've really clicked with is Jing. And I'm good with that.

So I'm more than a little surprised (pleasantly so) that I've fallen in so comfortably with the wives, girlfriends, and female staff for the Cyclones. Sofia is obviously amazing. And from the moment I met Maddie and Reagan at the Thanksgiving game, they've made me feel nothing but welcome.

When Sofia invited me to join her "little get-ready get-together" before the Cyclones Christmas gala tonight, I didn't stress about it or let myself drown in doubts about attending a big group hangout.

I just said yes.

All the newfound good sleep I'm getting is clearly making me more sociable.

In hindsight, though, this was probably not my smartest move. Because that's how I've ended up in the middle of an upscale boutique, trying on dresses and modeling them for a room full of women, all intently watching me.

"Liv, that looks so good on you!" Maddie nods her approval as she takes in the long, sweeping midnight blue gown I'm wearing.

"I agree," Lena adds in her soft, lilting voice.

Stefani flashes me a thumbs-up and Reagan snaps a picture, because according to her, everything needs to be documented on camera or "it might as well not have happened."

This dress is not something I'd ever think of wearing. But when I arrived at Sofia's place earlier, she took one look at the garment I was planning to wear—which was about five years old and probably more suited for a beach wedding than a winter wonderland black-tie extravaganza—and shook her head in a staunch *no*.

She immediately made an appointment to get me "gowned up" at a dress rental place she often works with, and her other guests decided to come along.

After this, we're getting our hair and makeup done.

What is my life right now?

"Thanks, everyone." I try not to balk under the attention as I turn my eyes back to the mirror.

I'm not going to lie. Standing here, on the dress shop podium thing, with all eyes on me as I squeeze into fancy dresses is a scene straight out of my nightmares.

Although, that being said, my nightmares have been somewhat... different the last few nights.

Ever since I moved into the Marino Mansion a few days

back, I've startled awake every morning to the same pesky dream that leaves me very, very flustered and even more determined to lock down a new apartment, stat.

Sleeping just down the hall from Aaron is clearly messing with my mind.

Although he does make a much better roommate than I would have expected. And I have to admit I sometimes enjoy hanging out with him.

"Is this *the one*?" Reagan asks. It's the third dress I've tried on—I was bursting out of the first one like a sausage escaping its casing, and the second one was about a foot too short.

This dress fits well, and it looks pretty good. "Sure," I reply, very unsure.

Sofia stands in front of me, and she assesses my silhouette with her critical, fashion stylist's eye.

"I don't know," she says thoughtfully, tapping her long fingernails against her thigh as she thinks. "Can you try on one more for me, Liv?"

I look around at the other girls for signs of boredom or frustration, but they all look pretty relaxed. Genuinely happy to be here, sipping champagne and watching Sofia dress me up like a life-size doll.

Sofia ushers me back into the changing room, helps me out of the blue dress, and then slips out to return a moment later with another garment, which she peeks around the curtain to hand to me. "Try *this* one."

"Red?" I squeak, staring at the crimson satin sheath on the hanger.

Black, white, beige, gray—those colors are comfortable, safe, neutral.

This dress already appears to be *anything* but those things.

"Just trust me." Sofia winks, then ducks out.

After a moment of hesitation—during which time I consider

pretending I somehow ingested an almond to get me out of this situation—I give it a go. The girls have been supremely supportive today. Even if this dress looks totally absurd on me, I have a feeling they'll be nothing but sweet about it.

I lumber around the fitting room like a baby elephant as I attempt to pull on the slippery piece of material. But I'm surprised to find that, instead of being tight and making me feel lumpy, the fabric is smooth. So smooth, it almost feels like liquid cascading over my body. The zipper glides up my back without any help needed, and when I spin to look at myself in the mirror, my eyes widen in shock.

I would have never picked this dress for myself.

For one, as a redhead, I avoid wearing red like the plague. For two, it's got a plunging neckline that is entirely out of my usual wheelhouse.

But it's... *perfect.* The spaghetti straps are delicate and pretty, and the fabric flatters my body in a way I didn't even know a dress could. The rich, vivid color is striking against my pale skin, and my copper waves complement rather than clash with the tone.

I look nice. Pretty, even.

"OHMYGOSH OLIVIA!" Sof squeals as I tentatively step out of the fitting room.

"Woah," Stefani says, her mouth hanging open. "You look like a freaking supermodel."

"Aaron is going to lose his *mind* when he sees you in that," Reagan adds.

"It's not a real date, remember?" I remind her. The ladies have all been briefed on the plan for tonight, and they've promised to keep an eye out for Brandi and would have my back in case of any shenanigans.

"He's still gonna lose it. Scratch that—every man in the room is gonna lose his mind."

I have to laugh. "That's kind of you to say."

Reagan scoffs. "I'm never kind for the sake of it. You look hot, Olivia."

I look in the mirror again, and then, for some reason, I picture how Aaron might react when he sees me wearing this later. Let myself envision the way his eyes might widen, pupils dilating. The thought of his approval isn't unpleasant and I watch a blush start to color my cheeks.

Dangerous waters, indeed.

"Thanks, Reagan." I give my head a shake, shaking off all thoughts of Aaron and his confusingly hypnotic eyes in the process. "I *feel* good in this dress. Maybe once I'm done bidding on Aaron, I can use it to find a man who's an actual romantic possibility." I look over my shoulder to waggle my brows at her jokingly. "Surely, there'll be some eligible bachelors at the gala tonight."

Reagan raises a brow. "Sorry. Remind me again why Aaron himself is not a romantic possibility?"

For many reasons, I want to say. But I start with the most objectively obvious one. "Well, because we don't like each other, for one."

"That's crazy talk," Maddie pipes up, looking thoughtful. "Aaron's great. I think he'd actually make a really good boyfriend. I even set him up on a date a few months ago."

I snort. "Did she happen to be a beautiful brunette he ditched at a nightclub?"

"Yes." Her lips slide into a big smile. "But one correction. *She* ditched *him* because she was completely and utterly in love with my brother."

"What?" I stare at her.

"Yup. Going out with Aaron helped her see how she truly felt about Jax. They're engaged now. And now that I think about it, I haven't seen Aaron with a woman since."

I remember what Aaron told me about how he isn't dating right now due to the Brandi drama and focusing on his captaincy, but I don't add this to the conversation. It feels like something he told me in confidence, and for some reason, I don't want to betray his trust, if that's what it was.

"Well, romantic possibility or not, he certainly looks at you differently than he does everyone else," Sofia chimes in.

And dammit if my heart doesn't pick up speed. "What do you mean?"

"He looks at you like he's studying you. Like he's trying to suss you out."

"Like he wants to jump your bones," Reagan adds with a wink.

I laugh, but it comes out a little shaky. "Probably just trying to figure out how to annoy me."

But even as I say this, I feel something inside me stir at the thought of him looking at me differently than he does everyone else. Looking at me like he *wants* me.

I've clearly got to keep my head on straight. My assignment is to outbid Brandi at the auction. Nothing else.

Simple, right?

26

AARON

Strings of twinkling white lights are draped along the ceiling, casting a soft, golden glow that makes the entire room feel enchanted. A towering Christmas tree easily twice as tall as the one in my living room glitters in the far corner of the ballroom, next to a roaring fireplace decorated with emerald green garlands and red velvet bows. A grand piano flanks the other side of the fire, and a player in a Santa suit runs his fingers over the keys while crooning Frank Sinatra.

Men in tuxedos and women in striking gowns mingle around the ballroom. The clink of glasses and the hum of laughter carry through the air, alongside the scents of pine and cinnamon. The atmosphere is festive and perfect, full of the same contagious holiday cheer as in those cheesy Hallmark Christmas movies my family loves to watch and I love to complain about. All while secretly enjoying the hell out of them, of course.

It truly is a Winter Wonderland. Spectacular in every way.

But all of this beauty pales next to the sight of Olivia in that dress.

She's a vision. A straight-up masterpiece of crimson satin

and copper curls and scarlet smiling lips. Red is my favorite color right now, and I have a feeling it'll stay that way.

We've been here nearly a damn hour already, and although I should be feeling anxious about seeing Brandi and also having to sweeten up Lieberman at some point tonight, I can't tear my eyes away from Olivia long enough to care.

That dress is doing things to my insides that they have no business doing. I can't concentrate on anything going on around me, because in my mind, I'm tracing the edges of that dress, smoothing my fingers along the shimmering pale skin exposed by the deep neckline and low, scooped back of the dress. I want to follow my fingers' path with my mouth, tasting and licking and kissing her bare skin until she's begging me to claim her mouth...

"You okay man?"

I startle out of my reverie to find Jake peering at me, eyes narrowed. *Whoa, my mind got away from me there.*

"Oh. Yeah. Yeah, I'm good." I yank my gaze away from Olivia, standing a few feet away at the bar with Sofia.

"You sure?" Triple J pipes up. "You're, like, super red. Redder than our jerseys."

"You running a fever or something?" Dallas asks as he begins to back away from me. "If so, you should go home. You definitely don't wanna get us all sick. We play Toronto in two days."

"I'm fine," I insist. "It's just hot in here."

"No, it's not," Triple J says with a shake of his head. "I'm actually a bit cold."

"Me too," Jake adds, his expression nothing short of suspicious.

"What are you boys talking about?" Sofia appears beside me, Olivia trailing a step behind.

"How Aaron's face currently looks like a beetroot," Dallas says cheerfully.

Red is no longer my favorite color, I decide. But then, my gaze flits back to Liv and I have to retract my retraction.

"I got you a club soda," she says, a crooked smile on her lips.

"Thanks," I accept the glass, accidentally-on-purpose letting my fingers brush against hers. I'm gratified to see the hitch in her breath as I do.

"And for the record, your face is more the color of a tomato," she adds helpfully, her eyes flashing with mischief. All at once, I am mentally hurtled back to the other night in my kitchen, when she covered my naked torso in washcloths.

I let my eyes sweep over her stunning form, and then they capture hers again. "I might be in need of some more first aid."

"Aaron!" Reagan suddenly darts up and grabs my arm. Peeking behind me, her expression registers relief. "And Olivia, good. Just the people I wanted to see. Can I have a word with you both in private?"

Every ounce of casual flirtation in me disappears as I look around to see if Brandi has arrived. But to my relief, I don't see her anywhere. "Sure thing, Reags."

I glance sideways at Liv, but she only shrugs as we follow Reagan and her flouncy, neon-pink dress out of the ballroom.

Once in the hallway, she surreptitiously looks left, then right, like she's a freaking spy or something. Then, she opens a door and ushers us into...

A coat closet.

Although, she ushers Olivia a little too fast, causing her to trip over her heel. I place my hands on Liv's waist for a moment to steady her. I can't help but let them linger there a moment too long, before reluctantly pulling them away and turning to Reagan.

"I assume this is about Brandi, but was the closet really necessary?" I arch a brow.

"Yes. We are on a covert mission."

"I think it was a nice touch," Olivia adds with a smirk, and Reagan grins.

"Thanks, girl." Reagan then looks at me. "I have news that I think you'll like, Aaron."

"Well, now that we are safely among the mink furs of the rich and glitzy, please do tell."

Olivia snorts with laughter at this, and we share a small smile before Reagan clears her throat. Dramatically.

"I decided to do some digging on Brandi before tonight."

I tense. I've been so wrapped up in being at the gala with Olivia, I'd almost forgotten why Olivia is here with me in the first place.

"Has she arrived?" Olivia asks tentatively.

"I haven't seen her yet, but she will be here, I'm sure of it." Reagan's eyes widen conspiratorially, and she takes a long pause for dramatic effect, I'm sure, before she adds, "This is what she does."

I frown. "I'm confused."

"Look at this."

She hands me her phone, and right there, on her screen, is a social media post dated several years back. The account that made the post is called CrazyforCarterCallahan and the picture unmistakably features an almost unrecognizable, bright blond Brandi holding up a signed poster from one of the star's movies.

What the hell?

I happen to know Carter Callahan—the Cyclones have worked with his charity in the past. I also know that he lives here in Atlanta.

I'm trying to figure out what this all means when Olivia

peers at the screen, too. She sucks in a breath. "She's done this before. You're not her first target."

"Good sleuthing, Sherlock," Reagan praises her before smirking at me. "You, however, were slow on the uptake there, Marino."

Olivia snickers, and I give her a little nudge as Reagan swipes her phone out of my hand. She then pulls up another post, this time an old and defunct fan account for an Atlanta-based pro-baseball player. And then, another for a rap star also based in this city.

"I contacted all of these people's PR teams, and they confirmed that their client had been harassed by Brandi in the past. She comes after her victims by creating negative press, and then essentially blackmails them into paying her to disappear."

"That is wild." I shake my head. "But I don't understand why you seem so happy about this. Surely, this is bad news—the woman is clearly a freaking professional at shakedowns, which means that I'm screwed. Who knows what she might pull tonight."

I cast a sideways glance at Olivia, anxiety suddenly churning in my gut. I shouldn't have brought her into this.

What if Brandi does something to her? The very thought makes me sick.

But Reagan's laughing merrily, sounding not unlike a movie villain. "Here's the thing, Aaron. In the past, she attacked her targets from multiple angles, but for you, she chose to focus on your love life. Probably because you've never really dated anyone seriously, and so that's what she exploited. She could make you look so fricking callous." Reagan's eyes move mischievously to Olivia. "But what I believe she *didn't* count on was you being linked to someone else."

Next to me, Olivia shifts her weight a little. I am also starting to have a distinct feeling about where this is going, and I want nothing more than to peek at Liv's face. Try to read her expression.

"So," Reagan continues, nonplussed. "If you were to be seen at a high-visibility event, perhaps... with someone serious in your life... someone you're living with... then Brandi's stories would no longer hold any weight. She would no longer be a victim in the eyes of the media, but just a jilted, bitter ex. And if she were to try anything crazy, it would be seen, and reported, as such."

"And therefore clear up any lingering doubts Dennis Lieberman has about me and my character," I finish, my mind reeling.

She gives me a little finger gun and a wink. "Bingo, my friend."

"Genius," Olivia adds, sparkling at Reagan. "You should really be working for the CIA rather than the Cyclones."

She snorts. "Nah, my talents scouring social media archives would be entirely wasted at the CIA."

Olivia laughs, and I watch as her face lights up..

"But Olivia and me... we're not actually together." Nor would she ever want to make it look like we were. She agreed to be my plus one tonight, nothing more.

"Duh." Reagan purses her lips. "But you're here together tonight, right?"

She looks from me to Liv, and we both nod.

"And you're both young, and hot, and otherwise not romantically entangled, right?"

Olivia's skin is the color of her dress. "Yes," she says unevenly.

"So, if you make it look real tonight, Brandi will have no choice but to fade into the background. Or risk looking like a hysterical brat having a tantrum." Reagan mimes dusting her shoulders off, then gives us an upward nod. "Another cracked case by the Cyclones' resident super sleuth! Now, if you'll excuse me, I have an auction to prepare for. I'll see you on-stage in five minutes."

And with that, she exits the coat closet, leaving Liv and me alone.

I rake a hand through my hair. As perfect as Reagan's solution might appear to be, there's one very important factor here. "I'm sorry, Liv. This wasn't part of our agreement. You are, in no way, obliged to go along with Reagan's plan."

I honestly expect Olivia to look as horrified as she did when she saw my Christmas tree at the prospect of acting like more than just my auction-bidder tonight. But there's a smile playing on her lips. "I'll do it."

"You will?" I blink at her.

"Sure."

"Why?"

Her smile grows, and despite how focused I am on sorting out this Brandi stuff, I can't help but notice how beautiful she is.

"Because you've done me more than a few favors lately." Her brows furrow slightly as she adds, "And because what Brandi's doing is pretty gross, and I'd like her to be stopped. There are so many women—so many *people*—who have actual terrible relationships. Her pretending you treated her badly just to blackmail you is horrendous."

"Well… thank you. This means a lot."

"And I am poised and ready to spend a lot." She bounces her eyebrows up and down. "A lot of *your* money."

"All to win the date of a lifetime with me," I tease.

"We'll see about that," she says with a laugh as she puts her hand on the doorknob. "Now, let's get you auctioned off."

She throws open the door and we tumble out of the closet to find Sadie Lincoln—AKA the right-hand reporter for Satan himself—standing in the hallway. Reflexively, I reach for Olivia's hand.

Sadie's pencil-thin brows shoot up. "Hello, Aaron."

I nod brusquely. "Sadie."

She snaps straight into pitbull mode, pulling her lips back in a grimace. "Just the man I wanted to see. I had some follow-up questions regarding Dennis Lieberman's dissatisfaction with— "

"Whoa," Olivia cuts her off with a sweet smile. She gives my hand a squeeze, while placing her other one on my chest, gazing up at me adoringly.

I'm momentarily stunned by the liquid hazel depths of her eyes. It's a look she's never directed at me before, and I want to drown in it.

"You promised me we wouldn't talk about work tonight, honey. Tonight is about raising money for the children, remember." She pouts her bottom lip, then looks up at me seductively. "And for spending time with me."

"I remember," I say solemnly, shaking my head like I've been reprimanded. "Sorry, my love."

Sadie practically topples over in shock.

Honestly, while I'm apprehensive about seeing Lieberman tonight, Olivia's presence is making me feel much better about whatever he might have to say to me.

So much so that I turn back to the reporter and arrange my features into a bashful grin. "Sorry, Sadie, the boss has spoken. And she's right—tonight's about the children. So you'll have to save those questions for our next pre-game media chat. Have a good night."

With that, I put my hand on the small of Olivia's back, just like I did in my fantasy earlier. I direct her back into the ballroom, reveling in fact that I now know what her silky soft skin feels like beneath my palm.

I'm going to need zero help making this look real tonight.

27

OLIVIA

"Ten thousand dollars!" I hold up my little bidding thingy as I declare the number grandly. I then shoot a smile to Brandi, who's glowering back at me.

"Ten thousand five hundred," she says, her face pinched.

Unreal. If she's bidding this much to win a date with Aaron, I can't even imagine how much she was planning to shake him down for afterwards.

"Eleven thousand," I say, almost bored. On stage, Aaron's eyes are dancing.

The auction so far has been hilarious. Dallas was claimed by a tiny old lady who looked sweet and innocent at first, but smiled like a Cheshire Cat when she placed the winning bid. Jake ended up causing a bidding war between a cougar-type in her fifties and a guy with a very determined glint in his eye. Bonnie Lieberman, Dennis Lieberman's wife, ended up winning Triple J. And Maddie did the same for Seb as I'm doing for Aaron—paying the big bucks to win a date with her own husband.

"We have eleven thousand, going once, going twice—" Reagan crows in her auctioneer voice.

"Eleven thousand one hundred." Brandi tosses her auburn-red hair haughtily, and I can't help but grin.

"Twenty thousand dollars!" I declare, air-toasting Aaron with my champagne flute.

Damn, that's a crazy amount of money. Money I would have no idea what to even do with, but hey.

Brandi scowls. Aaron still looks like he's trying not to laugh.

As captain, he's the last to be bid on, and I'm glad to see that he looks like he's enjoying himself. The gala has been way more fun than I imagined. Everyone is merrily tipsy and having a great time, me included.

Plus I'm sure the info Reagan shared earlier has put Aaron's mind at ease. And while I'm also relieved that he has a solution to his problems, I'm reeling that said solution involves us looking like we're together for real tonight.

Because it sure feels real right now.

I can still feel the imprint of his hand, hot on my bare back, as he led me back to the ballroom. And I'm remembering the way his pupils visibly dilated when he first saw me in my dress earlier, all made up and with my hair styled...

"Wow," he said in a way that made my core clench in the most unwelcome yet exciting of ways. "Red is *definitely* your color, Livvy."

Now, hours later, he's standing on stage, cocky and confident as ever, looking at me like he knows exactly what I'm thinking about.

Beside me, Sofia snickers, snapping me out of my wayward thoughts. "Good thing he's rich."

"It's for the children," I tell her giddily, thinking back to that moment outside the closet with that awful reporter woman. The memory of her shocked face makes me feel even more giggly.

"Twenty thousand dollars for a date with Aaron Marino!

Going once, going twice, and SOLD to Olivia Griswold!" Reagan crows, throwing her hands up.

"Yay!" I clap my hands. My whole table cheers wildly, and Aaron catches my eye for a moment, then tips his head upwards in a nod, like he's saluting me.

In the corner of my eye, I notice Brandi rise from her table and slink away. I hope this is enough to keep her away, permanently.

"And that concludes our auction!" Reagan booms into the mic. "Can I please have the winners come up to stand beside their prizes?"

We file onto the stage, and when I get in line next to Aaron, he looks down at me almost fondly. "Atta girl."

"I think you mean 'thank you,'" I whisper. "To which I would respond, 'you're welcome.'"

"Nah." He smiles lazily. "I think I'll just tell you how good you did. Brandi didn't stand a chance."

"Was the sudden leap to twenty k a bit much?" I ask, suddenly feeling a little guilty for spending his money so freely.

But he grins. "I would've been happy to watch you bid ten times that, so long as you ended up on stage next to me at the end of it all."

"Now!" Reagan announces bouncily. "For the next part of our auction... This has been kept a mystery, totally top secret, until now. Even our players don't know what's about to happen." She holds up a box. "In the spirit of festive hijinks, in this box, I have a selection of dates up for grabs. Each winner will draw one, and that's the date they will be going on."

Oh. Not what I expected.

"Winner's choice." Reagan holds out the box to the cougarish lady with her hands wrapped around Jake's arm.

She reaches into the box and extracts a piece of paper, which she hands to Reagan.

"Congratulations!" Reagan yells. "You've won a—drumroll please—life drawing class, with Jake Griswold as your model!"

The lady shrieks in delight.

"What?" Jake demands, his face aghast.

Reagan holds the mic away from her mouth for a moment. "Payback for you guys vetoing my sexy charity calendar idea last year," she says with a smirk before speaking back into the mic. "Don't worry, you'll be provided with a tasteful sprig of holly for your private bits. Remember, it's all for a great cause!"

Jake looks vaguely murdery, Aaron is shaking with silent laughter beside me, and Sofia is practically convulsing in her chair, wiping tears from her eyes as she looks up at her enraged boyfriend.

Reagan moves down the line: Bonnie Lieberman wins a couple's massage and spa day with Triple J, while Dallas's elderly suitor picks out a festive couple's yoga class. Dallas, to his credit, gives the old lady a high-five and a big grin.

By the time Reagan reaches me, my palms are sweaty. I rub them together to avoid accidentally rubbing them on my dress.

"Olivia, you're up!" She winks at me.

I dig my hand in the box, and then pass the paper to Reagan.

"Your prize is a... ooh, you win a festive private skating lesson from Aaron Marino!"

I let out a shaky breath, thanking my lucky stars that I didn't choose something that involved nudity. And that I can already skate, although I haven't done it in ages.

Everyone is cheering and applauding as Reagan finishes her speech, revealing the amount that's been raised so far and encouraging people to keep their donations coming.

I glance up at Aaron. "What constitutes a festive skating lesson?"

"I don't know, maybe some Christmas lights and music in

the background." His eyes gleam. "Or maybe I'll wear my elf costume."

"That's hot."

"The tights really show off my glutes."

"Wow, even hotter." I laugh, but I'm blushing at the thought of that admittedly fantastic behind of his in a pair of tights.

"Like I said, get ready for the best date of your life," he says, confident as can be.

"We'll see about that." I smirk at him.

His eyes find mine. "We definitely will."

28

OLIVIA

The dance floor is crowded and the atmosphere at the gala has done a sweeping one-eighty from upmarket and classy to a full-on party. It's late and a lot of the older benefactors have taken their leave. Now, the drinks are flowing, the lights are dimmed, and the classy piano playing has turned into a full DJ setup spewing raunchy pop songs.

It's the Christmas party of the year. Of the *decade*.

And I'm... enjoying myself. Immensely.

Turns out, Christmas ain't so bad when it involves bidding on a sexy hockey player and sipping just enough vintage champagne to feel a little giggly. But not too much, because I have a flight tomorrow.

"I can't believe you organized this!" I yell over the music to Reagan, who's bouncing up and down next to me on the dance floor, her face as pink as her dress. "You absolutely killed it."

"I know!" she yells back. "It's my biggest achievement yet. All the videos I've been posting throughout the night are blowing up like crazy." She clicks her tongue and smiles evilly. "Aaron's Army is currently very jealous of you, Miss Griswold."

Ha. I wonder how jealous they'd be if they knew that I'm

currently living in his bedroom and have applied cold compresses to his bare chest at night.

"I'm glad it's been good publicity for him," I say. And I mean it.

Our plan seems to have worked—Brandi has made herself scarce the rest of the evening.

And, after the auction concluded, Aaron introduced me to Dennis and Bonnie Lieberman, who were nice, if a little snooty.

We chit-chatted for a few minutes, and Dennis looked impressed when I informed him that I'm Jake Griswold's sister. Before he swept off to talk to the Cyclones' coach—who was passing by holding two towering plates stacked with hors d'oeuvres—Dennis nodded at Aaron and clapped him on the shoulder.

"Well kid," he said solemnly as he looked Aaron up and down. "As long as you keep your love life out of the media from now on, we should be on a better trajectory. Don't drop the ball, because no matter how much Coach Torres might sing your praises, I, for one, would like to have a captain in place who has a respectable reputation that aligns with our family-friendly franchise."

It wasn't praise, exactly—it honestly sounded like a *warning* to me—but Aaron looked almost relieved as he smiled and said, "No worries there, Mr. Lieberman. I plan to date only Olivia from here on out, and I'm sure the media doesn't care to discuss our boring old monogamy and commitment to each other."

This made Lieberman harrumph with pleased laughter, and made me almost choke on my drink. It was obviously a line, but dammit if it didn't give me butterflies.

After Lieberman departed, Aaron yanked me onto the dance floor and we've been here ever since, dancing the night away with the team. Aaron stays close to me, and even when we're all dancing as a big group, he's by my side.

Jimmy, as it turns out, is an extremely accomplished dancer. The man has busted out the foxtrot, merengue, and a full-blown waltz in between bouts of twerking. I bump hips with Reagan and give her a twirl, but then the music dips, and the DJ announces the last song of the night.

The upbeat Christmas song that was playing fades into a slow, smooth, sultry beat.

My heart feels full as I watch Jake pull Sofia into his chest, whispering something in her ear that makes her laugh. Maddie loops her arms around Seb's neck, gazing up at him like he hung the moon. Triple J wastes no time whisking Reagan into his arms.

I, meanwhile, decide this is a great time to go and get a glass of water. I turn around and find Aaron standing directly behind me. His eyes are full of a raw intensity I've never seen before as he steps forward, looking like an absolute snack in that tux of his.

He holds out a hand. "Dance with me, Olivia."

In true Aaron fashion, it's a statement, not a question. And I'm here for it.

I take a step forward slowly, almost cautiously. But he catches my elbows and gently pulls me towards him so that my body is flush against his.

"That's better," he says as he looks down at me, mouth quirked.

"Mmpf," is all I manage in response.

His body is warm and solid, and his hands drag up my arms before they make their way down my back, finally anchoring at the base of my spine. I suck in a shaky breath as his fingertips slowly, purposefully, draw tiny circles on my bare skin.

We begin to move together, swaying to the song. My entire body is taut with anticipation, yet strangely at ease in his arms.

Aaron's green gaze stays on me, tracking over my eyes before dipping down to my lips, which automatically part.

His own breathing is labored, and I can feel his heartbeat throbbing against my body where we're touching.

He looks at me for another moment, like he's considering, before he slowly—almost hesitantly—leans down and touches his forehead to mine. It's a gesture that seems entirely more intimate than it should.

"Have I told you how incredible you've been tonight," he says. Another statement. I can smell the mint on his breath and I swallow, my head swirling and my skin hot and tingling. My insides almost ache with something akin to longing.

We stay like this, so close yet somehow still so far, orbiting each other as the song goes on and everything else fades into the background. I'm hyper aware of the heat of his body, the incredible scent of his cologne mingled with that distinctive Aaron smell I always catch on his sheets.

"I don't want the night to end yet," I admit.

"It doesn't have to," he replies, and the implication makes my stomach swoop dangerously.

"More slasher movies?" I tease, my heart pounding in my throat.

"Mmm." His fingers are still drawing torturous circles on my skin. "Maybe a game of dirty word scrabble or two."

"I like the sound of that," I tell him as the song comes to an end and the lights begin to come up.

Aaron peels himself away from me, almost regretfully. "Well then, let's get you home, Miss Olivia."

I nod, but before we take a step, Dallas appears out of nowhere and claps Aaron on the arm. "You up for an afterparty?"

At the mention of the word *afterparty,* Jimmy looks up eagerly. His gaze moves from Dallas to Aaron, and he immediately puts two and two together to make seven. "Afterparty at the captain's house!" he cries.

"Hell yeah," Colton chimes in, moving towards us.

"We're in," Sofia adds, her arms around Jake's waist.

Aaron looks around at all of them, and then looks down at me, his face unreadable. "What are we gonna tell them?"

A flicker of disappointment moves through me—as fun as an afterparty sounds, I was looking forward to some TV stabbings and trying to beat Aaron's perfect Scrabble record. That game is growing on me like a rash.

And, okay, if I'm being *very* honest, I was looking even more forward to spending some alone time with him tonight. The tension between us feels loaded, heavy and thick in a way that's tangible. It's got my head in a spin, because I'm becoming acutely aware that I'm feeling a certain kind of way about Aaron. It's a feeling that almost scares me.

Maybe this is for the best. We can have fun with the others for the rest of the night, and by the next time I'm alone with Aaron, my feelings will hopefully be more in order.

"I say we tell them to come ready to party," I declare.

This makes him smile. "Raincheck on the movie and Scrabble night?"

"Deal."

OLIVIA

It's after midnight, and the party at Aaron's place is going strong. Most of the Cyclones have shown up—save for Seb and Maddie, who went home to relieve their babysitter—as well as a bunch of other people. Some I recognize, some I don't.

Music is pumping from the speakers, the Christmas tree is glittering in all its glory, and the drinks are flowing freely. Someone ordered several pizzas, which are now stacked haphazardly all over the living room. A few people are locked into rowdy, festive party games.

Usually, an event like this would make me feel uncomfortable and have me moving from group to group like a rogue puzzle piece, trying way too hard to fit somewhere.

Not this party.

After a couple glasses of champagne at the gala, I've switched to Diet Coke because of my round-trip flight tomorrow, along with the fact that I'll be looking at apartments in the morning. But I find I don't even need the social lubricant of alcohol to take the edge off right now.

"Go go go go go!" I cry, howling with laughter as Stefani stands on a chair and attempts to wiggle another gold hula hoop over Aaron's head. He's already spinning two, his hips gyrating wildly, and it might be the funniest thing I've ever seen.

Jake, on the opposing team, is somehow successfully spinning three, and Colton and Lena are attempting to slip yet another hoop over his head.

The game is called Five Gold Rings, and the object is to get someone from your team to spin five hula hoops at once. It's ridiculous in the best way.

"Add a fourth one to his arm!" someone calls out, and Triple J throws a hoop to Aaron. He sticks an arm out and somehow manages to catch it, which makes everyone cheer uproariously.

"I'm going to need a video of this," I say with delight. "Be right back."

I duck out of the living room and head to the kitchen, where I left my phone charging. I'm walking around the corner, still chuckling to myself, when a couple of quiet voices in the hallway stop me cold.

A man whose voice I don't recognize is comforting a woman. A peek around the corner confirms that I don't know either of them, but I can *also* confirm that she is a very, very pretty redhead.

"I don't know why you care so much about her, Tessa." The man shakes his head. "She'll be old news before you know it."

"She's Jake Griswold's *sister*," Tessa hisses back and I become even more still and quiet. They're talking about me? "He must be serious about her. He'd never just screw with his teammate's sister."

I startle, taking a step further back so I'm fully out of sight.
What the hell?

Who even is this Tessa? And why on earth is she apparently so bothered about me?

"Okay, look." The man drops his voice further. "I heard this through the grapevine, but he's just using her for appearances after that story blew up on Thanksgiving. She's a cover so he looks good. Basically his beard. Rumor has it that the team's GM was really pissed about the whole thing so this—*she*—is purely for optics."

"You think?" Tessa asks, her question sounding hopeful in a way that makes my stomach churn. "That would make sense. I mean, she's not even that pretty. She was looking at him tonight like a lovesick puppy, and don't get me wrong, I'm sooooo over him, but I just don't understand what she can offer him that I couldn't."

The guy snorts. "Maybe she's a nice person?"

His voice is laced with sarcastic laughter and Tessa laughs, too. The bitter, high-pitched, mocking sound makes me feel like my skin is burning.

"Oh, yeah," she agrees. "Because Aaron Marino is *so* into women's... personalities."

The guy snorts. "He never stays long enough to find out if a woman even has one."

"You definitely don't want to catch feelings for him," Tessa says. She's still laughing, but I can't help but hear how her voice cracks slightly. "Because he sure won't catch them for you."

I take another step back, and another. And when I know I'm out of earshot, I bolt for the stairs, thanking my stars that I ditched my heels earlier.

I run to Aaron's bedroom and duck into the ensuite, my heart pounding.

When I look in the mirror, I'm horrified to see tears dripping down my face. And I can't stop sniffling. I quickly turn on the shower full-blast to drown out any potential noise in case this pesky tearfulness turns into a full-blown ugly cry.

It's probably an unnecessary precaution to have the shower going—the party downstairs is loud and raucous—but I'll be damned if I let Aaron Marino hear me cry.

That was just so... *humiliating.*

Letting out a shaky breath, I try to let my logical self beat out my emotional one:

I have no reason to be upset. Tessa's mean friend wasn't wrong when he said that this was just a cover and I'd be old news soon. I knew all along that this wasn't real; tonight was just about making it look *real, and I was dumb enough to confuse reality with acting when we were dancing together earlier and Aaron rested his forehead against mine.*

We clearly did a good job pretending because Tessa— whoever she is—sure seemed to buy it.

So, you know, go us.

But then, something horrible happens. Because the more I try to reason with myself, the harder the tears fall. And I know, deep down, that this is about more than the conversation I just overheard—hurtful as it was about the way I look.

There's a sudden knock at the door.

"Olivia?" Aaron's voice carries over the rush of the shower water.

"I'm showering!" I yell back. "Go away."

"Are you naked?" he counters, not going away.

"People are usually naked when they shower, yes."

"That doesn't answer my question." He pauses. "Plus, you don't sound like you're in the shower, you sound like you're right on the other side of the door."

"I'm, uh, about to get undressed. For said shower."

"So, you're fully clothed."

"Um. Not no?"

"Okay, hold up. I'm coming in for a minute."

"No, I—"

The door swings open. "You said you'd be right back and then you disappeared so I came looking, but I can't say I understand the logic of showering during a pa—"

His words come to an abrupt halt when he sees me, and the teasing grin on his face falls right off.

"Livvy," he says roughly. "What's wrong?"

He's discarded his tuxedo jacket and bowtie, leaving him in his dress pants and a perfectly tailored white button-down with the top button popped, showing off a little triangle of tanned skin. His hair is mussed and his eyes are heavy-lidded, and he looks so perfectly, exquisitely handsome that it makes my stomach clench. "Nothing."

He comes to stand in front of me, his face creased with worry, and he gently puts his hands on my arms. "Don't lie to me. What's wrong? Did something happen?"

His voice has taken on an almost tender quality, and for some reason, this makes me mad.

"No, I just..." The tears start to fall again, hot and angry this time, and I furiously blink them away. "Who's Tessa?" I find myself asking.

He looks totally thrown off by the question. "Tessa? She's someone I briefly dated last winter. Why?"

"She's here tonight."

"Oh, yeah. She works in communications at the RGM, so she knows a bunch of people." He narrows his eyes. "Did she say something to upset you?"

"Honestly, it sounds like you broke her heart and she doesn't understand why you ended it with her."

Aaron scrubs a hand over his face. "Ah, yeah. We went on a couple of dates, and she wasn't happy when I ended it. But it wasn't going anywhere. We had nothing in common, and I had a feeling that she liked the idea of dating a hockey player more than she liked *me*. It was around that time that I realized I was getting sick of casual dating, and I didn't want to prolong something with Tessa that would never amount to anything."

"You thought she wasn't good enough for you," I say flatly.

"I thought she wasn't *right* for me," he corrects. "Olivia, I promise I'm not a callous guy. I know you'd like to think I pick up and discard women as it suits me, but that's not the case. It's not that I believe people aren't *good* enough for me."

"Apart from me." It's a stupid thing to say, but my emotions are still getting the better of me.

His eyes flicker in surprise. "What?"

"You thought I wasn't good enough for you."

"What the hell makes you think that?" he demands.

"That night when you almost kissed me, then took off like a bat out of hell?" I reply, then immediately cringe at my own words. "Look, I know it's dumb and petty of me to even bring it up, because we were just kids back then and a lot has changed since. I know you're different now. But, I guess, hearing Tessa tonight reminded me of that whole situation and how it made me feel, even though it's ancient history." I sniff snottily, waving my hand. "This is so embarrassing. I'm such a mess for no reason."

He closes the gap between us and captures my wrists in his hands, moving my hands away from my face so he can look at me. "You think I left that night because I thought you weren't good enough for me?"

I nod.

He swears.

"Livvy, I left that night for the exact opposite reason. I panicked because I realized how much I liked you, but also realized that I was about to leave for Atlanta to start training camp. And on top of that, you were my best friend's little sister and he'd be furious with me for making a move on you."

"What?"

"The next day, I was going to talk to you about what almost happened, but then, you made some comment about how you'd gone temporarily insane. I thought you'd done the whole thing to mess with me. So, I did the same. Acted like I'd been messing around too, because I... I guess I was dumb enough to believe that was easier than admitting the truth."

"The truth?"

He swallows, his Adam's apple straining along the thick, tanned column of his throat. "That I was kind of obsessed with you."

My head is pounding with confusion. "You... what?"

Aaron gives me this sweet, almost vulnerable look that I've never seen before but is already a favorite of mine. "Liv, you know why I gave you the nickname 'Lil Griz'?"

"To make me crazy," I reply with a dry smile.

"No. Because it was the easiest way to remind myself that you were Jake's sister, and therefore off-limits." His fingertips stroke my wrists, which are still wrapped in his hands. "I always had a crush on you. How could I not? You were so fun and feisty and interesting."

He closes his eyes for a moment, long lashes skimming his cheekbones before he opens them again and gives me the full force of his gaze.

"If one of us was ever not good enough, it was me. You were —and still are—so far out of my league."

His words dance all over my skin, making me shiver.

"Shut up, Aaron." My voice is half-hearted, my stomach full of nervous butterflies.

"I mean it. You're the most beautiful woman I've ever seen, and I wish you could see yourself the way I see you."

The look he gives me when he says this gives me goose-bumps, and it takes everything in me to keep my composure as I roll my eyes and gesture towards my face. "Even with puffy red panda eyes?"

He smiles softly. "Trust me—no other woman can hold a candle to you. Even with puffy red panda eyes and smudged lipstick." His smile slides into a sudden smirk. "Even when you're soaked to the skin like a drowned rat."

"Wha—?"

The word doesn't have a chance to leave my lips because, in one swift movement, he puts his hands on my waist, picks me up, and walks us into the shower until my back hits the wall.

The scorching water rushes over us, soaking us to the skin, and my hands dig into his shoulders as I squeal. "What are you doing? Your tux is going to be ruined!"

"You were shivering," he counters, running his hands over my arms as if he's attempting to smooth my goosebumps away. Unfortunately, the feel of his rough skin on mine has the opposite effect, and despite the warm water, I break out in about a million more goosebumps.

Steam billows around us in clouds and the satin of my dress sticks to my skin.

"You're beautiful all the time, Olivia." His voice is hot, his expression raw.

He cups my chin, his thumb moving to trace my bottom lip, and for a moment, all my nerve endings sizzle in exquisite white-hot bliss.

"But you hate me," I mumble stupidly, half-aware that I'm breathing way too hard.

Aaron looks at me through heavy-lidded, dark eyes as he tucks a strand of hair behind my ear, fingertips skimming my cheek. "The only thing I hate about you, Olivia, is having to be around you and not being able to do this."

He leans forward and carefully, measuredly, brushes his lips across mine, featherlight and teasing and warm and entirely perfect. It's somehow too much and nowhere near enough all at once, but too soon, he pulls back, his breathing ragged.

My eyes flutter open to find his fixed on me.

Watching me.

Waiting for me, I realize.

And apparently, all the blood has run out of my brain and flooded the rest of my body, because in answer, I close the gap between us and press my lips against his again.

A low groan comes from his throat and he wastes no time, his hand moving to my face, angling my chin so he can kiss me deeper.

As his tongue moves over mine, an anguished sound leaves my mouth and my hands struggle to find purchase on his chest, grabbing at his soaked clothes as I pull him impossibly closer.

The steamy water continues to pour over us, and all I can feel is the heat of liquid on my skin, the heat of Aaron's body against me, the heat of his mouth as it moves over mine in a rhythm that makes my head spin and my legs shake. In response, he slides his hands under my thighs, picking me up again so I'm pinned against the wall, my legs looping around his waist as he continues to kiss me so expertly, it makes me forget anything outside of him even exists.

I've never in my life been kissed like this. Had no idea kissing *could* be like this.

During my fantasies of one-upping Aaron and getting my retribution, my mind would sometimes run away with me and I'd somehow end up fantasizing about what it would be like to kiss him. In my mind, we'd be warriors sparring, fighting for control of the situation, using every weapon in our arsenal to one-up each other.

In reality, I am completely at his mercy.

I'm hot and flustered and drenched in desire, putty in his hands. He's kissing me wildly, with complete abandon, scrapes of teeth and tongue and total raw emotion. Yet there's something gentler underneath it all, driving the kiss. Like he's savoring every second, drinking me in as he kisses me senseless.

My legs tighten around him, and my hands move from the

wet shirt sticking to his skin to find his hair, tangling in it and pulling it. He kisses me harder, one arm wrapped under my thighs, while the other braces on the shower tile behind my head, holding us firmly together.

His lips break away from mine and I moan in disappointment, until his hot, wet mouth latches onto my neck. My back arches as he kisses from my pulse point all the way to my collarbone, which he nips with his teeth, then soothes with a kiss, before kissing his way back up again, a man on a mission.

"Do you know how long I've wanted this, Olivia? Do you know how many times I've laid in bed at night, thinking about you? *Dreaming* about doing exactly this with you?"

His words make my entire core feel like it's unspooling, unraveling, and all I can do is croak his name—a shaky, desperate *"Aaron"*—before I grab his face again. Like I solely exist right now to have his lips on mine.

He laughs softly, the sound deep and throaty. "The answer is too many times to count."

And then he kisses me again.

And again.

And again.

Until there's no here and now, or me or him. But just us, in this moment, soaked clothes sliding over our skin, and our mouths exploring and learning each other as we trace the lines of each other's bodies.

30

AARON

The morning after the gala, I don't go to the arena.

Instead, I lie in bed, eyes closed, replaying every moment of last night on repeat.

Because I kissed Olivia Griswold, and instead of punching me in the face, she *kissed me back.* With an intensity that told me she was as into it as I was.

I don't think I'll ever get enough of that sassy, pouty, perfect mouth of hers. I can still taste her. Still feel how soft her skin was under my hands. And I think I'll forever be undone by the sounds she made while I kissed her neck and explored, learning what she liked, what made her back arch, what made her whimper, what made her say my name like that.

My name has never, ever sounded so good.

When I asked Olivia to come to the gala with me to outbid Brandi, I would have never in my wildest dreams imagined that the night could end like *that.*

"Focus, Aaron," I mutter to myself, shaking off my lust-drenched thoughts and finally slipping out of bed.

I pad downstairs and pick up bottles and take-out pizza

boxes, cleaning up until all remnants of last night's party have been squared away.

Well, almost all remnants...

I still can't stop thinking about her. Can't wait to see her when she wakes up.

I want to do something nice for her.

Which brings me to my next task: make Olivia a breakfast burrito. She's viewing some apartments this morning before she does a round-trip flight to Miami.

My culinary experience is pretty much nil, with the exception of my soup extravaganza last week, but I'm feeling confident enough. I have no idea how Olivia is feeling after last night, but I do know that she can't feel worse in the face of her favorite breakfast.

I can't believe that, for years, she thought that *I* thought she wasn't good enough for me. The very notion is absurd. Although it explains so much, and I'm glad to have set the record straight. I wish I could have done so a long time ago. Saved us years of unresolved tension.

But the past is in the past. All I can do now is move forward with whatever this is, or could be, between Olivia and me.

Telling Lieberman we were together last night felt *good*. And while I was relieved to see that the GM wasn't too displeased with me, I was more focused on how Olivia blushed when I declared that I only want to date her from now on.

Which is actually very true.

Because whatever this is between us, I'm here for it.

As I crack eggs into a bowl, my phone buzzes with a Face-Time call from my mom.

"Morning," I answer, propping my phone up on the counter.

"Good morning." Mom blinks. "Why are you at home?"

"Well, I do live here." I start to add some twists of black pepper to my bowl of eggs.

"Hardly!" she scoffs. "I almost forgot what your kitchen looked like. And since when do you cook? First, you call Nonna for help with the soup that I know you never, ever make. And now, you're whipping up..." She squints at my bowl. "An omelet?"

"Breakfast burritos," I say with a chuckle as I walk to the fridge in search of breakfast sausages.

"Hmm, I see," my mom says suspiciously.

"Just over a week until I'm home," I change the subject. "I can't wait. Any snow in the forecast?"

"Tons of it." Mom looks excited. I didn't get my love of Christmas from nowhere—my mom is its biggest fan. "Rachael's boys are so excited for Uncle Aaron to come sledding with them."

We always had a million festive traditions when I was growing up: sledding with my dad, uncles, and cousins, then stuffing our faces with Nonna's panettone; attending a candle-light Christmas Eve carol service, followed by a feast of seafood; watching *Miracle on 34th Street* on Christmas morning with hot cocoa topped with extra whipped cream.

In case you haven't heard, we Italians love our food.

Speaking of which...

"Dammit!" I yelp. The eggs are burning and I hurtle towards them, grabbing the pan off the stove, but it's too late. They smell terrible.

And then, I hear the creak of a bedroom door opening upstairs.

"Mom, I've got to go," I tell her as I stare at the burnt eggs. Gross.

"Why?" she prompts. "Is 'Nobody' there with you?"

I laugh, remembering our last conversation. "No, Mom. She's definitely not nobody."

Far from it. I want Olivia to know what last night meant to me. How serious I was when I said I'd dreamed about her so many times.

Tomorrow afternoon, she flies to Southeast Asia for a few days, so today is the last time I'll be able to spend proper, quality time with her until right before I go home for Christmas.

"I knew it!" Mom announces triumphantly. "Do I need to add a place at the Christmas dinner table?"

"No, no, Mom," I say, hearing footsteps on the stairs. "It's not like that."

But a part of me wonders if it *could* be like that. The thought of Olivia sitting here alone at Christmas while I'm with my massive family just feels wrong.

I know she wouldn't accept an invitation to fly to New Jersey with me for the holidays, but I wonder if there's anything I can do to soften some of her bad memories by replacing them with better ones.

Just like I want to put the past in the past and show her how much I like her, I also wonder if I can help her put the past in the past with the holidays.

Suddenly, I get an idea. A damn good idea that will help me achieve both of those things.

"Well, what *is* it like?" Mom demands, eyes glinting.

Like nothing I've ever experienced.

"I'm not sure yet," I say, the most honest answer I can speak aloud.

Mom gives me a terrifying wink. "Well, if you really want to impress her, I'd toss those eggs in the trash and order takeout."

Laughing to herself, she hangs up just as Olivia enters the kitchen.

At the very sight of her, my heart picks up speed. She's barefoot with her face free of makeup, dressed in an oversized Giants hoodie and leggings. Her hair's in a top knot, she's wearing her glasses, and the sight of her does something to me on such a deep level, I'm knocked off-kilter for a moment.

"Hi," she says, her voice soft and throaty. "Am I interrupting something?"

"Oh, no. It was just my mom on the phone." I point sheepishly to the mess on the counter. "I was, uh, trying to make breakfast. Failing, too."

"I can see that." She laughs, her face shining. All I want to do is make her laugh for as long as I can. "Do you need some help?"

"Do I look like a man who needs help, Griswold?"

She raises a smug brow as she studies the mess in the kitchen. "Yes."

"Well luckily, I have a better idea," I tell her. "Before we check out your apartment options, wanna hit up Essy's?"

"Now you're speaking my language, Marino."

31

OLIVIA

"Last but not least, this is the bathroom," says the landlord, a burly guy named Kris, as he pushes open the door to a small, but clean, room with white tiled walls.

I follow Kris into the space, Aaron right behind me. It's a squeeze for three people, especially when one of them is as big as Aaron. I try not to notice the heat radiating off his body behind me, but every time I so much as breathe, I catch the now-familiar scent of his skin—warmth and clean laundry and the hint of some deliciously spicy, masculine cologne.

I refocus my attention squarely on the task at hand, which involves appraising this teeny, tiny but bright bathroom. Luckily, given my rather nomadic lifestyle lately, I don't have many toiletries to take up space in here. My stuff takes up a laughably small corner in Aaron's master bath.

At that moment, my eyes zero in on the shower, and I tumble back to last night.

His white shirt, wet and plastered to his muscular chest. His eyes on fire. His hands on my body...

Kris, who looks to be in his mid-forties and lives with his

wife and kids in one of the building's top-floor apartments, frowns. "Is it not to your liking?"

"Oh, no. It's nice," I say quickly, my voice a little shaky. I can't let my wayward thoughts of Aaron's mouth on mine distract me, because this place is perfect. It's not a huge apartment, by any means, but everything is clean and well-kept, there's a communal laundry room in the building, and it's close to transit connections to the airport.

Most importantly, it's a one bedroom, which means *no more raving roommates.*

"*Very* nice," Aaron adds with a note in his voice that gives me goosebumps and makes me wonder if he's looking at that shower thinking the very same thing as I am. I crane my neck around to look at him and find him looking back at me, that same fire from last night sparking in his eyes.

I swallow thickly and turn to Kris. "I'd love to fill out an application form."

"Great." He looks pleased, but then, his expression morphs into one of concern. "Are you feeling okay, Olivia? You look a little hot. Would you like some water?"

Fml.

"Yes, Olivia, would you like some water?" Aaron echoes with a smile in his voice that makes me want to simultaneously slap him and drag him into this shower to test out its kissing capacity.

Last night, after kissing me senseless in his shower, Aaron and I returned to the party like nothing happened. Well, *he* acted like nothing happened. I, on the other hand, blushed like a tomato and lied about having pizza stuck in my hair when Jake —who had been super distracted with Sofia all night—suddenly took a keen interest in why my hair was wet.

A story which made Aaron smirk at me in a secret way that left me breathless.

For the rest of the night, he'd go out of his way to surreptitiously trail his fingers on my arm in passing, and there were a few moments where I found him watching me from across the room with such an intensity, it made me lose my train of thought mid-conversation.

I'm not sure what it means, exactly, or if anything like that will happen again. But one thing's for certain: that was the best kiss of my life, hands down.

And more than that, as Aaron and I went from breakfast at Essy's to three different apartment viewings this morning, I've realized that something has fundamentally changed in the way I feel towards him.

It's been difficult, lately, rectifying the fun I've been having with Aaron and our meaningful, surprisingly deep conversations, with the loathing I've been carrying towards him for so many years. It was like I couldn't put the pieces of him together to form a whole person that I had one opinion about.

But after what he said last night, it's a little easier to blend the *then* and *now* versions of Aaron in my mind.

Although, never in my wildest dreams could I have imagined him kissing me like *that*.

I'm about to make some veiled comment about wanting more water—because I'm still wondering if Aaron is thinking about last night as much as I am, and if he's not, I want to remind him. But when I look at him, he's taken his phone out of his pocket and is texting someone at lightning speed.

"Um, no, thank you," I tell Kris instead, once again trying to redirect my thoughts. "I'm good for water. I'll just take the application form."

I filled out an application for the first apartment we looked at, too, but this one is superior in every way. I'm feeling relatively excited about it as Kris leads us down to the lobby. He gives me a form, and then heads into his office. I look up at Aaron, wanting to ask his thoughts on the place and confirm that it's a good find—because I do actually kind of care about his opinion—when his phone rings.

He checks the screen and moves towards the door. "Uh, I'll be right back."

I turn back to my form and fill it out dutifully, but I can't help but wonder who he's talking to and if it's the same person he was texting a minute ago.

"I can't believe that you're currently living with Aaron Marino and you're applying to move *here*," Kris says from behind me. He's left his office and is now watching Aaron pace outside with wide eyes. He managed to keep his inner fan hidden pretty well during the viewing.

"Trust me, I find it hard to believe I live with him, too," I mutter as I continue down the form.

And that's when my heart falls.

There's a security deposit, but it's more than I was expecting to pay. This building also requires the first and last month's rent in advance. And the rent itself is at the top end of my budget.

Which means that, even if I *do* get it, this apartment is not going to work for me, financially.

I swallow thickly as I finish the form anyway. It would be awkward not to, especially with Kris standing over my shoulder.

"All good?" Aaron asks when he ducks back inside.

I nod, biting the inside of my cheek. "Yup. I'm ready to go."

We each shake Kris's hand, and then leave the building. I'm feeling a little downtrodden, and the worst part is that I'm not sure if it has more to do with not being able to afford that apartment, or not knowing who Aaron was talking to so urgently.

Clearly, I need to give my head a shake and snap out of it.

"You seemed to like that one," Aaron says as we stroll down the sidewalk. "I did, too. The building looks safe and the landlord seems like a good guy."

"I don't know if it's going to work," I tell him, pasting on a small smile. "Bit of a stretch for me. But, it's fine." I wave a hand as we approach his car. "The first one we saw was a good option, too. And it's within my budget."

"Well, I wouldn't write it off so fast. You never know what might happen." I could swear there's a twinkle in his eye, but he turns away to open the passenger door for me too quickly for me to be sure.

"You have to say that. You're basically the epitome of golden retriever energy."

He laughs—cackles, really—as he gets in on the driver's side. "Alright, I might have an idea to cheer you up."

"What's that?"

"How tired do you think you'll be after work today?"

Weird question, but I shrug. "Shouldn't be too bad. It's just a quick turnaround."

"I was thinking of cashing in on our skating lesson date."

"Tonight?" I ask in surprise.

"Yeah." His eyes glimmer. "If you're up for a date tonight."

He says this so easily, pleasantly, like this date isn't an obligation for him to fulfill. I raise a brow at him. "If I remember correctly, I was the one doing the bidding, and you were the bidd*ee*. Ergo, I am the one who gets to 'cash in' on the date."

"I remember no such thing," Aaron declares. "Look. I just got off the phone with Reagan and she's happy to let me do the date my way rather than what she originally organized. So yes, I'd love to take you out tonight, Olivia."

My heart does a little jump, and I have to remind myself not to get carried away.

Because he was talking to Reagan earlier about taking *me* on a date.

One that he organized himself instead of sticking with the one organized for him.

And the way he's talking right now, the way he's looking at me, this almost feels like it might not be a total obligation.

In a desperate attempt to play it cool when I am quite literally the opposite right now, I laugh. "Okay. Let's do it."

He grins, looking impossibly handsome for a moment, but then, grin turns cocky. "Hope you're ready for a serious ass-kicking, Lil Griz."

I fix him with a confident stare. "You won't even know what hit you, Marino."

He laughs deeply. "I'll meet you at the airport later with your skates."

His words make my stomach go fizzy. I've been a flight attendant for eight years, but this will only be the second time that I get picked up at the airport after returning from a trip.

The first time was two weeks ago.

Aaron again.

It means more to me than I would have ever imagined.

As Aaron pulls away from the curb and heads towards home, I tilt my chin up at him playfully. "So, let me get this straight, you organized this whole date without asking me. What if I'd said no?"

"Then I would've obviously had to assume that you're such a terrible skater, you've deemed yourself unteachable." His eyes sparkle. "Or I would've invited Jing to come with me in your stead."

"Insufferable as ever, aren't you?"

"You know you love it, Griswold."

Excitement flutters through me, and I have to take a moment to regain my composure.

I press a hand to my forehead. I must be getting sick. And am possibly delirious.

For years, Christmas has been, for me, the most hateful time of year, and Aaron Marino, my most hated person. Yet here I am, impossibly excited about the thought of a Christmassy date with him.

32

AARON

"Wait, aren't we going to the RGM?" Olivia asks as she squints out the passenger window at the turn we'd normally take to get to the arena.

I stop at a red light. "Nope."

Olivia frowns at the road ahead, and I take a moment to let my eyes roam over her, taking her in.

After she said yes to our date earlier, I drove her home, and she got changed for work while also packing a bag of clothes for this evening. She met me at Arrivals twenty minutes ago wearing black leggings, a soft fleece jacket, and a baby pink beanie hat that complements the pink of her cheeks. Her waves are soft and loose around her face, and I can't get over how incredible she looks.

She has no idea what I *actually* have planned for tonight. I'll admit I'm nervous about it—it's more than a little out of her comfort zone.

She finally turns her gaze on me, meeting my eyes. "You're not going to tell me where we're going, are you?"

"Also nope."

"Hmm." She screws up her nose. "I brought you candy from the airport, but now, I'm thinking I might keep it all for myself."

"You dare hold the airport candy hostage?"

"I do."

Olivia raises a brow, challenging me, but I refuse to take the bait, giving her a shrug. "Suit yourself."

She makes this noise in the back of her throat. Sort of a growl-groan thing that unexpectedly makes my blood heat. "Insufferable man."

"Impatient woman."

"Maybe I'm excited," she counters.

"Me too." I grin. "But I'm still not telling you."

She crosses her eyes at me, and we share a smile before she whines, "Fineeee. But if you're not going to tell me where we're going, at least tell me how Jake's life drawing date went?"

This makes me laugh. Jake's dreaded date happened this afternoon and I obviously had to stop by his place afterwards to make fun of him mercilessly—*uh*, I mean, find out how it went.

"You'll have to ask him yourself because the story will be way, way funnier coming from him. But let's just say that the woman who won the date titled her finished artwork 'Jingle Balls.'"

Olivia bursts out laughing. "No way!"

"Way. Jake said that she's planning on framing it and putting it above her fireplace." I grin at the memory of his horrified face. "Then Sofia started heckling him, saying she was jealous and she wants to go back there with him so she can paint her own version."

"That's amazing." Olivia howls. "I cannot wait to make fun of him about this for the rest of our lives."

"I will be joining you on that," I say, and then immediately want to swallow those words because she was obviously talking about her and Jake's lives, not her and mine.

Way to be cool, Aaron.

But if I'm being honest, nothing about me is cool when it comes to Olivia.

She makes me feel... different. After a few weeks living together, I know her better than I ever have. There's this ease about the way we laugh and banter with each other, yet challenge each other, too. Like always, her energy fuels me. I feed off of it, crave it when she's not around. She *fits* with me in a way that I didn't think was possible.

Luckily, she seems to miss my complete lack of chill and just chuckles as she stares out the window at the traffic signs while I merge onto the 85.

"We're not too far," I tell her, answering her unasked question. "Well, not too far-ish."

She smiles softly at me. "I can wait."

I can, too, I realize. Maybe a part of me has been waiting for her, all this time.

Forty-five minutes later, I pull into a parking lot and cut the engine. Olivia looks out the windows into the darkness. "You brought me to a random parking lot in an even more random small town outside of Atlanta?"

"Correct. Except for the random part. It's not random at all."

"You researched the best place to dispose of a body without getting caught, then?" She looks up at me with her chin tilted at an angle that's half the fiery Olivia I know and adore, half downright flirtatious. It's an all-together new look for me to experience and love on her.

And it's doing things to me. Like making me have to reluctantly resist the urge to kiss her breathless, right here in the parking lot.

I force myself to stick to the task at hand.

"Not quite that either."

I get out of the car and come around to her side, opening her door and offering my hand to her. After a second's hesitation, she accepts, threading her fingers through mine as she climbs out. Her palm feels warm and soft and small as it presses into my hand.

I lead her towards a dimly lit pathway to the side of the parking area. "It's maybe a little less murdery and a little more Christmassy. Which I know isn't to your usual taste. But the rule was a festive skating date, so..."

She looks up at me solemnly. "It *is* very important that we follow those iron-clad gala rules."

"Glad you take the rules as seriously as I do," I tell her with a snort as we continue down the pathway and around the corner, where the community rink I've rented awaits.

I lead her to the edge of the rink, and then, I flip the power on.

All at once, the area around the rink is alight, illuminating the darkness.

"What on earth?" Olivia gapes.

We're standing at the edge of a seasonal outdoor rink set up in the town's park—apparently, they set one up every Christmas and use a refrigeration system to keep it frozen in the typically mild Georgia winters. I loved the idea of outdoor skating so much, I booked the entire place for the evening so that we could be alone.

Multi-colored lights and strands of tinsel decorate the canopy overhead, and a light machine casts a pattern of a million snowflakes onto the untouched sheet of ice. The surrounding trees are strung with more lights that shimmer and flicker in the darkness. We're far enough away from Atlanta's city lights that the stars are visible overhead, and from the speakers, the opening bars of Coldplay's "Christmas Lights" begin to play.

But I'm barely noticing or appreciating any of this, because *she* is all I can look at.

Olivia's eyes move over the entire scene, like she's analyzing and cataloging everything she sees.

"You ready?" I ask, and she looks at me. Her eyes are shimmering hazel and gold, rivaling the glow of the lights. She nods, but right before we move to put on our skates, I drop her hand to collect my bag. "One more thing."

From inside the bag, I produce a crumpled sweater and hold it up in front of her. It's the most hideously awful festive-looking sweater that money could buy: a bright-green, knit number with lights wired into it and tinsel cuffs.

Oh, and an image of Santa Claus riding a T-rex on the front. No idea why.

I give her a sly look. "The rules did say 'festive date,' and so I am most definitely planning to wear this."

She takes one look at the sweatshirt and bursts out laughing. "That is the ugliest ugly Christmas sweater I have ever seen in my life."

"Mission accomplished." I wink at her and shrug off my coat so I can pull the sweater over my head.

She just rolls her eyes. "You look ridiculous."

"Wanna join me?" I have a spare sweater in my bag, but it might be a step too far to expect her to dress Christmassy.

She bites her lip, then shakes her head. "Thanks, but I'll leave the poor fashion choices to you. I think that sweater slots in somewhere between your old MILF t-shirt and that terrible hairstyle you had in high school."

This makes me laugh, even as I groan and place my head in my hands. "You remember the faux-hawk."

She looks at me impishly. "I could never forget the faux-hawk if I tried."

We sit on the bench beside the ice and lace up our skates. I might do this all the time—it's my literal job—but I'm lagging behind Olivia, too distracted catching her eye and watching her smirk at my sweater.

When we finally step out on the ice, it's just as I hoped it would be. The atmosphere is a perfect mix of tacky, festive, and fun.

"It's been forever since I skated," Olivia mutters.

Almost experimentally, she does a little twirl on the toe pick of her figure skate. She used to figure skate as a kid—long before I knew her—but just like everything having to do with Olivia, my brain clearly saved that special little tidbit.

She grins as she exits the twirl, like she's proud of herself. "Still got it."

"Show off," I tell her as I skate backwards in front of her. "I believe I'm meant to be giving you a lesson right now."

"The rules said a skating lesson with Aaron Marino. Didn't specify who was teaching who."

I skate over so I'm standing right in front of her, so close that our chests are practically touching. "Show me what you've got then, Griswold."

A slow, sexy smile creeps over her face, and suddenly, she's skating away, fast. She stretches her arms out elegantly as she executes a little jump, twisting in the air and impressively sticking the landing—there's just a small wobble, which corrects swiftly as she punches a victorious fist in the air.

Her face is red from the cold, but her eyes are warm as she takes a goofy bow. Frick, she's cute. I'm going to miss the hell out of her when she flies to Asia tomorrow.

"Haven't done that in years." She puts her hands on her hips. "You're up, Marino."

I skate fast and hard for a few strides before jumping and attempting to throw my body in a twist. The result is a bizarre kind of airborne pirouette, my arms flung wide and sloppy as I propel my weight around.

I overshoot slightly, and then flail like a madman after trying (and failing) to stick the landing in toe-pickless hockey skates. The front of my skate hits the ice first, which makes me stumble forward, hands out. But I manage to regain my balance at the last moment, still wobbling as I windmill my hands to steady myself.

"Nailed it!" I cry as I raise both arms in victory.

When I look at Liv, she's doubled over with laughter. "That was incredible. I can't believe you landed that in hockey skates," she cackles, but her face freezes. "Actually, thank goodness you did. Your coach would have killed me if his captain got injured on my watch."

I lean forward, sticking my back leg out and skating around on one foot, arms flung out dramatically like I'm a damn swan. "Not even a possibility, Griswold. I'm the best male figure skater out there."

"You ever figure skated before?"

"No," I admit, "but I'm sure I'd be a natural. In fact..." I skate over to her and place my hands at her waist. "We're doing a lift."

She struggles a little in my arms, but doesn't skate away. "Don't be ridiculous. You can't lift me."

"Watch me."

And then, with absolutely zero grace or poise or form or anything else needed to figure skate, I lift Olivia into the air, holding her up like she's Simba in the freaking Lion King.

"This isn't regulation!" she squeals, clinging onto my arms for dear life.

I've been skating since I was three years old and have spent most of my life in skates. It feels as natural to me as walking. So much so that I'm entirely confident in every move I make, knowing that I've got her. Knowing I could never let her go.

I could do this forever.

"It's a brand-new move," I shout. "The Aaron Marino Masterpiece."

"Put me down, you fool!"

"And the crowd goes wild!" I yell instead, skating backwards with her in my arms.

She's laughing, her palms now spanning my hands around her waist. The lights above us are sparkling, and the Christmas music is swelling, and it's a picture-perfect moment that I hope she'll remember for a long time.

I know I will.

33

OLIVIA

I can't remember the last time I laughed this much. Or hurt this much. I haven't busted out my figure skating moves since I was about twelve, so after an hour of messing around on the ice with Aaron, twirling and jumping and generally acting like idiots, I'm sore all over.

"Ready to call it?" he asks. His cheeks are pink, and his green eyes are shining, and minus the ridiculous sweater, he looks like some kind of prince from a storybook.

But a sexy, naughty version who's about to ravage you. Like the ones in those books Jing reads.

One can only hope.

Apparently my mind is still firmly on last night's kiss. Or as Aaron would say, in the sex gutter.

"Yup," I say with a smile that I hope masks my thoughts.

We change into our shoes, and I'm expecting us to walk back to the car, but he puts a hand on my elbow and steers me in the other direction. "This way."

I chuckle as he leads me to the far end of the rink. "Let me guess, you're not going to tell me where we're going."

"Damn straight." He smirks at me, and then offers me his

arm. I loop my hand through the crook of his elbow and let my fingers splay on his bicep as we walk along a dark pathway once again, walking further from the car.

"That was really fun, Aaron," I say, and I mean every word. "Thanks for setting it up."

His eyes twinkle in the darkness as he looks down at me. "The date isn't over yet."

A few moments later, we step off the pathway and onto a quiet street that looks like a Christmas bomb exploded on it.

It's the sort of street that would belong in the same fairytale book in which I was just picturing Aaron, complete with old-fashioned street lamps and cobbled walkways. Quaint store-fronts with intricate window displays feature fake snow, and nativity scenes, and toys from *The Nutcracker*. White Christmas lights are strung above us, glowing like stars. Hidden speakers along the street play an old Christmas hymn, which floats through the crisp night air.

At the end of the street, a majestic Christmas tree with a huge star on top towers over a bustling Christmas market.

"Where are we?" I gape at Aaron for what feels like the millionth time this evening.

He looks down at the cobble for a moment before looking at me, his eyes suddenly cautious. "Helen, Georgia. Also known as the Christmassiest town in the state. Which I'm not sure is a word, but should be."

"Should it?" I ask dumbly. I'm not sure what to think. I could tell that he planned our ice skating date tonight to show-case the tacky, fun side of Christmas, and I thought he'd done that to keep things light, seeing as he knows I don't like the holidays.

But this is something else entirely. This is nostalgic, whimsi-cal, *storybook* Christmas. The sort of place designed to deliver that specific type of Christmas magic feeling I've been running from for so long.

Why would he take me here?

For a moment, I'm thrown back to the past, remembering the last time I let my guard down with Aaron, and then felt like a fool for doing so.

But I stop that line of thought in its tracks. Because I know that he's not the guy I thought he was. Back then, or here now.

I trust him, I realize. Trust him with my feelings. Trust him with what I've shared. Something within me seems to recognize this on a fundamental level. Recognize that he's here for me.

He stops walking and spins me around to face him. When he sees my expression, his mouth presses in a line.

"If it's too much, we can go. But I had a thought..." He swallows, his Adam's apple bobbing. "Did you know that my dad died while I was playing a hockey game?"

I dip my head. "I had no idea. I'm so sorry."

"It was a long time ago." His eyes focus on mine. "My first season with the Cyclones. After a game, I got off the ice to learn that I had a phone call and it was an emergency." He takes a breath in through his nose, and then out. Quietly, subtly, but I notice the pause. "He'd been sick for a long time, so I knew it was coming, but I wasn't ready, you know? I don't know if you can ever be ready for something like that."

I stroke his coat sleeve, feeling overcome with the desire to comfort him. Wishing I could somehow make things better, but all I can offer is, "Of course not."

"I took time off for the funeral and to help my mom out, but when I got back to Atlanta and started playing again, I wasn't in a great place." He sets his jaw. "My dad and hockey were, like, linked in my brain. I'd never known one without the other. My dad taught me to skate, he bought me my first hockey stick, and after he died, I'd get anxious every time I stepped on the ice. Felt like something bad was going to happen." His brows furrow together. "It messed with my head, and it began messing with my game, too."

"That's completely understandable." I'm surprised that he's sharing all of this with me, but I'm glad that he feels he can. I like seeing this more vulnerable side of him, even though I'm sad to learn what he went through. I have a few vague memories of Aaron's parents from high school—mostly seeing them at hockey games. They seemed so different from mine; always smiling, always looking happy together.

They looked like a unit.

I'm upset for his, and his mom's, loss.

"Understandable personally, yes," Aaron says with a shrug. "But not professionally. If I wanted a career playing hockey, I had to get my head back in the game and stop associating stepping out on the ice with my dad dying."

"How'd you do that?"

Aaron's lips tip up slightly at the corner. "My whole career, he had these little leather notebooks where he'd jot stuff down while I was playing. After my games, he'd call me and talk me through his thoughts. The good, the bad, and the ugly. We'd review it all together."

He pushes back his sleeve and holds up his hand to show me the black leather bracelet looped around his thick wrist.

"I missed talking to him so much after my games, and I couldn't exactly carry his notebooks around with me. So, I had this bracelet made from the cover of his last notebook, and now, it's like my dad's with me every time I skate." He fingers the bracelet absentmindedly. "While I couldn't change what happened, I didn't have to be stuck in that moment forever. Instead, I could carry the past with me and honor his memory, while moving forward and making new memories with hockey that he would be proud of."

"Aaron, that's... beautiful." He's talking about his grief so candidly. Who knew that, under that confident, unruffled exterior, there was such a strong, yet soft, man. Masculinity at its finest—being unafraid to be vulnerable, and understanding that vulnerability can be a strength in itself. "Thank you for sharing that with me."

His small smile shows a mixture of hesitancy and hope. "I thought, maybe, we could do the same tonight. Or a version of it, at least. You can't undo the past, or change it, or make those memories of Christmas any less real or painful. And you don't have to forget them and how they shaped you. But you can add to them. Create new memories of this holiday that are happy and peaceful." He reaches for my hands, wrapping them in his. "They can exist together, the before and the after, and both be equally true. It's okay to have complicated, mixed feelings."

I stare at him for a moment as his words sink in. I can hardly believe the extent of his thoughtfulness and care.

"You are an amazing man, Aaron Marino," I say quietly.

"Nah." He scuffs the toe of his boot on the sidewalk. "I just want you to be happy."

"I am." I suddenly realize how true this is and have to swallow a lump in my throat.

Seeing how overcome I am, Aaron gently smiles and points towards the Christmas market at the end of the street, redirecting the conversation. "And food would make you happier right now, no?"

The mood lightens and I grin. "What are we waiting for?"

And so, we walk through the market, hand in hand, as crowds of happy, laughing people surround us. We stop to watch carolers sing, and to purchase spiked hot chocolates and Bavarian pretzels. And to buy a handmade tree ornament from a craft store—a single skate, to remember this night, and to mark honoring the past while still moving forward. I plan to hang it on the tree in the living room the second we get home.

My heart feels heavy, but in a good way. Full of happiness and joy and memories in the making.

It almost feels too soon that the vendors are packing up and we're meandering back to Aaron's car. My face hurts from smiling and stings from the cold, though I'm feeling warm inside. My arm is tucked through Aaron's, and I feel relaxed and comfortable at his side.

"Hey, Livvy?" he asks as we approach his car.

"Yeah?"

"I leave for Jersey on Christmas Eve and my last home game before the break is on the 23rd." He pauses for a moment. "I was wondering... would you come to the game?" Another pause. "For me?"

My answer is easy, said without hesitation. "I wouldn't dream of being anywhere else."

Something weird is happening.

I'm sitting at a rooftop cafe in Ho Chi Minh City, a steaming bowl of pho in front of me and the vibrant city splayed out below me. There's not a hint of Christmas anywhere, but instead, a million motorbikes zoom down busy roads and among street markets. Vendors on every corner sell banh mi and shrimp rice paper dumplings, the savory scents carrying through the hot, humid morning air. The mingling sounds of taxi horns and children's laughter from the park feels pleasantly bustling.

It's beautiful, and chaotic, and perfect.

My layover in Ho Chi Minh City was one of the stops I was over the moon to land this month, and yet...

I'm ready to go home.

I dig my chopsticks into the huge bowl and gather some rice noodles, processing this foreign feeling. Not only that I want to go back, but also that there's a *home* to go back to. I've been gone for a few days now, and while I'm loving taking in all the sights and sounds and smells, I feel ready to be grounded.

Ready to be in one place. For a few days, at least.

I miss Aaron's comfy bed. Miss his amazing shower, which is all the more amazing now that it holds a certain spine-tingling memory. Miss his car, which drove us to that annoyingly—okay, *adorably*— festive little town. I even miss his dartboard-defaced Christmas tree.

And, dammit. I might just miss him, too.

I've been thinking about my magical Christmas date with Aaron (there's a string of words I never thought I'd put together) almost constantly during this trip to Asia.

On a whim, I snap a picture of the view and text it to him. We've been texting throughout my trip.

> Good morning from Vietnam! Having a rooftop breakfast. Beats Essy's view of a strip mall parking lot, doesn't it?

> Looks beautiful. But I'm 100% sure that's only the second best view on that rooftop.

A giggle—yes, a damn giggle—escapes me.

Another text comes through, and my giggle catches in my throat.

It's a picture of Aaron, shirtless and clad only in gray sweat-pants and his black baseball hat, sitting backwards on his head. He's sitting on a huge bed in a hotel room, right next to a half-eaten sub sandwich sitting on its checkered paper wrapping. In the back of the photo, Jake and Dallas are on the couch, stuffing their faces with their own sandwiches.

> My current view. We won our game tonight, so we're celebrating with Philly cheesesteaks. You know what they say, when in Philly...

> I woke up early and caught most of it. Congrats! Nice goal in the second. But serious rookie move getting peppers on your sandwich

> I am going to ignore your shockingly poor taste in cheesesteak toppings because I have much more pressing matters to discuss. Namely, did you jump to your feet and cheer for me again when I scored?

A question that would have once made me incandescent with indignance now makes me snort with laughter. For so long, I thought that Aaron acted the way he did because he was arrogant and pleased with himself. And while I do still believe that he is (at least a little) arrogant and pleased with himself, he's a different person than I once thought.

A person that I like. A lot.

> I was cheering for Perez, of course.

Perez, who I happen to know was out with a strained ligament for the game.

I'm hilarious, I know.

> Of course you were.

> Also, it's tomorrow morning for you right now, which means that you are in the future. What's it like?!

I open my phone camera and turn it to selfie mode, snapping a picture of myself backlit by the sparkling morning sun.

> The future is bright.

> The future is breathtaking.

This makes me blush like crazy, and I'm in half a mind to fan myself with the menu.

> Stop flirting with me, Marino.

No.

Seriously can't wait to be home.

> Guess I can live with that.

We fly home from Philly tomorrow morning. When do you fly back?

> Tonight, Vietnam time. I'll arrive in Atlanta with plenty of time to make it to your game.

I can hardly believe that tomorrow is December 23rd, and the last Cyclones game before the Christmas break. Following that, Aaron and I will have the night together at his place before he flies to Jersey the next morning for the holidays.

And when he comes back? Well, it'll almost be time for me to move out.

I ended up accepting the first apartment Aaron and I looked at last week, and I'm due to move in on the first. I loved the one that Kris showed us, but the numbers simply didn't add up. Plus, when I looked up the listing again, it was gone. The place must've been leased to someone else, which was disappointing, but ultimately allowed me to make my peace and move on.

I'm sure the one I took will be just fine. I've been looking forward to having my own space for ages, yet after a few weeks at Aaron's, there's a part of me that doesn't feel like it wants the space anymore.

I'm shaken out of my thoughts by a new message.

You gonna turn up wearing my jersey, Griswold?

A thrill runs through me at the thought of turning up to a Cyclones game wearing a number 22 jersey. But I'm pretty sure Jake would blow a fuse.

I'm about to text this to Aaron, but then, a store just below me catches my eye.

A custom clothing store.

No. I'll be wearing something even better.

35

OLIVIA

"That was amazing!" Jing gushes, flinging her arms—which are surely being weighed down by the bells attached to the sleeves of her ridiculous Christmas sweater—around me. "That man is incredible to watch on the ice."

I grin as we walk through the sea of crimson jerseys in the arena's concourse. "Which one?"

"Well, all of them," she concedes, poking her tongue out at me. "But I was specifically referring to the hottie with a body that you took a very sexy shower with recently. Not to mention the date he took you on that was straight out of a Hallmark Christmas movie."

"Shh!" I hiss, flapping my hands at her as I glance around to see if anyone overheard. Lucky for me, nobody is paying attention.

The entire arena is buzzing right now off the back of a Cyclones win, and the feel of Christmas in the air.

I'm not going to lie, when I landed in Atlanta earlier, I was so excited that I took a break from my usual Americano with oat milk and instead bought Jing and myself peppermint mochas.

Which is *insanely* festive, in my book.

"So what are you and The Stallion doing after the game tonight?" Jing asks, then gives a huge, exaggerated wink. "Or is that question off-limits?"

"We're just gonna chill," I tell her.

Our actual plan—crafted over text—is Italian takeout, wine, and dirty word Scrabble in front of the fireplace. In the spirit of the holidays, I've also agreed to watch *Miracle on 34th Street* instead of a slasher flick. And I got him a little Christmas surprise that I plan on revealing on the way home tonight.

Least I can do after his thoughtful attempt to help me make new and improved Christmas memories.

"Netflix and chill," she responds with a leer, and I give her a shove, but it's an affectionate one.

When we get to the entrance for the MARTA, I pull her into a hug. "Well, Merry Christmas, Jing," I tell her. "I'm so happy that I met you this year."

She pulls back, laughing. "That man is turning you into a total softie, isn't he?"

"No," I protest.

"He is, and I'm here for it." She stands on her tiptoes and kisses my forehead like I'm a child. "Merry Christmas, my softie little friend."

"See ya in a few days."

"Tokyo, baby!" she responds, and then melts into the crowd headed towards the subway.

I pretty much sprint to the players' area, more than a little excited to see Aaron again after the days we spent apart. But instead of waving me through, the security guard—an older guy who often works on this door and certainly knows me by now—asks me to wait. He then says something on his radio that I can't hear.

A few moments later, Aaron ducks through the door clad in his soft gray sweats and a black Cyclones hoodie. He's also sporting damp, freshly showered hair and a determined expression. And dammit if my heart doesn't skip a beat or three.

"Thanks, Mac," he says with a nod to the security guard. "Merry Christmas."

"Same to you, Aaron." The guard's wrinkled face shows something like amusement.

"Hey Livvy," Aaron says to me, and I realize how much I love it when he calls me that. Nobody else does, it's just him.

"Hey," I reply, smiling. "Didn't want me to come in?"

"I was actually trying to get out." He nods at the door behind him. "There's a ton of people in there chatting, and I didn't feel like sharing you tonight."

This sends my stomach into a flurry of butterflies. "I'm glad."

"Plus, that Scrabble won't play itself."

"You are such a nerd," I tease.

"You love it," he counters. "And you have no idea how much I missed you."

Then, he grabs my hand and we run to the underground parking, giggling like we're a pair of teenagers sneaking out at night.

We ride home with Justin Bieber's Christmas album cranked, shouting out random half-snippets of lyrics while I order cacio e pepe, lobster ravioli, and browned butter and sage gnocchi on UberEats. We're breathless and laughing and having fun, but all the while, I'm hyper aware of Aaron stealing glances at me that are loaded with almost as much heat as I currently feel from being back in his vicinity.

It gives me that fizzy sensation in my stomach that makes me half want to wrap my arms around myself and squeal, half tell him to pull over so I can climb on top of him.

Luckily, I manage to control myself, and instead settle for

continuing to feel hot and bothered and giddy as his eyes continue to skim over me.

But by the time we pull into his driveway, I'm feeling a strange sense of... something else. Something deeper.

I should be excited. An evening with Aaron, just the two of us, followed by four blissful days of alone time to apply face masks, watch *New Girl* and *Schitt's Creek,* and stuff my face with chocolate.

I should be excited, but I'm not. Which is crazy.

I spent eight years living in London all by myself, and now, I'm feeling some type of way about being home alone for *four freaking days*?

Jing's right. I'm clearly turning into a big ol' softie.

And I must not be hiding it well, because as soon as we get out of the car, Aaron looks at me peculiarly. "What's going on, Livvy?"

"Just thinking."

"Sounds dangerous."

I swat his arm playfully as we climb his front steps.

"Kidding. Kidding." He laughs. "But seriously, what's on your mind?"

"I'm just..." I pause as I search for the words. I feel like there's so much to say, but I don't know how to vocalize any of it. And this isn't the time to say anything anyway, so I finally settle on: "I'm happy we have tonight."

His eyes go soft. "I plan on making the most of every moment."

We're standing on his front porch now, just looking at each other. Neither of us makes a move to open the front door. He's so close that I can feel the heat of his body, smell that enticingly manly, spicy cologne on his skin in a way that's making me dizzy with want for him.

"I got you something."

His brows rise and his lips slide into a funny little half smile, like this surprises him. "You did?"

"Wanna see?"

"I do."

Holding eye contact, I slowly begin to undo the big, round buttons on my peacoat.

"Olivia!" Aaron's voice is both sharp and ragged in the sexiest way, and his eyes go from emotional to flaring with heat. He quickly catches himself and glances around. "Shouldn't we get inside?"

I grin as I undo the last button.

"Get your mind out of the sex gutter, Marino."

I let my coat fall to the ground...

Revealing my very own hideous, fluffy Christmas sweater.

And when I say hideous, I mean *hideous*. It's baby pink and made of that shaggy furry material that gives muppet vibes. It's also covered in embroidered ice skates, and snowflakes, and baby snowmen. Across the front, in swirly, glittery script, are the words "Proud Member of Aaron's Army."

Aaron's eyes go huge, and as he reads the words across my chest, he sputters an incredulous laugh.

"I was going to get one that said 'Santa's Favorite Ho' but they were all sold out," I joke, then smile up at him. "But in all seriousness, I want to take this opportunity to admit that I was very wrong about you for a very long time, Aaron Marino. And I want to thank you for making the worst time of the year a little— well, a *lot*—better for me."

He shakes his head, and when he speaks, his voice is thick. "You never cease to amaze me, Olivia Griswold."

Then, he brushes his lips against mine.

The contact is electric, casting sizzling sparks all across my skin. My body's reaction is immediate, and I stand on my tiptoes and wrap my arms around his neck, tugging him towards me so impatiently, it's a little embarrassing.

I kiss him harder, and he leans in, his tongue in my mouth and his hands twisting in my hair.

I'm floating off into the happiest place in the world when he groans and pulls back a little. "I wasn't going to do this," he says against my mouth, his breathing labored.

"Do what?" I blink up at him and try to ignore the sudden doubt that maybe this—*I*—was too much. Maybe after a few days apart, this wasn't what he wanted.

"I missed you this week, Olivia. *You.*" His eyes bore into mine. "And I told myself a million times that I was going to be patient tonight. That I wasn't going to jump on you and kiss you senseless the second I saw you. Because even though I've been going half-crazy the entire drive home thinking about your lips, I wanted to show you that this is more than just physical. That I haven't just been waiting to get you home, but that I've been craving your company as much as touching you. Your laugh as much as your gasps." He chuckles softly, his minty breath whispering over my lips. "But then, you had to go and wear *this*"—his hand fists in my sweater—"and make me lose the last shred of my resolve. I couldn't help myself, Olivia."

"Good. I don't want you to," I tell him, and his eyes flicker. That crazy luminous green. Those long, dark eyelashes. And within his eyes, a raw, stripped emotion that makes me suck in a breath before his mouth claims mine again.

I expect the kiss to pick up where it left off, for him to devour me wildly, leaving me breathless and gasping and clinging to him.

Instead, he surprises me. He backs me against the front door, one big hand next to my head, the other cupping my face, effectively pinning me in place. His body presses against mine, and I arch into him as he kisses me with what I can only describe as the physical communication of that raw emotion I saw in his eyes.

He kisses me slowly, carefully, but with total dedication to the task. Like we have all the time in the world, but that's not enough. Each movement of his lips is fraught with pure, unbridled *feeling*, and it's somehow impossibly hotter than the frantic kiss we were sharing a moment ago.

Saying everything, all at once, without uttering a single word.

He deepens the kiss, angling my face up, and a strangled, almost anguished noise escapes my throat as his tongue brushes over mine. Seeing stars, I grab him by the lapels of his coat and pull him closer, fully losing myself in him.

I let my hands move over his body, exploring. They trace the shape of his big shoulders, then travel over the planes of his chest and the ridges of his abs. This elicits a delicious shiver from him.

"Livvy." His stubble scratches my jaw as he presses a kiss to the sensitive skin there. "We should really take this inside."

"Yeah," I pant, my fingers sliding under the bottom of his sweatshirt, skimming across his warm, taut stomach. "We should."

But instead, he makes a deep noise in his throat and moves his mouth back over mine again.

And that's when the front door opens.

36

AARON

My wildest dream is turning into an unhinged fever nightmare, real fast.

Because honestly, the last person in the world you want to see while you're locked in a passionate embrace with your dream woman is your freaking *mother*.

Oh, and bonus points for seeing your grandmother, too.

But, here we are. Somehow.

"Mom," I gasp in a daze, one hand locked on the doorframe, which I caught literal seconds from tumbling head over heels into my house. Thank the good Lord for my hockey reflexes. My other hand is wrapped tight around Livvy's lower back, catching her from landing on top of Nonna. "What on earth are you doing here?!"

Mom's delighted eyes slide from my disheveled form to Olivia's mussed-up hair and swollen lips and shocked expression. She smiles knowingly. "Surprise!"

"We're here for Christmas," Nonna announces, looking as wickedly gleeful as my mother does.

"What?" I choke out as I run my fingers through my hair,

which I'm sure is sticking up straight from Olivia locking her fingers in it. Not that I'm complaining.

For the past hour, I've been trying to process how amazing it feels to see Olivia again. How I missed her way more than I even thought I would, and was counting down the moments until I could see her again.

Now, I'm additionally trying to process the fact that my mother and grandmother are standing here, right in front of me. "I'm meant to fly to Newark in the morning."

"Not anymore, you're not," Nonna tuts as her wrinkled hands clasp around Olivia's arm. "Hello, sweetheart, come on in. I'm excited to hear all about this 'not nobody' that Aaron keeps going on and on about. Can I expect any great-grandbabies in the near future, may I ask?"

"Pardon me?" Olivia squeaks as Nonna—all five feet and one hundred pounds of her—practically drags her through the front door and down the hallway.

If this wasn't all so insane, it would be comical. Olivia, in her heeled boots, is about a foot taller than Nonna, and yet, she's being pulled through the house like a wayward puppy being leash trained.

I step into the entryway in an attempt to free Liv from Nonna's clutches, but Mom intercepts and pulls me into a huge hug. "So good to see you, my boy."

"It's good to see you too, Mom," I tell her as I try to figure out what the hell is happening, alongside the news that I'm apparently not going home for Christmas.

"Sorry we didn't make it to your game. Tonight's flight was the only one before Christmas Day with two seats left."

I look down at her. "Ma, don't get me wrong, I'm glad that you and Nonna are here, but... *why* are you here, exactly? And why is Nonna interrogating Livvy about babies?"

"*Livvy* is her name, then." She has straight mischief in her eyes—it's a well-known fact in my family that I got my love of teasing from my mother. She goes on to explain, "You were so insistent on coming home for Christmas, but I wanted to meet the woman you kept talking in circles about. So, Nonna and I decided to come here instead. Spend Christmas in the city you've been calling home for the past few years. Probably about time anyway."

"Would've been nice to have a heads-up," I tease, but honestly, I'm happy to see them both a day early. No matter how misguided and schemey they are.

And this means I won't have to leave Olivia.

As excited as I've been to see my family, the thought of leaving Olivia here by herself for the holidays felt wrong. Not only did I not want to be apart from her again, but I know how difficult this time of year is for her.

I was planning on talking to her tonight and offering for her to come to Jersey with me, or for me to stay here with her. From the beginning, she stated that she wanted to spend Christmas by herself—that was part of our original agreement—but I wanted to offer an alternative, just in case her feelings had changed.

Now, I don't know how she'll feel about my family gate-crashing.

And the last thing on earth I want to do is break a promise I made to her.

Mom and I walk to the kitchen (okay, I practically sprint there while my mom cackles behind me), and we find Olivia making tea while Nonna sits at a barstool, eyes glinting. "I like this one, Nipotino," she tells me.

I have to smile as Liv's eyes meet mine. "Ah, she's all right."

"And he's not *entirely* insufferable," she fires back cheekily. "Also, what's Nipotino?"

"Grandson," I explain to her. "It's an affectionate term in Italy."

"Cute." Liv gives me a wrinkle-nosed smile that I commit to memory forever.

"So, how did you two meet?" Mom sits next to Nonna and spreads her hands on the counter, silver bracelets jingling from her wrists. She eyes Olivia's sweatshirt curiously. "Are you a fan?"

"Oh yeah, she's my biggest fan," I reply, and watch with delight as Liv's face flares as red as Santa's suit.

"Not a fan, no. This was just a little joke for Christmas. I'm not crazy or anything..." she trails off, worrying her teeth into her bottom lip like she's physically trying to contain her ramble.

"Mom," I say, saving her while throwing myself in the firing line. "Livvy's full name is Olivia Griswold. You know, from high school."

Her reaction is exactly what I expect.

Mom squeals. "Really?"

Nonna claps her hands to her powdered cheeks. "Oddio, it's a Christmas miracle!"

"Olivia Griswold! This makes so much sense now." Mom beams at Liv. "You know, he never shut up about you. It was always 'Olivia this' and 'Olivia that.' The poor boy was completely under your spell, my dear." She winks at me. "What a marvelous surprise. I'm so happy we came."

I can physically feel the blush creeping up my neck as I look at Olivia, who's staring back at me. She puts her hands on her hips, a sassy grin on her face. "Never shut up about me, huh? Now who's a fan of who?"

I shrug a shoulder. "Told you I was a bit obsessed with you."

Still am.

I take in her sparkly eyes and glowing expression. *Probably always will be.*

Just then, the doorbell rings and I let out a groan, suddenly picturing my huge extended family of uncles and cousins and step-cousins standing on my doorstep with their billion suitcases to join my mom, Nonna, and me for Christmas. "Who could that be?"

"That'll be our food." Olivia looks at Mom and Nonna. "We ordered a ton, if you're hungry."

"Starving," Mom confirms, then pats Olivia's arm downright affectionately. "Thank you, my dear."

"Um, we'll go get the food," I say quickly. "*Both* of us."

With that, I put my hand on Olivia's lower back and usher her into the hallway.

When we're safely out of earshot, I let out a big breath. "I'm so sorry. I promise I had no idea they were coming for Christmas."

"I know." She smiles. "I saw your face when you realized that your grandmother witnessed you with your tongue in my mouth."

"Right," I groan. "Almost successfully managed to block that out. So thanks for that."

"You're welcome," she singsongs.

"Anyway. I know you originally wanted to spend Christmas alone, and if that's still the case, I want you to know that I'm gonna fix this." I bite my lip, thinking fast. "I'm sure I can get them on my flight to Jersey tomorrow morning with me."

Olivia casts a sidelong glance towards the kitchen, a funny look flitting over her face. "No. They should stay. *You* should stay."

I blink at her, taking in her gorgeous hazel eyes, her pretty, slightly flushed cheeks. "Are you sure?"

"I'll go back to my old apartment for a few days. I'm still on the lease 'til the end of the month," she offers. "Give you some family time."

"Absolutely not." I pin her with my gaze. "You are *not* going back to that dump under any circumstances."

"Okay, we'll all stay then." She shrugs, but I could swear there's a twinkle in her eye. "You can show me a Marino family Christmas."

"You seriously want to experience that?"

"Yup."

"I'd love nothing more than to spend Christmas with you. And my family," I tell her, hardly believing how this is all working out right now. "But promise me that you'll let me know if it gets to be too much for you. Okay?"

"Okay," she agrees. "I'm sure it'll be fine, though. A little bird once told me that I needed to make new Christmas memories."

I grin. "What a smart bird. Bet he was handsome, too."

"Plus, your mom and grandma seem hilarious." She wrinkles her nose at me. "Way funnier than you."

"They are their own special brand of something, let me tell you." I look towards the kitchen to see my mother noseying in the pantry. Probably for a bottle of red wine. "Mom likes you already, I can tell."

"She does?" Olivia whispers back. Her face is lit up, and the fact that she cares about what my mother thinks makes me feel warm, like I've already had a glass of wine.

"How could she not?" I respond softly as I find her hand. As our fingers interlock, hers brush over my bracelet.

"My dad would've liked you, too," I add quietly, and I mean it. My dad was honest and no nonsense and an incredibly good judge of character. He would've loved Olivia and her fiery side. I tug on a strand of her coppery hair. "He also would have said I have good taste."

Liv sticks her tongue out at me. "He would have been right."

I squeeze her hand, her small palm pressing against mine as we walk back around the corner to join my mom and Nonna in the kitchen.

"Where's the food, Nipotino?" Nonna demands.

"Right. The food." I start, jerking a thumb over my shoulder. "I'll get it."

"This is what happens when we're too busy making out in the hallway!" Nonna's cackles follow me as I grab the food from the delivery man, giving him an apology in the vein of "please excuse my nutjob family."

By the time I get back to the kitchen, Olivia's clearly placated my heckling grandmother and they're setting the table while Mom pours the wine. Nonna goes on to take the foil containers of food directly out of my hands and sniff them before announcing that we need to find a new Italian place because this one doesn't smell authentic enough.

We finally sit down to eat all together in the dining room, and the lights on the Christmas tree shine bright behind us as Nonna says a blessing. The whole scene is entirely festive and cozy and domesticated, and dammit, I am here for it.

When Olivia raises her head, her eyes are full of an emotion that almost makes me wrap my arms around her and carry her upstairs. Not to do anything that Dallas would approve of, but to just hold her.

I've never brought a woman home to meet my family. But as I watch Livvy Griswold—the woman I've thought about for so many years—chat with my mom and ask my grandma about her favorite recipes, while every so often smiling at me across the table, it's like my family has come home to meet *her*.

And it feels more right than anything ever has.

37

AARON

"You're wrong, Mom," I say, checking the dictionary propped open in my lap. "Zaxes *is* a word—technically, the term for tools that cut roof slates." I lean forward to count the points. "And it's on a triple-word score, which means that Olivia and Nonna win."

"Yes!" Olivia high-fives my grandmother, and Nonna grasps Olivia's hand to hoist it above her head in a victory pose.

"Take that, losers!" Nonna crows, which makes Liv laugh.

"Yeah, loser," she parrots, eyes dancing as she levels her gaze on me. "In your face!"

"Such a gracious and humble winner you make, Griswold."

"Such a sore loser *you* make, Marino. I bet you're dying inside. You never lose Scrabble."

She's right, I don't. But I'm happy to lose to her.

I can't look away from her sparkling eyes, her smiling lips, the way she gestures wildly as she and my grandmother celebrate their winning word. One that Nonna somehow happened to know and which makes me wonder what tricks she might have up her sleeve.

Literally. The woman has been known to shove tiny Scrabble cheat sheets up her shirtsleeves.

"Ah, well," Mom says and I look over to see her smiling at me, a knowing glint in her eye. She clearly caught me in the act of gazing at Olivia. "Can't win 'em all."

I toss my fingers through my hair with a sheepish smile before starting to collect everyone's dessert plates.

Earlier tonight, I was feeling torn about going home to New Jersey. But now, I have everyone here with me, in one place.

In addition to this, we won our game earlier tonight, so the Cyclones are officially on a winning streak. I also haven't heard from Brandi since the gala, and my love life has most definitely not been in the media—which means that Lieberman is placated and my captaincy is no longer being questioned.

A perfect end to the year, if you ask me.

Frick, I love Christmas.

Now, after an evening of pasta and wine and lots of gossip about Uncle Dino's new hair plugs that he absolutely insists he did not get, we call it a night. Olivia gives Mom and Nonna big hugs before she heads to bed, but instead of following her, they wait until she's upstairs and out of sight before turning to me with huge, matching grins.

"She's a keeper, that one," Nonna says in a satisfied tone, hands on her hips.

I load the last glass into the dishwasher, then turn to face them. "I know."

"What does her brother make of all this?" Mom tilts her head curiously.

I'm a bit rattled by the question. I've kissed Jake's little sister twice now, and I haven't talked to him about it. Haven't told him how I feel about her.

Which probably makes me a terrible friend.

"We, um, haven't told him yet," I admit. "This thing

between us is pretty new, and Olivia and I haven't even had a chance to talk about what we are, let alone tell other people."

Mom frowns, her dark eyes scrutinizing. "What do you mean you don't know what this is between you? You're clearly head over heels for her."

"Hopelessly so," Nonna adds cheerfully. "You should see your face when you look at the girl. You're a lovesick fool for her."

"That's rude." I chuckle.

"No, it's accurate. And it's not an insult. That's exactly how I imagine I look at Patrick Dempsey, especially when he's playing McDreamy." Nonna sighs.

Mom puts a hand on my arm. "Word of advice. If you're as serious about Olivia as you seem to be, I'd recommend telling Jake sooner rather than later. He's your oldest friend."

She's right. I know she's right.

The longer we—I—put off not talking to Jake about this, the worse it might look when he finds out.

Because it really is a question of *when*. I'm not going anywhere, and I will gladly do this thing, whatever it is, with Olivia for as long as she'll have me.

After Christmas, I promise myself. I'll talk to Olivia first, and then we can talk to Jake accordingly, and I'm sure it'll all be fine because he will understand that I have nothing but the best intentions and I will treat his sister like a freaking queen.

"I will, Mom." I nod, appreciating her concern for me, but also for Jake and Olivia. "Thanks."

Nonna yawns loudly, and we take that as our cue to head upstairs.

It's only when we get to the top of the stairs that I realize I've been so distracted tonight, I've forgotten a very important detail...

"Where are you guys gonna sleep?!"

"Hmm?" Mom says. "I put my bags in the room full of your hockey stuff, and Nonna's in the other room, just like usual."

"But Olivia—"

"Is in your room, no?" Mom asks innocently, though her eyes are shrewd.

"Well, yes," I stammer. "But I've been staying in one of the guest rooms."

She snorts. "Do you think I was born yesterday?"

"No, really. It's not like that," I tell my mother firmly. "Olivia's staying in my room because I thought she'd be more comfortable. We're not staying in there together."

"Oh, come on, Aaron." Mom tuts. "We're not that old and fuddy-duddy that you have to pretend for us. We're under no impression that you two don't share a room."

"Indeed." Nonna folds her arms. "Don't even try to fool us, my boy. I saw that scene on your doorstep earlier and it was like something out of a movie. The racy kind. You can't fool us into thinking that you've been sleeping in separate rooms after we witnessed *that*."

I scrub a hand over my eyes. This is *not* a conversation I expected or wanted to have with my mother and grandmother, ever. Let alone now, when I'm tired and it's late. I just want to go to bed, but instead, I'm standing in the hallway, locked in a stalemate.

"It's true, Mom," I insist, trying to think of how to solve this. "Look. What if I book you guys into that nice hotel a couple blocks away? That way, you have lots of space, and you won't have to sleep in rooms filled with my hockey stuff or a bunch of crochet animals."

"But I always sleep in the room with all your hockey memorabilia," Mom says with a wicked gleam in her eye. She's enjoying this way too much.

"Family does not sleep in hotels, Aaron. I won't hear of it,"

Nonna scolds with a slightly terrifying wink. "So, off you go. Scamper on back to that beautiful girl of yours, and we will see you both in the morning for a nice Christmas Eve breakfast."

Oh, dear Lord in heaven.

Part of me wants to argue, but deep down, I know it's a lost cause. My mother is more stubborn than an ox, and Nonna is going to be mortally offended if I offer to pay for a hotel again.

Clearly, the easiest thing to do is give them the guest rooms, and I'll crash on the couch for the remainder of their stay.

Merry Christmas to me.

"Okay," I say as I idly wonder if there are any clean blankets and pillows in the linen closet.

"Good. It's settled then." Mom bids Nonna and me good-night as she steps into her room with a knowing little smirk.

"And don't worry about keeping the noise down," Nonna says as she gives me a big smacking kiss on the cheek. "Your mother brought her earplugs and I plan on taking a sleeping pill."

With that, she steps into her room, giving me another one of those terrifying winks as she goes.

I doubt I will ever be able to scrub my brain clean of that particular image.

Once they're safely out of sight, I head to the linen closet in search of a spare comforter and pillow.

I'm rummaging around when the master bedroom door pops open and Olivia peeks out. "You look like a man who needs a place to stay tonight. Which is very Christmas-story-esque, actually."

I groan. "Please tell me you didn't overhear that conversation."

"What conversation?" She blinks innocently. "Oh, you mean the one where your dear, sweet grandmother sent you off to have a night of wild sex with me?"

I groan again. "Yes."

"Nah. Didn't hear a word."

Our eyes meet, and we both laugh. "I'm sorry about them. They're just so desperate for a couple of Aaron Juniors, they can't think straight."

"I think it's very sweet." She opens the door wide so her flannel pjs are on full display. She looks cute as all hell. "So, you coming in or are you planning on standing out there all night?"

I hold up the comforter I found at the back of the closet. "I'm gonna sleep on the couch," I tell her, even as I peek past her into the bedroom. "Might just need to mooch a pillow or two."

She bites her full lower lip. Which is more than a little distracting, let me tell you. "I'm okay with you staying here. You know, if you want to," she says quietly, almost timidly. "I wouldn't mind the company."

Olivia's gaze is angled down, away from me, in such a way that I have to reach out and gently tilt her chin back up so her eyes meet mine. "Me neither."

Truth is, I'm still aching to hold her.

So, I do.

I climb into bed next to her and wrap my arm around her, and it feels like the most natural thing in the world. Instinctively, I draw her close so I can smell her shampoo and feel her soft breaths—first shallow, and then deeper, as she falls asleep in my arms.

And right there, in the darkness, I realize with startling clarity that I have, indeed, fallen head over heels in love with her.

38

OLIVIA

I was twelve when my dad got arrested on Christmas Eve.

That day, he drank so much that he got in a fight outside of a local church during a freaking Christmas Carol service.

Very classy, I must say.

Jake and I were meant to stay with him that entire Christmas period, but when he got hauled off to jail to dry out and clean his act up, the two of us ended up at my mom's new place at the eleventh hour.

Mom had remarried, and this was her first official Christmas as Mrs. Jones. Her new husband, Mr. Jones, was a nice enough man, but he also had two kids and they were staying with them for the holiday.

Meaning that Jake and I were given air mattresses and assigned to sleep in the living room.

My mom hadn't counted on us being there, so she hadn't bought enough food to cook for six people. The house also wasn't big enough for all of us to stay comfortably, so we were pretty much on top of each other the entire time Jake and I were there.

The situation put me on edge, and when I talked to Mom

about it, she kept insisting that it was totally fine that Jake and I had crashed her Christmas.

Yup. *Crashed* her Christmas.

She was almost apologetic for our presence—like being around her kids from her first marriage would taint her new, happy family.

When Dad finally sobered up, got out of jail, and came to pick us up on Christmas evening, I felt... *relieved*. If I went back to his place, I wouldn't be in the way anymore. Wouldn't be taking up space somewhere I didn't belong.

I hoped that, maybe, we could have a do-over Christmas. Have a second dinner, the three of us, and everything would be fine because we were following our original plan. And then, next year, when we were scheduled to go to Mom's place, she'd be prepared to host us, and that would be fine, too.

What *actually* happened was the opposite of fine:

Mom followed Dad out to the car, yelling at him for being selfish. He drove us home in silence, and the minute we got back, he went straight to the nearest bar.

Jake, who was fourteen at the time, was kind enough to watch *Elf* with me while we shared a box of Lindt truffles he'd swiped from Mom's house. But I knew that he would've rather gone to see his friends, and the second the movie was over and I was getting ready for bed, he went out on his bike, pedaling off down our snow-covered cul-de-sac in the glow of the streetlights.

That night, I got into bed in an empty house, closed my eyes, and vowed to never celebrate Christmas again. Vowed to never get excited for a holiday that would just let me down, that did nothing but highlight the fact that I didn't fit in anywhere.

The next morning, I woke up with a clear sense of relief—both because the holiday was over, and because I'd put a wall up to protect myself from ever feeling that way again.

Fourteen years later, Aaron Marino is breaking down those walls, brick by brick.

On Christmas Eve morning, I wake up snuggled into his chest after having the best night's sleep I can remember. We make a pancake brunch for his mom and Nonna and the four of us go to Lenox Square Mall so Nonna can buy us all matching Christmas pajamas—something she insisted upon. After that, we head to a fresh fish market to load up on seafood for the Seven Fish dinner, which I learned is an Italian-American tradition the Marino family honor every year.

In the evening, we drive around the city and critique the Christmas lights, scoring each display. When we come home, Aaron lights the fire and we gather in the living room wearing our new pajamas to feast on the massive seafood platters that Aaron's mom, Natalia, prepared for us.

It's perfectly cozy and lovely, but there's something deeper than that. A feeling of family. Togetherness.

And I don't know if it's Aaron, or this house, or his family's warmth, or whether I've had a total brain transplant, but I feel a part of this togetherness. Like I belong here, in this scene.

I fall asleep on Christmas Eve wrapped once again in Aaron's arms and feeling totally content. Full of delicious food and great conversation and cozy memories and that sense of warmth and *home* that has always evaded me—especially around the holidays—but is now, unbelievably, more and more present in my life.

And then, on Christmas morning...

"SNOW!"

My eyes flutter open and I groan, confused and disoriented after being unceremoniously yanked from a deep sleep. But when I fully open my eyes and sit up, I'm greeted by the sight of a shirtless Aaron standing at the window, looking like... well, looking like a kid on Christmas morning.

He turns around and gives me a guilty smile. "Oh, would you look at that. You're awake," he says lightly, and I throw a pillow at him.

"Thanks to your ten-thousand decibel meteorology report," I retort, but I'm laughing.

"Sorry," he says, sounding not the least bit sorry. "But now that you're awake, come look!"

I roll out of his bed and make my way to the window to see the blanket of white on the ground outside. It's sparse, but it's there.

"Woah. It's weird seeing snow here." I press my hand against the window. The condensation feels cool against my palm.

"Best." Aaron stands behind me and gently moves my hair aside so he can kiss my neck. "Day." He kisses my neck again, and my entire body melts into him. "Ever." Again, my head is spinning.

"We've barely even gotten out of bed," I say with a laugh, looking back at him.

"I know. And my statement still stands." He then claims my lips once again. When he pulls back, all too soon, his green eyes are soft. "I love snow. And I love that I get to spend today with you."

My lips slide into a smile. "Merry Christmas, Aaron."

"Merry Christmas, Olivia."

And honestly, I feel it.

Merry, I mean. So much so that I dress in a cute sweater and a short skirt, and I even wear the snowmen earrings Nonna insisted on buying me at the mall yesterday. I braid my hair and apply the smallest amount of makeup, because photos on Christmas Day are a thing, right?

By the time I get downstairs, Aaron's pouring coffee and has already started prepping for the "huge breakfast feast" he warned me was his family's staple on Christmas morning. Seriously, I have never seen, nor eaten, so much food in my life. Nonna and Natalia are nowhere to be seen—they must have slept through the early morning snow memo.

As I pad over to Aaron and he hands me my coffee, I notice that he's wearing his stupid T-rex Santa sweater again.

He's never looked better.

"Hey, while we're still alone." He pauses, looking a little hesitant. "I got you something."

It's only then that I notice the gift-wrapped square package on the counter next to him. My eyebrows raise. "You got me a gift?"

"Fair warning, it's nowhere near as good as your Aaron's Army sweater."

"Well, nothing could top that." I laugh, but I'm touched.

Aaron passes the gift to me, and I open the package to find a set of white queen-size bed sheets.

One-thousand-thread-count Egyptian cotton.

"Exactly the same as mine, but for a queen bed," he explains as I run my thumb along the soft, luxurious material. "For your new apartment."

"Thank you, Aaron. This is so thoughtful!"

It really is.

I just don't have the heart to tell him that the apartment I'll be moving into on January first is furnished with a double bed, and not a queen bed. It's the thought that counts, and Aaron clearly put thought into this gift.

He bites his lower lip as he watches me gently stroke the incredible fabric. "Open the card."

"Oh!"

I hadn't noticed the red envelope tucked into the side of the packaging. I slide it open and out falls not a card, but what appears to be a folded document. A legal-looking document.

I squint at it. "It's a... lease?"

Aaron nods. "For the apartment you wanted, the one in Kris's building. Starting January first."

"What?" My jaw drops open as I look at the paperwork again in confusion.

But, there it is.

My name is on the lease. Damage deposit, plus first and last month's rent, are fully paid.

"You don't have to take it if you don't want," Aaron says, apparently misunderstanding my silence. "I just knew that you hadn't paid the deposit on the other apartment yet, and I could tell that you weren't excited to live there. I didn't want this one to get snatched up by someone else. But obviously, feel free to throw this in the trash and live where you please."

The paper goes slack in my hands as I process this. For so long, I've been on my own and looking out for myself. But here I am, on Christmas morning, no longer alone but living in the house of my former nemesis, who is now giving me a gift that shows he's looking out for me, too.

"How did you do this?"

"I called Kris after we left and told him that I'd like to lease it in your name." His green eyes are boring into mine as he speaks.

"Naturally," I mutter, my head spinning. With the first and last month's rent and damage deposit all taken care of, this apartment is now viable for me. More than viable.

But this gift, it's just... *too much.*

It's beyond generous and kind and thoughtful and oh-so-Aaron. It also reminds me of the fact that the new year is less than a week away, and I'm going to miss being here, at his place, with him.

Is he going to miss me, too?

"I don't know what to say," I tell him honestly.

"You don't have to say anything right now." He shrugs. "This is your decision. I just didn't want you to lose the option of living there."

"And if I don't take it?"

"I'll sublease it, I guess." He grins suddenly. "Or use it to store all my hockey memorabilia. After living in that guest room for a couple weeks, I was a little sick of staring at my own face. Which I didn't think could ever happen, but here we are."

"Here we are," I echo, that now-familiar fluttery feeling gathering in my stomach once again. The Aaron effect on me, it seems. "Thank you. This is unbelievable."

It continually surprises me how intuitive he is, how well he reads me. How well he *knows* me.

What a guy.

No. What a *man*.

He slides a hand around my back, his fingers grazing the sensitive skin at the waistband of my skirt in a way that makes my entire focus zone in on where he's touching me. "I have a confession to make."

He says this in a low voice that makes the flutters grow tenfold. "Oh, yeah?"

"My gift wasn't entirely unselfish."

"Is that right?" I run my hands up his firm chest, reveling in the way my touch makes his heartbeat quicken. "Let me guess, you wanted to test out that shower, too?"

His chuckle is deep and dirty. "No. Well, yes, that *was* on my mind. But showers aside, I like the idea of you living in that apartment because it's so close to this house."

"So we can still have slasher movie and Scrabble nights after I move out?" I ask with a smirk.

His hand moves to cup my face, his thumb dragging slowly and sexily over my lower lip. "So I can spend as much time as possible with you."

And if that doesn't make my entire stomach swoop.

"Awh, you're going to miss me being your roomie," I tease, but my voice comes out all throaty. Because honestly, knowing that Aaron might miss me as much as I'll miss him when I move out feels like another incredible gift.

"I am. But I heard somewhere that it's best not to start a new relationship while living with the person." He smirks. "Apparently, that part usually comes later."

My breath catches. "Relationship?"

"That's what I want this to be, if it's what you want." His fingertips trace my jaw. "I just want to be with you, Olivia. Whatever you want that to look like, I'm here for it. I'm yours."

I'm yours.

He's mine.

We belong to each other.

"I think that's what I want this to be, too," I say, a lump forming in my throat.

Aaron's eyes are full of fire and tenderness, longing and desire. His hand presses firmly into my back, pulling me flush against his chest. And just when his lips are about to meet mine...

A squeal behind me startles me so much, I almost fall over.

"What on earth?!"

Aaron is laughing. "I think Nonna may have been eavesdropping on our conversation."

39

OLIVIA

"What would you think about going to the children's hospital this afternoon?" Aaron asks me as we clean up after an amazing Christmas breakfast. It's been a wonderful morning with Aaron's mom and Nonna, and through every moment, I've been repeating the word *boyfriend* to myself, over and over, while glancing in Aaron's direction.

It feels good. And now that I've tried the word on for size, I want to wear it forever, like one of his oversized sweatshirts.

"Children's hospital?" I ask. "Any particular reason why?"

"Mom and Nonna are going to a carol service, so I was thinking of something we could do, too." Aaron shrugs. "I go there sometimes to chat with the kids and deliver gifts. I was going to stop in when I got back from Jersey, but now that I'm here for Christmas, I figured we could go today."

"You bring gifts to sick kids on the regular?" I ask him, eyes wide.

"It's mostly dumb stuff, like those crochet animals I make." He wipes down the counter, not meeting my gaze. "Don't go giving me a sainthood or something."

How on earth did I ever think this man was a terrible human?

"Aaron, that's not dumb at all. That's the nicest idea ever, and I'd love to go with you."

His smile is like sunshine. "Thanks, Livvy."

Just then, the doorbell rings.

"I'll get it," I say as I finish washing a serving dish and stack it on the drying rack. I pad into the hallway and open the front door.

I blink in surprise at the couple standing on the doorstep.

"Jake! Sofia!" I cry, unsure why they're here, but delighted to see them.

"Olivia." Jake's looking at me like I've lost my ever-loving mind for some reason, which might be related to the festive snowmen earrings I'm wearing and my Christmassy elf-print socks (also courtesy of Nonna). Then, he looks right past me to where Aaron is walking down the hallway, and his expression becomes carefully neutral. "Aaron."

Sofia and I hug as Aaron comes to stand beside me.

"Hey, guys. Merry Christmas." Aaron's gaze flickers to me, then back to Jake.

"I thought you were in Jersey," my brother says instead of repaying the greeting, and I hypocritically flick my eyes heavenward. Like I'm not an ex-disgruntled-Grinch person myself.

"Last minute change of plan," Aaron says.

"Very last minute!" I tack on quickly, feeling strangely guilty, like I'm a kid caught with their hand in the cookie jar. Which is dumb. I haven't done anything wrong.

Jake frowns. "Okay, what's going on here?"

"My mom and Nonna showed up unexpectedly after our game two nights ago," Aaron explains casually, running his fingers through his hair. "They wanted to spend Christmas in Atlanta."

"Did they now?" Jake's voice is... off. He's always a little grouchy, but right now, he sounds like a grumpy freaking robot.

"Well." Sofia's calm tone fills the slightly awkward silence in the hallway. "We came over because my parents are having a post-lunch siesta, and we thought you, Olivia, were alone and might want some company. Jake's idea."

My gaze lands on Jake. "Really?"

"It's been a long time since I spent Christmas with my only sister." Again, with the robot voice.

"Come on in, then." Aaron's cheery voice sounds almost forced as he ushers Jake and Sof inside. "Mom and Nonna are in the kitchen. They're gonna be so happy to see you."

As Jake and Sofia walk ahead, Aaron falls into step with me.

"Hey," he says softly. "I'd like to talk to Jake about us. I don't want to keep him in the dark, or make him think that we're trying to hide anything or go behind his back. I also want it to come from one of us before Mom or Nonna puts their foot in it. But I wanted to ask you if you'd prefer to tell him yourself or if I can?"

Always so considerate.

"Tell him," I say with a shrug. "We're all adults here. He can deal."

"Right." Aaron looks a little unconvinced. "You're right."

When we reach the kitchen, Natalia and Nonna are fawning over Sofia while simultaneously chatting Jake's ear off. He's nodding along politely, but his eyes are fixed on Aaron and me.

Slightly annoyed, I sidle over to him and tug on his sleeve. "What, Jake?"

"I didn't say anything."

I roll my eyes. "I mean, why do you look like someone shoved a stick up your ass?"

He huffs a laugh that has zero humor and folds his arms. He

then completely ignores my question, and instead says, "Aaron, may I have a word?"

A word?

Who does he think he is, Marlon Brando in the freaking Godfather?

"Uh, sure thing, man." Aaron gestures towards the French doors leading onto the deck. He follows Jake outside, and then gives me a lingering look before shutting the door behind them.

I whirl around to Sofia. "What's going on, Sof?"

Her cheeks flush and she starts playing with a tassel hanging off a cloth on the counter. "Er," she starts. "There might be a photo circulating that features you and Aaron. You know, um, together."

"What?" I squawk.

"There's a..." Sofia waves her hands in front of her uselessly, looking not unlike a dancing octopus or something. "There's a picture of the two of you. Kissing."

"What?! Where?" I squawk again like I'm the freaking resident parrot of the Marino household.

"Uhm, here, I think." She blinks, gazing around. "Oh, you mean where did we see the photo? That awful Brandi woman posted it on her Instagram."

My body feels like it's malfunctioning as my jaw drops wide open.

Nonna looks from me, to Sofia, to the men standing outside. "I'll fetch the Baileys."

Sofia nods gratefully. "A drink would be nice right now."

I don't reply. My body is apparently coming back online and I lunge for my phone. I open Instagram and search for the AaronMarinosMistress account.

Within seconds, I'm staring at an image that makes my stomach drop. An image of myself and Aaron that's been posted for the entire world to see. An image that somehow perfectly captures both of our faces in the porch light, so there's no pretending it could be anyone else.

Specifically, it's a picture of us pressed against his front door the other night while he was kissing me senseless.

Well. *This* can't be good.

40

AARON

Jake stomps out onto the deck and kicks at the snow with the toe of his boot.

"A white Christmas in Atlanta, who would have thought?" I ask lightly. I'm fully aware that he's pissed, though I'm not quite sure why. Jake sometimes gets into these grumpy spells, but this feels different. More directed.

To the point that I could almost believe he's jumped to some conclusion about me and Olivia that isn't even half of the real story.

But I know that's ridiculous. And I know my friend. I need to *ease* into that particular conversation. Take it slow and careful.

Otherwise he'll probably punch me in the face.

"Hmpf," he mutters, unzipping his jacket. "Dunno how it's snowing. It's not even cold out here."

He throws off his coat, and I can't help but snort when I see what he's wearing underneath.

"Nice sweater."

"Sofia made me wear it." He glowers down at his ugly Christmas sweater, which features several fluffy white kittens wearing Santa hats. He then turns that glare my way. "And speak for yourself."

I run a hand over my Tree Rex sweater. "I wore it of my own volition."

"You would."

I don't reply.

Jake looks at me.

I look at him.

He clenches his fists and narrows his eyes while I try to keep my stance as relaxed as possible, genuinely wondering at this point what on earth could be making him so upset and if he's somehow found something out about Olivia and me.

We stand there, on my deck, two huge hockey players locked in a freaking faceoff while adorned in ugly Christmas sweaters. I'm sure the sight would be comical for anyone looking.

"You move my little sister into your house and then start screwing her?" Jake suddenly blurts out. "What the hell is wrong with you?!"

"Woah, woah, woah. It's not like that," I say, trying to remain calm. "Look, I'm not sure where you heard that from, exactly, but that's not—"

"How do you explain *this*?" Jake thunders, whipping out his phone.

My eyes bug as I take in the picture on Brandi's Instagram—which has an annoyingly large amount of followers. It was posted earlier today with the caption:

"Looks like Aaron Marino got a brand new redhead for Christmas! But in true roachy fashion, his latest conquest happens to be his own teammate's little sister. How low will this guy stoop? Someone's definitely on Santa's naughty list this year #roachboy #donewithaaronmarino"

Fricking Brandi.

I was just thinking the other night that I hadn't heard from her in ages, and I was naive enough to believe that maybe she had moved on... but here she is again, popping up like the ghost of freaking Christmas past, dead set on haunting me.

"Well, first and foremost, I need you to believe me when I say that I'm not *screwing* Olivia, as you so eloquently put it," I tell Jake.

"I should punch you in the face right now!"

Called it.

"And as entertaining as it would be for my mom, my grandmother, your sister, and your girlfriend to watch you throwing down while wearing a litter of kittens on your chest, I'd prefer you didn't hit me until you actually hear me out," I say calmly.

"How dare you take advantage of her like that!" he rants on, clearly not hearing me.

"And how dare *you* turn up here on Christmas day under the guise of seeing her just to yell at me," I retort, my blood heating. "I understand that you're just trying to look out for her, and I appreciate that, but I'm not *taking advantage* of her. We're together. For real."

"You're *what*?" Jake spits out, eyes bugging.

"Together. And while that picture was obviously not the ideal way for you to find out, it's true. Olivia and I are a couple. We were going to tell you after Christmas, but now you know."

"I..." Jake narrows his eyes at me, but his fists finally unclench. "You don't date anyone seriously."

"There's nobody but Olivia for me."

"I don't like this one bit. You better not be playing with her."

"I'm not," I say.

It's entirely true. For months, I lied to myself. Told myself I'd stopped dating purely to focus on my captaincy. But I realize now that it was about so much more than just hockey.

"I care about your sister, a lot," I tell him. "But I get that you're not happy with me right now."

And I do. I'm not happy with me, either.

Our relationship aside, I was idiotic enough to put Olivia in a position where we ended up getting photographed, and now said photo is pasted all over the internet.

I should've known better.

"I want you to give Olivia some respect and talk to her about this, too," I continue. "She's an adult, and she's made a decision here as much as I have."

Jake's nostrils flare. "You're going to talk to *me* about respect when you were hooking up with her behind my back?"

I sigh. "I already told you, that's not what it's like."

To Jake's credit, he does seem to catch himself, scrubbing a hand over his eyes. "Right. You're *together*. I just... need some time to process this. You're supposed to be my teammate. My friend. Not my little sister's love interest, you asshole."

"I get it." I nod. "I'll give you some space to process."

"Good."

"Guess I'll see you in a couple of days for our game against Houston?"

"Guess so," he mutters. He turns and goes back in the house, leaving me alone in the snow with my racing thoughts.

41

AARON

"That was interesting," Olivia says after we see a grumpy Jake and an almost apologetic Sofia to the door. Mom and Nonna also left a few minutes ago on their way to church, with Nonna muttering to herself that she'd pray for our souls after Jake and I almost threw down on the Lord's birthday.

"I'll say," I reply as I study her face. She doesn't seem too fazed, but I'm trying to gauge if that's because she's genuinely okay, or if she's putting up some of those walls of hers again.

"He's not mad at you," I assure her, then attempt to crack a smile. "I think he just wanted to punch me in the face, to be honest."

She snorts. "The Griswold men do love a Christmas brawl."

"Jake was definitely dressed for a holiday throwdown," I add, but my voice must sound forced, because Olivia frowns.

"Don't worry about my stupid brother. He'll come around."

I sigh and scrub a hand over my face. "I mean, he was just being a protective big brother. I'd have done the same thing if I was him."

"Yeah," she says, hands on her hips. "But *you* would have been less of a dick about it."

"He was just worried about you getting hurt," I say as my fingers wrap around my bracelet. "It's nice that he was looking out for you. And you're right, he will come around."

"Stupid man-child," she huffs as she crosses her arms over her chest. Then, her expression turns thoughtful. "How do you think Brandi even got that picture?"

My frown deepens. It's been on my mind, too. "She must've followed us home from the game that night. I mean, we weren't exactly making out behind closed doors. She could've taken that shot from the street without even coming up the driveway." I wince at the thought, at the position I've put Olivia in. "I'm sorry, Liv. I never meant for you to get dragged into this."

I'm mad that Brandi targeted Olivia.

Mad that the world had to find out about the woman I love in this way.

Mad at myself for letting this happen.

The anger settles in my stomach, gnawing at me.

"Ah, I was in it anyway after coming to the gala with you." Olivia pulls a face. "I think this is her butt-hurt attempt at revenge after I foiled her auction plans. But on the bright side, according to that hashtag, she's done with you."

"Maybe," I say as casually as I can, but my skin prickles and my thoughts are still moving too fast.

Our game against Houston is in two days, on home ice. And yes, I care that Jake is mad at me, and that this photo could get back to Lieberman.

But I realize that, above all, I care about Olivia. How *she* feels with all of this.

I was trying to give her a good Christmas, but all I've done is get her splashed all over Instagram as gossip fodder.

"Shall we get ready to go to the hospital?" Olivia asks, and I'm grateful for a subject change.

"Do you still want to go with me?"

"Absolutely."

"Then I'll get everything packed up."

She lays a hand on my arm, and her touch calms me a little. "I'll help."

Upstairs, in the guest room Nonna is staying in, Olivia blinks as she takes in the cacophony of crochet animals lining the shelves. "This is..."

"Weird," I finish for her with a little smile.

"I was going to go with impressive, but weird works, too."

"It's my hockey tradition. More of a superstition, I guess."

She surprises me by nodding. "I remember the story—Aaron Marino had the game of his life after crocheting with his Nonna one day, and it's been his pregame-ritual ever since," she singsongs.

I balk at her.

Olivia mimes buffing her nails on her shirt, eyes twinkling. "What can I say? I remember some things about you too, Aaron Marino." She reaches out to touch the nose of the little red fox I was crocheting on Thanksgiving. "These are pretty awesome, actually. I bet the kids love getting them."

She turns to look me dead in the eye, and for a moment, I get the distinct impression that she sees me. *Really* sees me.

Not the hockey captain, not the supposed playboy, not the guy who has used humor and banter to get her attention for as long as I can remember.

But me. *Aaron.*

I feel almost vulnerable in a way that I'm not used to as she walks over and wraps her hand around my wrist, her fingers grazing my bracelet. "You don't strike me as a particularly superstitious guy. In fact, if this bracelet is any indication, I'd say you're more secretly sentimental than superstitious."

"You might be right," I admit. "Crocheting before games,

moving my hands, stops my thoughts from racing. Helps me feel calm and focused."

"Focused on the game?"

I frown at my bracelet. "Yeah. And focused on not letting anyone down."

"Who could you possibly be letting down?"

"My teammates. My coach. My old captain. My family. My dad's memory." I pause. Exhale. "You."

She blinks. "*Me?*"

"Yeah, you," I reply. "I've inadvertently dragged you into all this Brandi B.S., and now, she's coming after you."

"That's not your fault. You're not responsible for other people's behavior."

"I know, but I am responsible for the people I care about." I bite down on my lip. "My family worked so hard to get me to where I am, and my teammates and Coach Torres have put all their trust in me this season. I'm scared of screwing it up."

"I think you're carrying the weight of other people's expectations, and it's a weight you don't need to bear." Olivia shakes her head. "You've clearly worked hard to get here, Aaron, and there's a reason people have chosen to place their trust in you. Do you not see how much you deserve this?"

I know I've worked my ass off, and I'm endlessly grateful for my career. So much so that I feel stupid even thinking any of this, but sometimes I don't feel worthy of being where I am and get convinced that I'll never live up to my own hype.

Imposter syndrome, I think it's called. I googled it once, and it resonated with me. The stress of being in the spotlight. The huge shoes Malachi left for me to fill as captain. Fulfilling my dad's goals for me and making his memory proud.

"I just want to be someone that people can believe in."

It's the first time I've ever said this aloud, and for a moment,

I want to take the words back and paint on a teasing expression. Be strong for her, instead of admitting my weaknesses.

But Olivia steps forward and wraps her arms around my neck. Tugs on the back of my head until I'm looking at her.

She smiles and she's so achingly beautiful, I can hardly stand it. "I believe in you, Aaron."

When she says it, I almost believe it, too.

42

OLIVIA

"Thank you again for bringing me Princess Sparkles, Mr. Aaron."

"You're so welcome, Miss Chloe. Merry Christmas." Aaron's eyes crinkle at the corners as he smiles down at the little girl, who's laying in bed hugging the pink and white crocheted cat stuffie he gave her—now officially named Princess Sparkles.

We've spent the last three hours at the hospital, and I've had a lump in my throat since we walked through the front door. There are decorations hanging everywhere, and the nurses are wearing Santa hats with their scrubs, but somehow, all this seems to do is highlight that these kids are spending their Christmases here instead of at home.

As we moved from room to room, chatting with the kids and passing out crochet animals, gift cards, signed 22 jerseys, and an array of candy, I've felt a spectrum of emotions. Aching sadness for those who can't be with their families today. Tentative hope for the kids who are on the road to recovery. A sense of bittersweet joy for every little face that has brightened at the sight of Aaron coming to see them.

Right now, it feels like that pesky throat lump is about to

take up permanent residence in my esophagus because as we leave Chloe's room, Aaron turns to me with another crinkly-eyed grin. "Cute, huh?"

"She was adorable," I say, then gesture down the hallway. "Where to next?"

"Okay, so I know I'm not meant to have favorites, but I saved this kid for last because he is one of my all-time favorites."

"Lead the way," I say, a little misty-eyed as Aaron envelops my hand with his and we walk together to the next room.

I hang back in the doorway, watching as Aaron crouches down beside the bed of a skinny pre-teen boy and gives him a fist bump.

"Parker, my man! How's it going?" he asks in the exact same tone that he uses to speak to his teammates.

"Aaron!" The kiddo's smile stretches all the way across his face. "I'm so happy you're here! I thought you couldn't come visit today."

Aaron shoots me a look that makes me feel tingly all over. "Last minute change of plan," he says as he forgoes the chair by the bed and instead sits on the floor right beside the machine Parker is hooked up to. He stretches his legs out, the picture of ease. "I'm glad I could make it. This is Olivia, by the way." He jerks his thumb towards me.

"Hi," I say softly, still hovering by the door.

Aaron beckons me inside the room, then grins cheekily. "Santa got her for me for Christmas." He drops his voice to a stage whisper. "Isn't she pretty?"

Parker looks me up and down, dead serious as he considers Aaron's question. "She is," he finally concludes.

"What did Santa get you this year?" Aaron asks.

I think he's made a faux-pas for a moment, because Parker is clearly too old to believe in Santa, but the kid laughs. "I asked him for new kidneys, but he just got me the new Madden for Playstation instead."

"Madden?!" Aaron demands. "Santa's lost his ever-loving mind. He was meant to bring you NHL 25 so you could play as me."

Parker smirks and shakes his head. "Bo-*ring*."

Aaron widens his eyes in mock-horror and then looks over and shakes his head at me. "I visit this kid all the time, we're the best of friends, and yet he's still a diehard Falcons fan. Couldn't care less about hockey, no matter how hard I try to convince him that it's clearly the best sport."

"Football is a far superior game," Parker claps back. "Both in video game format and in real life."

"But my avatar in the new NHL game is a total stud." Aaron pouts.

"Still. Bet he can't throw a spiral to save his life."

This insult makes Aaron howl with laughter, and Parker's eyes gleam happily at having made him laugh like that. Meanwhile, I'm trying to soak in the whole scene. Parker clearly adores Aaron, and it's clear that one of the things he loves is the way Aaron's treating him. Like he's not hooked up to a million machines and clad in a hospital gown.

Like they're best buddies. Hanging out, and having a chat, and ragging on each other.

The lump in my throat gets bigger, my eyes more misty.

"Olivia, back me up!" Aaron calls, patting the floor next to him.

"Nah, Olivia looks smart enough to be on my side." Parker bats his eyelids at me.

"Hey, stop flirting with my girl!" Aaron chastises with a grin, before winking at me. "Future heartbreaker, this one."

Parker's scrawny chest puffs with pride, while my own feels

like it's constricting with more emotions than I know what to do with.

"And also, she's not *that* smart," Aaron tells Parker, winking at me. "Do you know that she used to hate Christmas? Can you believe it?"

Parker gasps in horror, and as I slide down to a cross-legged seat next to Aaron, he places a casual hand on my knee as our conversation turns to the holidays. Parker tells us about his baby sister's diaper exploding when his parents visited earlier today, and Aaron fills Parker in on Natalia and Nonna catching us kissing at his front door, which makes the boy cackle.

Seriously, who is this guy? How could anybody not adore him?

My prior self was clearly insane, because now, I see who he really is: a man who invests endless time, effort, and energy in the people who are important to him. Who faces up to his challenges and tackles his problems head on, because the people who matter to him are worth fighting for and believing in, even when he barely believes in himself.

It's inspiring. When I look at myself, I see that, in contrast, I've been living in fear of investing in important relationships in case those people don't invest in me, too, and caring about someone turns into something painful. And keeping that emotional distance from people left an emptiness. A loneliness.

For years, I tried in vain to fill that void with work and travel and escape. And while those things have been great, in and of themselves, they did nothing to satisfy the fundamental ache in me for connection and belonging.

Not things, not experiences, but deeper relationships that were truly meaningful.

I realize that, in this moment, there is nowhere else on earth I'd rather be than sitting on this cold linoleum floor next to Aaron, celebrating Christmas by spending time with these incredible kids, then going home to his place to spend the evening with his family.

Because it *means something*.

Over the past few months, I've felt happier than I have in years, and it's all due to the people in my life. I have a wonderful friend in Jing and budding friendships with the ladies I've met through the Cyclones.

And then, I have Sofia. My brother. Aaron.

People who matter to me so much that I'm willing to risk putting myself out there and simply *letting them* matter this much to me.

For the first time in my adult life, I'm going to take a leaf out of Aaron's book and fight for what—*who*—I love.

Which means I need to talk to my brother, stat.

43

OLIVIA

I feel like I'm getting a taste of the Brandi life as I skulk in the underground parking lot at the RGM. And let me tell you, it's not the life for me.

For one, it's freaking cold down here.

For two, my legs hurt from crouching beside Aaron's car like a criminal.

Although, it's given me a lot of time to examine that dent in his driver's side door and reflect on just how much this man has done for me in such a short span of time.

Which is why I'm currently doing this for him.

For *us*.

It's the first opportunity I've had to face this head on, because Aaron's mom and Nonna kept us occupied from the moment we came back from visiting the kids in the hospital, right up until they walked through security at ATL last night.

It felt weird to be on that side of things—to not be the one leaving, but the one saying goodbye. To people who, strangely enough, already feel like family.

And as I walked out of the airport hand in hand with Aaron, ready to go home, I felt complete.

Bright headlights flood the parking lot and I look up to see that Jake's forest green SUV is finally pulling into the lot.

About *fricking* time.

I jump up and run over to his assigned parking spot, so I'm waiting, arms crossed, when he clambers out of his vehicle in his game-day suit. It's a nice one—charcoal gray and perfectly tailored. Sofia must've picked it out.

"Looking good, big bro."

Jake jerks his head up in surprise. "Liv, what the hell are you doing down here?"

"Waiting for you."

"Why?"

"I need to talk to you before your game."

His mouth twists. "Couldn't you have just called me?"

"No."

Well, yes, actually. But pointlessly crouching behind a car and then surprising him seemed like a better plan. You know, for dramatic effect.

"What's going on?" Jake eyes me suspiciously. "Is this about Marino? Because if it is, I've already said my piece to him."

"But you haven't said your piece to me!" I burst out. "Me, your only sister. Who is a consenting adult and would like to be part of this moronic conversation!"

"The hell are you talking about?"

"I'm talking about the fact that Aaron's been your best friend for years, and he came home after your morning skate earlier and said you barely talked to him. Barely even looked at him. That all the guys seem to think he's been taking advantage of Jake Griswold's poor, sweet, innocent sister."

"Huh. So Marino ran home to tattle to you. How cute."

This makes me a little enraged. It's been two days since Christmas, and Aaron's been nothing but nice about Jake and his so-called protective-big-brother motives. But I haven't heard a peep out of Jake to prove that theory right. "I forced him to tell me! He keeps covering for you, saying he'd be the same way if he were in your position."

"Damn right he would," Jake thunders. "You're my sister, Olivia. And Aaron might be a nice guy, but the women he dates don't tend to stick around for awhile, if you know what I mean."

"Duh!" I say. "I am aware. And I'm also aware that neither did the women *you* dated. Until Sofia."

This makes Jake flounder for a moment, but his glare darkens. "Not the same. I didn't move Sofia into my house and seduce her behind her brother's back. You always seemed to hate Aaron so much, I figured I'd never have to worry about you two." His eyes flicker to my hair. "Despite the fact that Aaron typically goes for women that look like you."

I pause, momentarily caught off guard.

Looks like Aaron Marino got a brand new redhead for Christmas!

The words from the caption of Brandi's Instagram post come back to me, but I'm surprised to feel... *nothing*.

The old Olivia would have stumbled over this. Would have spiraled thinking about how pretty Aaron's redheaded ex Tessa is. How, when I first saw Aaron again at the club all those months ago, he was on a date with a brunette that he declared a "total nonstarter" and approached a redhead later that same night. How even freaking Brandi appears to have dyed her previously blond hair auburn to get Aaron's attention in the first place...

How his exact words to me the day I packed up my apartment were that he was "always more into redheads."

In the past, I would have pieced all this together to form an incomplete picture that ignored the most important thing: what was actually real and true below the surface.

But I am not that Olivia anymore. I'm not that person who's

rootless and looking for an excuse to run at the first sign of trouble.

"Do you hear yourself right now?!" I cry. "First, my relationship—and most importantly, *why someone is dating me*—is none of your business. And second, to be honest, this noble big brother act of yours is wearing a little thin. I like Aaron, and he likes me, and if you have a problem with that, it's *your* problem. Not mine. Not Aaron's. So stop putting it on him."

I know my place with Aaron. I know who he is and how he feels about me, no matter what I look like. And I know how I feel about him, too.

I'm in this. All in. I choose to be with him, and to let the chips fall where they may. I might not know what the future holds, but I know that choosing to take a chance on this—on *us*—is worth the risk.

I'm not Aaron's type, I'm his *person.*

And he's mine.

"I—" Jake starts, all fired up, but then, his face falls. "Wait. What do you mean 'noble big brother act?'"

I wipe my nose with my sleeve. "What I mean is that I've been on my own for years now and you never cared about what I did, or where I was, or who I dated. And then, I start dating someone you like and admire, and you lose your ever-loving mind about it. Like, grow up, Jake."

Jake's face slackens. "Is that what you really think?" He swallows. "That couldn't be further from the truth. I care, Liv. I've always cared. Our parents put us through so much crap and I wanted to be there for you, but I know I fell short. Didn't try hard enough. You were always so hell-bent on getting as far away from our family as possible—which I understand, and I was glad you got out—but I always felt bad that I couldn't look out for you. I was so fricking happy when you moved here. I thought it would give us a fresh start. Give me a chance to be the brother I wasn't."

I have to bite my lip as tears fill my eyes. "That's what I wanted too," I say quietly. "I chose Atlanta specifically to be closer to you. And when I came here and saw you and Sofia together, a part of me felt like I was intruding. Like you had your own thing going here. And so, I guess I kept my distance, emotionally."

Jake looks downright aghast. "You would never be intruding, Liv. You're my family, and I love you. No matter what."

"Same." The tears are flowing freely now, and Jake's blinking rather quickly.

He opens his arms and wraps me in a hug—something we don't do, ever. I hug him back fiercely. My only brother. My family.

I pull back after a moment and look at him through my tears. "We're a sorry pair, huh?"

"We are," he agrees. "I guess I might have overreacted a *smidge* to you being with Marino. I was trying to make up for lost time. So many years of not threatening to kick all your old boyfriends' asses."

I snort with laughter. "Please. I could've kicked their asses myself, if I'd been so inclined."

This makes him smile, and he ruffles my hair. "I know. You're a badass, Liv. But that checks out, because you're related to me."

"A sorry pair of badasses, indeed," I agree.

"Hey, look." He pulls a pained face. "I love you, and Aaron's the best friend I ever had. I trust both of your judgments, and if you're saying that this is real for you, I believe you. Sure, it's a bit weird for me—and probably will be for awhile—but I'm not going to be a jackass about it anymore. You can look out for yourself, and I respect that."

"Thanks, Jake."

He nods. Draws his brows together. "But in the interest of looking out for both of you, you should probably know that, given everything that's happened this season, that photo might not be great for his image."

Jake's words remind me of what Lieberman said at the gala about Aaron keeping his love life out of the media, but I shake my head. "I think that photo just shows that we're together, rather than being a catalyst for more negative stories."

"I hope so. Plus, I've never seen him react the way he did about this."

"React like what?"

"Like he was more worried about *you* than what it might mean for his hockey career."

My stomach simultaneously soars and tightens at Jake's words. I'm overjoyed to hear how much Aaron seems to care for me, but at the same time, I'd never want to negatively affect his career.

Before I can fully process this, Jake smiles. "But I *will* kill him if he hurts you, no matter how much I like the guy. Understand?"

"I do." I smile back at him. "But you won't ever have to. Because he won't."

"Good."

"Now get out of here." I give my brother a shove. "You have a game to win."

And with that, my brother gives me a wave and exits the parking lot towards the players' area. Meanwhile, I run back to the arena entrance. I'm ready to sit in the friends and family box as both girlfriend and family of Cyclones players, and watch my boys kick some ass on the ice together.

44

AARON

Sixty minutes of gameplay, and it's all come down to the last sixty seconds.

We're tied 1-1, but the game's been frustrating from the moment the puck dropped. We're outplaying and outshooting the Houston Dragons—one of the worst ranked teams in the league right now—but their behemoth goalie has evaded us from actually *outscoring* them tonight.

Which is the metric that actually matters, at the end of the day.

It's our first game back after Christmas, we're on home ice playing for a packed arena, and the woman of my dreams is in the crowd, cheering for me.

I want to *win*, dammit.

Before the game, I managed to avoid the press. I didn't want them bringing up Olivia and that photo that seems to be everywhere. I figured I'd get out here on the ice, play a hell of a game, and give them something else to talk about.

Make my team, my coach, and her proud.

We might have less than a minute left, but I'm not giving up yet.

The guys on the second line skate towards the boards and I stand, ready to jump back on the ice for my last shift.

Colton, Seb, and I skate into position. Then, time simultaneously speeds up, and slows right down.

Dallas steals the puck from one of Houston's D-men and snaps it forward to Seb, who skates furiously ahead. He's fast, fast enough to outskate the Houston guy flanking him, and I hold my breath for a moment—can feel the entire arena hold its breath—as he swings back his stick and takes the shot.

It soars through the air at lightning speed, a beautiful shot, but it misses its target by mere inches, soaring past the net.

The crowd lets out a collective groan, but I barely hear it. Instead, I'm tearing down the ice, stick outstretched, to claim the puck. I get there first, hook it with my stick, and maneuver around another Houston player, my skates biting the ice as I turn.

I'm behind the net, the Dragons' goalie only a couple of feet away, and adrenaline pumps through my body as I shift my weight, sizing my options.

I can pass it to Jake, who's wide open. Or, I can pass to Perez, who's right by the net on the goalie's weak side, and he'll have a chance to sneak it in if we catch the goalie off guard.

It takes me a split second to determine that Perez currently has a better chance of scoring, so I neatly send it Colton's way. He makes contact, and does exactly what I hoped he would do: attempts to edge it in behind the goalie's right skate.

He's unsuccessful, and the goalie intercepts the puck and sends it flying down the ice, where it hits a Houston forward's stick. He skates fast and hard, propelling his body forward effortlessly, dekes out both Dallas and Jake, and then, the moment he has a clear shot on net, lines up and lets it fly.

The puck streaks towards the net, and time stands still as Lars launches himself into a dive.

I can only watch as the puck grazes the edge of his glove... and lands smack in the back of the net, just as the clock runs out.

The Houston guys throw their gloves up in victory, and the entire RGM lets out a groan that I feel in my bones.

Final score: Houston—2, Atlanta—1.

We lose.

It's our first game back after Christmas. We're on home ice playing for a packed arena. The woman of my dreams is in the crowd...

And we lose.

Immediately, my mind goes straight to familiar anxious thoughts: *You screwed up and made the wrong decision, Aaron. You just lost your team the game.*

I try to shake off the thoughts as we file off the ice, lifting my head to see if I can spot a familiar copper-haired figure.

When I locate her, everything else stills. Calms.

She holds up her hands in the shape of a heart.

I believe in you, Aaron.

Her words brush over my skin and I feel them sinking in. Hitting their mark.

My eyes remain on Olivia's as I hold up my own gloved hands and make a heart in return. The girl with fire in her eyes that fuels my own fire. The girl I once desired, who grew into the only woman I have ever truly wanted. The reason I understand the feeling of being so far gone for someone that there's no hope nor want of return.

I love Olivia. I don't know if it's chemistry or astrology or damn alchemy that dictates that, and frankly, I don't care. I just know it's *right*.

So much so that I don't give a damn what anyone else thinks, or what they might say about me reacting to losing a game we should have won by looking at her and doing this.

I care what *she* thinks. I care about her.

Us.

The voice in my mind that always tells me to do better and reminds me of all my shortcomings can take a damn backseat, because Olivia belongs at the forefront.

⁂

Back in the locker room, morale is low like it always is after a loss. But instead of doing what I might have done in the past and apologizing for what I believed was my mistake, I act like the damn captain they appointed me to be.

"Good game, Ferrar," I tell one of our rookies who's unlacing his skates. "That shot on net in the second was a thing of pure beauty."

He beams. "You think?"

"Absolutely."

I then move on to congratulate Seb on his goal at the end of the first, and Lars for an incredible save at the start of the third. I sit with Colton and assure him that what happened wasn't his fault—nor mine, nor anyone's. The other team getting that breakaway was simply a lucky fluke, and it was an admittedly gorgeous shot that won Houston the game.

"We played well tonight," I address the room. "And next game, we'll play better. We got this. One loss does not define who we are."

The guys cheer in agreement and I'm happy to see the mood improve. I flop down on the bench and am surprised when Jake comes to sit beside me.

"Nice speech," he says with a chuckle.

"Thanks. Want a pep talk, too?" I joke.

"Nah. Olivia already gave me the talk of a lifetime earlier."

My brows shoot up. "She did?"

He nods. "Full-blown stalked me in the parking garage, then verbally chewed me up and spit me out."

I break into laughter. "Classic Liv."

"You're gonna have your hands full with her," Jake says with what looks to be a genuine smile.

"I know. I can't wait." I grin back, and just like that, everything is good between us again. I know that, with time, Jake will come to see that not only is Olivia the best thing that's ever happened to me, but that I can be good for her, too. I vow to do everything in my power to be.

"Marino!" Coach Torres's booming voice calls through the room.

"Yes, Coach?"

"A minute."

I promptly get to my feet and follow him to his office. I wonder what he has to say, and usually I'd be anxious as all hell about the fact that he wants to talk to me right after a loss. But I hold my head up and stand firm on my new truth.

"What's up?" I ask as I sink into a chair opposite him.

"I saw you boosting the guys' moods back there. I wanted to tell you that you're doing a good job."

"Thank you," I say, surprised. Not what I'd been expecting him to say at all.

"You're a good captain, Marino," Coach tells me. "You've only been in this role for a few months, and already, the guys respect you. Want to hear what you've got to say."

"Glad you think so."

"I do." Coach's piercing eyes bore into me as he steeples his hands on his desk. He clears his throat. "But I also wanted to give you a heads up that the press have swooped in like vultures on the news of you getting together with Griswold's sister."

My heart sinks. This isn't surprising to me. That damn picture is everywhere.

"I figured they might," I say slowly. I'm already thinking about how I can best protect Olivia from what will surely be an onslaught of questions and assumptions.

"They're asking more questions about your role here. Lieberman is not one bit happy, and I have a feeling that he's going to amp up his campaign to get you replaced. Whatever happens, I want to let you know that I'm on your side. I believe in you."

I appreciate Torres's words immensely, and that he's in my corner, but I can read between the lines: if Lieberman really pushes back, Coach's hands might be tied.

"I do, too, Coach," I say with conviction. "And for as long as the Cyclones organization lets me, I'm going to continue to be the best damn captain I can be."

"That's what I like to hear, Marino," Torres says with a nod. "I suggest you go find your girl and enjoy the rest of your night. I'll handle the media storm that's brewing out there."

And that's when I know exactly what I need to do.

"Actually, Coach," I say. "Can I join in on the press conference?"

His bushy brows fly up. "You *want* to speak to the media tonight?"

"I do."

No more imposter syndrome. Lieberman can skewer me all he wants after this, but for now, I'm still this team's damn captain.

And I have something to say.

45

OLIVIA

It's a beautiful moment.

Aaron, on the ice, looking up at me with his gloved hands in a heart shape and publicly declaring me *his*.

It's the sort of thing I would have hated and shied away from until recently. Now, I'm living for it.

The damned magic of Christmas is real after all. And this holiday season is one I will savor forever.

"That is freaking adorable!" Reagan exclaims, squeezing my arm as the Cyclones start to file off the ice. "He's obsessed with you."

On my other side, Sofia laughs. "If he proposes to you before Jake proposes to me, I'm gonna riot."

My eyes widen at the prospect, and she laughs. "I'm kidding. Mostly just wanted to see the look on your face at the thought of you being the future Mrs. Marino."

I open my mouth to make some witty-adjacent remark, but what comes out instead is, "It's not the most terrible thought in the world."

"Ahhh," Maddie croons. "She's just as obsessed as he is." Her expression takes on a mushy, sentimental quality as she continues, "You guys remind me of Seb and me when we first got together. Seb was just like Aaron—hockey, hockey, hockey. He was eating, sleeping, breathing it. And then, he was different. I see that same change in Aaron." She shakes her head slowly, her eyes now on her husband, who shoots her a wink before ducking out of sight. "Amazing what can happen to a man when he makes room for love in his life."

I glance down at Aaron, who's the last to disappear towards the locker rooms, and he gives me one more sweet, lopsided smile before leaving the ice.

I smile back, feeling warm inside. Until my gaze snags on Lieberman.

He's talking to Coach Torres by the players' bench, his face red and his expression... well, *pissed*.

I'm not too sure why. The guys lost tonight, but they've been on a winning streak recently. And Brandi's powerless now that Aaron is officially off the market. As scandalous as that photo she posted was, and as much as it got people talking, it ultimately did nothing but confirm that Aaron and I are together.

Nothing illegal or un-captain-like about a man kissing his girlfriend on his own damned front porch, is there?

Even so, as I'm watching him, it almost looks like Lieberman says the word *Marino*. And he doesn't look happy about it.

"Come on," Sofia suddenly says, looping her arm through mine and shaking me out of my thoughts. "Shall we go to the players' area to meet our men?"

I push away my uneasiness about Lieberman—maybe he's just a generally pissed-off guy. And I'm sure I imagined him saying Aaron's name. He's done talking to Coach now anyway and is walking off.

"Absolutely," I reply.

We make our way with the rest of the guys' partners

towards the players' area, chatting easily while we wait. Eventually, the locker room door opens and the guys begin to come out. Seb makes a beeline for Maddie, his eyes bulging out like cartoon-hearts. Lars goes to greet Lena. Dallas makes his way out with his head dipped, looking uncharacteristically gloomy.

Jake comes out a few moments later, hands in his pockets. He walks over to us and kisses Sofia, and I avert my eyes towards the locker room doors for a moment to give them privacy.

Soon enough, I realize that no one else is coming from the locker room. All of the Cyclones are out now, save for one.

I turn to Jake. "Where's Aaron?"

He shrugs. "He went to Coach's office after the game to talk to him. Not sure why. I figured he'd be out by now."

"Is that normal—to get called to Coach Torres' office after a game?"

"Usually ain't a good thing. And besides, Coach should be on his way to the press conference by now." Jake scratches his beard. "I'm sure it's fine."

"Maybe he's taking an extra-long shower."

This makes Jake chuckle. "He does love to wash that luxurious hair of his." His gaze suddenly darkens. "Unless..."

"Unless what?"

"Unless Aaron's going with Coach to do postgame press." Jake shakes his head. "Can't imagine why he'd wanna do that, though."

"Would Coach have requested Aaron speak to the press with him?"

"Doubt it. Especially with that, you know..." He clears his throat gruffly. "Uh, you know, that *photo* that doesn't bear thinking about. Aaron hates talking to the media about his personal life."

"I don't think anyone's going to care about a photo of Aaron kissing his girlfriend. I'm sure way worse photos of most of you have surfaced."

"True. You should've seen the video of Dallas that got leaked last year..." Jake goes off into a story, but I find myself tuning out, looking back at the locker room doors for Aaron again.

He really *is* taking a while. Everyone else is out here.

Could he actually be going to do postgame press?

Just then, the door to the players' area opens and Reagan appears, her heels click-clacking on the tiles. Her face is a neutral mask as she looks around until her eyes zero in on me. She makes a beeline for our little group.

For some reason, my stomach sinks.

"Everything okay?" I ask her.

She worries her teeth into her lower lip before she lets out a sigh. "Everything's fine, but I do want to make you aware of something."

"Oh?"

Reagan's clutching her phone in her hand and she holds the screen up towards me. "The photo of you and Aaron that Brandi posted on Christmas Day has become a topic of discussion tonight, and unfortunately, not in a good way."

"What do you mean?" I tilt my head, then repeat Aaron's words from the gala, "I'm sure the media don't care about our boring old monogamy."

I say this with a jokey smile, but Reagan frowns.

"Yeah," she says. "But because Brandi's last story on Thanksgiving got so much traction on social media, people were already questioning Aaron's leadership. Now, they're saying that you're just his latest fling and it's not a good look because you're his teammate's little sister." She holds up a hand. "Not that I believe that, obviously, but it's what people are saying. The commentators mentioned it earlier during the game as well, saying that it's causing a rift between Aaron and Jake that's affecting Aaron's play."

"Not true, in any way," Jake says immediately, which I appreciate.

Sofia rubs my arm. "'Course not."

I suddenly recall Lieberman's pissed-off expression and the way I could've sworn he grumbled *Marino* when talking to Torres.

The team's GM isn't happy. The media are questioning Aaron about his dating life again, when Aaron assured Lieberman at the gala that they wouldn't. Coach is off to talk to the press, and there's no sign of Aaron coming out of the locker room.

Has that stupid photo of us actually thrown Aaron's captaincy into question again?

This is so dumb. A total lie that's not fair to Aaron at all. He's the most committed, passionate, loving human I know.

"Where?"

"What?" Jake blinks.

"Where's the press conference taking place?"

Reagan gives me directions towards the media area, and I take off running.

I'm not sure what Aaron's going to say, but I know that I want to be there for him. Jake's words about Aaron putting me before hockey are at the forefront of my mind, and I'm beyond annoyed that he's being questioned again over a photo of the two of us in what *was* an intimate, special moment.

I want to be there to show him that I believe in him, no matter what.

I throw open the door to the media area, but a security guard I don't recognize steps in my way.

"Sorry, lady. Press only from this point onwards."

"I'm Aaron Marino's girlfriend," I explain hurriedly, turning to show him the MARINO printed across the back of my number 22 crimson jersey.

The guard only guffaws. "Like that proves anything. There are thousands of fans in here tonight wearing that jersey." He narrows his eyes skeptically. "Let me guess. You're one of those 'army chicks,' aren't you?"

"The term is Aaron's Army," I correct him proudly. "And yes, I guess I am. But seriously, I'm Aaron's actual girlfriend. And Jake Griswold's sister. I need to get in there."

He crosses his arms. "No media pass, no entry."

This almost makes me laugh. Running into this press conference is the exact kind of thing I would have run *from* in the past. Because if Jake and Reagan—and my gut instinct—are correct, I'm walking into a room full of people talking about me, critiquing me, making me feel like I don't belong.

And today, I'm running *towards* all of that.

Because if Aaron's there, I *do* belong. And no matter what they're saying about him—saying about *us*—showing up for him is what matters.

My mind races as I try to think of a way to get this brute to let me through. But at that moment, that Sadie Whatshername woman walks up behind me, looking very sharklike in a navy-blue suit and stilettos.

"Oh! She knows me!" I point at Sadie. "She can vouch."

Sadie's icy eyes narrow on me, then flick to the guard. "What's going on?"

"I need to get in there," I tell her.

"Isn't that sweet? You want to be there when your boy-toy talks to the press." She laughs dismissively, clearly intending to saunter on by without helping.

Then, her eyes take on a gleam and she stops. Turns back towards me.

"Actually, she's right," Sadie tells the guard. "She's Olivia Griswold—Jake's sister and Aaron's current flirtation."

"Girlfriend," I correct tightly.

Sadie waves a hand. "Semantics. She's with me, Clark. She can come in."

"Okay, Miss Lincoln." Clark nods and lets us both inside.

The room is packed with cameras and reporters all jostling and bustling around chaotically, speaking over each other in a cacophony. While Sadie stalks up to take a seat in the front row, I hang back, crossing the room to slide into a chair near the back corner. I don't want to draw any unnecessary attention—I just want Aaron to see that I'm here supporting him. That we're in this together.

A few minutes later, Aaron walks into the room flanked by Coach Torres and another one of the Cyclones' coaches. He doesn't spot me right away, but I'm sure he's not expecting me to be here.

They take their seats at the front, and almost immediately begin answering questions about the game tonight, their thoughts on the loss, and how they played.

It's all very civilized...

At first.

"So, Aaron." Sadie stands and gives him a slick smirk of a smile. "How do you think tonight's game went?"

"I think our guys played great. We worked well as a team, got a lot of good shots on net, but the outcome of the game was unfortunately not what we hoped for." Aaron looks calm, poised and confident. The look of a man in total control, the look of a *captain*.

It's a very good look, indeed.

But Sadie's expression turns sickly sweet. She beams around the room before looking back at Aaron. "So you'd say you made the correct call on who to pass to for what could have been the winning shot?"

Aaron's eyes flicker for a moment, but he sets his jaw. Clears his throat. "Yes. Perez was in an ideal spot to score, and I made a calculated decision to pass to him."

"Teamwork, right?" Sadie's looking even more shark-like, her eyes gleaming.

Aaron frowns, like he's trying to figure out her angle. "Right."

"Would you say the Cyclones are tight as a team?"

"Absolutely."

"So your involvement with Jake Griswold's sister *isn't* causing a rift between you two on the ice? Splitting up the Cyclones' former 'dream team'?"

Coach Torres opens his mouth to answer, but Aaron gets there first.

"No." His eyes are stone cold.

"But it will cause problems once it ends, right?" Sadie almost taunts. "Risky for team morale to have a fling with your teammate's sister. Something a good captain should consider."

"Enough!"

Aaron bangs his fist on the table, making the twitchy journalist in front of me jump in his seat.

A hush falls over the room as Aaron continues in a calm, commanding tone. "Olivia Griswold is *not* a fling. And I don't give a damn what you all have to say about whether I'm fit to be captain of this team, because the fact is, I *am* the captain at this moment. A captain my coach and teammates elected. And while I don't care what you have to say about *me*, I'm here to set the record straight about Olivia so you vultures can't spin any more ludicrous stories and drag her name through the mud, too."

Sadie snorts, her professional facade cracking. "Says the guy who has endless flings with endless redheads. What the hell makes this one different?"

"She's not just another redhead." Aaron's voice doesn't waver as he looks around the room. Finally, his gaze lands on me and his lips slide into a genuine smile. "I love her. I'm hopelessly, completely in love with her. I think I might have always loved her."

I sit there, in my rickety chair at the back of the media room, stunned.

Because Aaron Marino loves me.

This incredible man loves *me*.

My heart feels buoyant. About to burst with happiness.

"I love you, too!" I yell like a fool, jumping to my feet. "I love you too, Aaron!"

And though I know that everyone is looking right at me, I don't care. Because Aaron's eyes light up at the sight of me on my feet and causing a scene for him, and his is the only opinion that matters.

Cameras start clicking, people start talking, and Sadie Lincoln's face falls as her plan to humiliate us backfires. Lieberman, standing off to the side of the room, looks surprisingly calm and composed, and I swear I see a twinkle in Coach Torres's eye as Aaron gets to his feet, hops over the press table, and jumps off the stage in one swift motion.

He muscles his way through the crowd until he reaches me.

"It's true." I smile up at him. "I love you. I'm *in* love with you."

"I love you isn't enough, Olivia." His arms circle around me. "The way I feel about you is all-consuming—it's everything. *You're* everything. I've been in love with you forever, and I'll continue to love you forever, and then after forever ends."

"I'm not just another redhead?" I tease, grinning up at him. "I'd hate to think that I was just your type."

He shakes his head with a smile. "The only reason I was drawn to women with red hair in the first place was because of you. I never forgot you." He pauses, then lowers his voice to an intimate level meant only for my ears. "Want to know the actual reason I didn't date anyone for months?"

"Because you were focusing on your captaincy... until you fell for me, of course."

"Because when you walked back into my life again all those months ago, and I saw you standing in that club in that silver dress looking like you were straight out of my wildest dreams, I knew, deep down, that there was no one else for me. That dating other people was now entirely out of the question, because anyone else would pale in comparison."

My heart speeds up to double time. "Come on, Marino. Don't feed me that old line about how I'm not like the other girls."

"But you're not, Griswold." He smiles a smile of pure sunshine. "You're *you*."

And then, he kisses me. I kiss him back fiercely, not giving a damn who's watching.

Because this, right here, in his arms, is exactly where I belong.

EPILOGUE

AARON

"I miss her," I complain as I take a sip of my beer—yes, beer, because it's New Years Eve, and this is a party, and tonight, I'm relaxing and having a drink with my teammates.

"It's been three days, bro," Jake responds with a scowl, but his eyes are twinkling. "What time does she get in tonight?"

"Around 11:45. She'll probably drop by here after, if she's not too tired."

I was looking forward to ringing in the new year with my new girlfriend, but we both have jobs that take us to different places, and right now, she's on a plane flying in from Tokyo. Tomorrow, we'll move her into her new apartment. I'm excited to see how things play out from there, because no matter what, we got this.

Our relationship, no matter how it started—going from hate to love and living together before we were even dating—will always be *ours*. A story that's completely unique to us. *Right* for us.

I even sent her an invite to Words With Friends so we can play Scrabble when we're apart. She's going to make fun of me for that and call me a nerd, and I'm going to love it.

Nothing could make me stop loving her.

"And let me guess, if she *is* too tired, you'll leave the party and go home to her," Jake says drily as he cracks open another Dos Equis.

My lips slide into a smile. "Busted."

"Whipped as all hell, my man."

"Takes one to know one," I say with a smirk, because even as he says the words, Jake's eyes are firmly on Sofia, who is currently dancing up a storm with Lena, Stefani, and none other than Coach Torres.

Our coach lets his hair down precisely once a year: at our annual team New Year's Eve party. This year is no exception—the guy's wearing a pair of huge, sparkly comedy New Year's glasses and absolutely dominating the dance floor. Like, to the point that I'm worried he might sustain a groin injury.

"I'm gonna get another drink," I tell Jake, but he's not listening. He's making a beeline for the dance floor to scoop Sofia into his arms.

As I make my way to the bar, I notice that Reagan and Triple J are cozily whispering together at the edge of the dance floor. I also spot Lieberman and his wife slow dancing to a pulsing rap song, which is pretty hilarious to witness.

The GM sees me and gives me a nod, which I return, before he looks back down at his wife.

After the press conference the other night, I was pretty sure Lieberman was going to insist I be demoted, but I ultimately knew that, no matter what happened, I would never regret speaking the truth about the woman I love.

Turns out, he was impressed with the way I dealt with the

press. Apparently, one of the main reasons he vouched for Slater as captain in the first place was because Seb's a family man and he believed Seb would bring the same maturity and commitment to the role as Mal did.

Lieberman went on to admit that I've shown much better leadership than he thought I would, and that I clearly have a team-first mentality. He said I've shown myself to be a man who fights for what he loves, and he respects that. We shook hands and left things on a good note that gives me hope for the rest of this hockey season and beyond.

And honestly, I see what he meant. After the guys on the team heard my impassioned speech—because, of course, it aired absolutely everywhere—they seem to have even more respect for me. Faith in me.

They believe in me, and I believe in myself too. I know I won't let them down.

At the bar, I'm surprised to find Dallas—who turned up without a date tonight—slinging back a shot, alone.

"Hey, Cap." He hiccups. "Let me buy you a shot."

I chuckle at my teammate's flushed cheeks and slightly slurred words. "Sure."

The bartender pours a couple more tequilas, and I down mine with a wince. Dallas, meanwhile, doesn't even flinch, and instead, he beckons the bartender for yet another.

I hold up a hand to signal that I'm good, then turn to my teammate with a brow raised. "Everything okay, Coop?"

He slouches against the bar. "Yeah, don't worry 'bout me, Cap."

But he isn't smiling.

Nope, he's staring straight into the bottom of his empty shot glass, lost in his thoughts.

Hmm. This is definitely out-of-character for sarcastic, confident, easygoing Dallas who's usually the life of the party. And usually flirting and dancing with every woman at said party.

Girl trouble, maybe?

I suddenly remember something he said on the way to the Christmas tree farm.

"Hey, whatever happened to that girl you met a few weeks ago? The one you talked to all night?"

Dallas laughs, but the sound is almost bitter, and I have a feeling I hit on something. His eyes fix on something—some*one*?—on the dance floor. I follow his gaze and am surprised to see that he's looking at Coach Torres. "A definite no-go."

I frown in confusion, but don't prompt him. Just wait.

He swallows. Scrubs a hand over his eyes. "Can you keep a secret?"

"Always."

"Turns out she's Torres' daughter."

"Caelin?!" I'm unable to keep the shock out of my tone.

Dallas turns his slightly unfocused baby blues on me. "You know her?"

"We've met. How in the hell did you manage to spend a whole night talking to her and not realize who she was?"

"I don't know," Dallas replies with a groan. "I swear I had no idea. She didn't seem to know who I was, either. But after the whole Sadie debacle, if Coach finds out that I made a move on his damn *daughter*, I'm gonna be traded in a heartbeat."

"No." I shake my head. "You're a hell of a player. You and Griz together on the same line are practically unstoppable. Coach knows you're a good guy, too."

"Doubtful." Dallas grimaces. "Do you know he hauled me into his office a couple days after the cockroach thing and tore me a new one?"

I bite my cheek. "No."

"He figured out that Sadie's apparent vendetta against you

was actually rooted in something *I* did." Dallas winces a little. "Which I'm very sorry about, by the way, dude. We did go out a couple of times, and after it ended, I suspected she wasn't happy, but I didn't expect her to go out of her way to take down anyone who might be seen as a playboy hockey player. You got caught in her crosshairs, and that was my fault."

I pause for a moment, letting his words sink in, and then shake my head. "Sadie's behavior was her choice, no matter what you did or didn't do."

This goes for both Sadie *and* Brandi.

The two have been quiet lately—we played Baltimore last night, and every question Sadie asked me before the game was actually related to hockey. As for Brandi, I had a high-tech security system added to both my house and Olivia's new apartment, in case of any future incidents.

I'm not too worried about her, though. Thanks to some leaked info by an anonymous source (who was definitely Reagan), TMZ did a big write-up about Brandi's antics and how she's blackmailed multiple celebrities and athletes. Meaning that pretty much any credibility she had is now in the gutter.

I can't say I feel one bit sorry for her.

Unlike for my teammate, who seems totally down in the dumps right now. I put a reassuring hand on his shoulder. "I'd never blame you for all that ridiculous media B.S. And neither would Coach."

"I think he does, though." Dallas looks stricken for a moment, but he shakes it off, his jaw setting. "I liked Caelin. We had a connection." He grabs another shot and pounds it. Wipes his mouth with the back of his hand and huffs a laugh. "But, oh well. You win some, you lose some."

My thoughts turn to my beautiful, fiery redhead, and my lips quirk in a smile. "Never say never, bro. If it's right, it'll happen. Even against all odds. Love has a funny way of showing up when you least expect it—and where you never dare to imagine it."

He snorts. "Maybe for you."

"Either way, you're a fundamental part of this team. And no matter what goes down, me and the guys have your back, always."

"Thanks, Marino." His expression softens at my words. "And speaking of all this mushy stuff, where's our Lil Griz tonight?"

"Yeah, where's Olivia?" Triple J appears beside us. He's wearing a party hat and is holding a huge fishbowl cocktail with an umbrella in it. Holding it with two hands, to be precise—he's carrying at least a gallon of liquid.

I explain to my teammates that Olivia's flying back from Tokyo and she might not make it until after midnight, if she feels up to coming at all.

Jimmy looks appalled. "Well, that's not good enough."

"What do you mean?" I tilt my head at him.

"I mean, we should all be together to ring in the new year." He nods firmly. "And whether she likes it or not, Olivia's one of us now."

"She is," Dallas agrees.

A slow smile starts to spread on my lips. "You're right. It's *not* right that she's not here." My mind is whirring with a sudden idea. "In fact, if she can't be here, I should be *there*."

"You should," Seb pipes up from where he's walking up behind me, an arm wrapped around Maddie's waist.

I face my teammates with a slight frown. "Would you guys mind if I bail on the party?"

Triple J takes a long, noisy suck of his drink through the crazy loopy straw. "Maybe we should come, too."

"What?"

"Yes." Dallas is grinning at Triple J. "Just like you have our backs, Cap, we have yours. So, let's go get your girl. Actually, let's round everyone up and we'll *all* go."

I chuckle. "So, what? Order a bunch of Ubers to convoy to the airport?"

Jimmy shrugs nonchalantly. "Or we could take the limo I hired for the evening."

OLIVIA

"Should old acquaintance be forgot for the sake of Auld Lang Syne!" Jing bellows tunelessly as we walk through a freakishly empty Hartsfield-Jackson airport.

She went on a couple of dates with a Scottish guy over the holidays, and as my only experience with Scotland involves Gregory the dreadful bagpiper, she's been hard at work trying to change my mind. For the entirety of our trip to Tokyo and back, she regaled me with every positive aspect she's learned of Scottish culture, including a complete rendition—with harmonies somehow included—of the song they like to sing at midnight on New Year's.

I check my watch. "You're four minutes early."

"I'm just getting started, baby." She loops her arm through mine as we board the little airport train that'll take us back to the main arrivals area.

"That was a long flight," I say as I sink into my seat.

I'm tired, but definitely not too exhausted to take a cab straight to the Cyclones' New Year's party, which is currently happening in a hotel downtown.

I'm beyond excited to see Aaron. Touch him. Kiss him.

Make up for lost time, because boy have I missed him the past few days.

But it's the good kind of missing someone. Not the lonely kind that feels empty, but that sweet ache in your stomach at the end of an amazing trip when you know you're coming home to the person you love.

That's what Atlanta is now. What Aaron is now. *Home.*

I can come and go, travel the world and back again, and I always have a place—a person—to return to that's mine.

"Too exhausted to give the Italian Stallion the night of his life?" Jing says with a big wink.

"Shut it, *Bing,*" I tell her with a laugh. She shoves me, and I add, "Maybe we could arrange a double date soon. Me, you, the Italian Stallion, and the Kilted Wonder."

"What's under his kilt really *is* a wonder," Jing says with a sigh. "His ass—or arse, as the Scots say—could rival your boyfriend's."

This makes me giggle.

I love my friend.

I love my brother and his girlfriend.

And I *really* love my boyfriend.

This past year has brought me so many amazing things, and I'm looking forward to the next one to bring deeper roots *and* more growth and adventure. Existing together, both equally true and valid.

The two of us pile off the train—we were the only passengers—and as we walk towards Arrivals, there's a similar quiet. It's a ghost town of an airport while everyone in the city rings in the new year with their loved ones.

Next to me, Jing does a little dance. "Just one minute to midnight."

I wonder what Aaron's doing right now. Jake joked that he'd

kiss him at midnight for me, which I actually kind of hope he does.

Smiling, I loop my arm through Jing's as we step through to Arrivals.

"SURPRISE!"

A deafening cheer fills the concourse and confetti flutters through the air.

"What the?!" I blink in shock, and as the confetti falls, I'm stunned to see about twenty hockey players, an array of spouses and girlfriends, and the Cyclones' staff and coaches. Everyone is decked out in party hats and new year's glasses.

"You were meant to wait until midnight to throw the confetti, dumbass," Dallas says to Triple J, who's beaming without a care in the world.

"I got too excited!" Jimmy responds, throwing his hands up.

Jake, too, has clearly gotten carried away with the premature celebrations, because he's blasting away on one those metallic party horns.

It's an absolute spectacle. A spectacle I can see security descending on very soon.

But there, in the middle of it all... *Aaron.*

He has a smile that makes him look even more impossibly, devilishly handsome than he did in my daydreams during our days apart.

"It's you!" I shriek, dropping my bags and running to him without a second's thought.

He catches me easily, like I weigh nothing, and pulls me into his chest for a hug. "I've missed you, Livvy."

"What're you doing here?" I ask as I inhale his sexy, familiar, comforting scent. Revel in the sensation of his strong arms around me.

"Welcoming you home."

Somewhere far in the background, I can hear everyone begin to count. "Ten! Nine!"

All my focus is on Aaron. Here with me. Always showing up when I need him, when I hope he will, and even when I don't believe for a second that he could.

"Happy New Year, Olivia," he says softly.

"Happy New Year, Aaron," I respond, anticipation rising in my stomach as he cups my face with his hands and gazes down at me.

"Four! Three!" the crowd chants.

"Ah screw, it," Aaron murmurs, and his lips are on mine. A couple seconds early and too perfect for words.

When we pull apart, I'm dizzy and breathless, but I manage a cheeky smirk as I tilt my head up to look at him. "Way to jump the gun there, Marino. Couldn't wait two more seconds to ravish me?"

"Absolutely not," he replies, the picture of confidence. "I've been waiting for this forever."

And then, he kisses me again, and I let myself melt into him.

Everything I want and need, now and always, is right here with me.

A NOTE FROM KATIE

Hello and happy holidays to each and every one of you!

It takes so many people to publish a book, and like always, I have many many thank yous to send out into the universe for this one being in your hands today.

First things first, I want to thank each and every of my readers. I love and appreciate you so much. Thanks for hanging out with Aaron and Olivia when there are so many amazing festive books out there to get lost in.

Alex, you're the best. Thank you for working tirelessly with me to improve and refine this story and for your patience with me. Eternally thankful to be able to work with you and also consider you such a great friend. Love you!

Leah - thank you so much for being the best author bestie a girl could ask for. I don't know what I'd do without our sprint sessions, endless voice notes back and forth offering moral support, and safe spaces to vent.

Emily S and Emily W, you ladies are amazing! You killed it with this launch, and I am so grateful to know you both and to get to work with you.

Madi, thank you for being you. Your feedback is always so spot on and your observations help shape my stories in so many ways. You're awesome, and your crocheting skills are top-notch... Aaron could learn a thing or two from you ;)

To my beta readers, who are absolute stars.

Dawn and Bethany, thank you for your fantastic suggestions and for helping me take this story to the finish line.

Megan, thank you for your meticulous attention to what I'll just call my grammar problem lol, and for keeping all the little details consistent! I'm so lucky to have you all in my corner.

Michelle, I so appreciate your comments on the flight attendant story in particular, and for helping me make that as realistic as possible. Jesse, thank you again for your hockey knowledge and for letting me pick your brain constantly on really dumb details.

Abby and Suzan, thank you for all your work with typo hunting. I so appreciate you both :)

A huge thanks to my launch team for helping me spread the word about Aaron and Olivia, and my wonderful ARC readers, for taking the time to read and review this book!

Thank you to Cindy, for your beautiful cover art, and to all of my author friends who are endlessly supportive. I am so grateful to be part of this community.

And last but definitely not least, thank you to my husband for putting up with my eternal cycle of spiraling over every book I write, and still loving me anyway.

Love always and a very merry Christmas from my family to yours,

ALSO BY KATIE BAILEY

The Quit List

Cyclones Christmas

Season's Schemings

Donovan Family

So That Happened

I Think He Knows

Only in Atlanta

The Roommate Situation

The Neighbor War